# THE KILL LINE

# THE KILL LINE

J.J. CAGNEY

CITY OWL PRESS

THE KILL LINE

CITY OWL PRESS
www.cityowlpress.com



Cover Design by MiblArt. All stock photos licensed appropriately.

Edited by Tee Tate.

For information on subsidiary rights, please contact the publisher at info@cityowlpress.com.

Print Edition ISBN: 978-1-64898-574-4

Digital Edition ISBN: 978-1-64898-575-1

CITY OWL PRESS
Escape Your World • Get Lost in Ours

*For Paul Hart,*
*Thank you for a lifetime of Yellowstone stories, generous advice, and insider knowledge that brought this novel to life. I hope I've done them—and you—proud.*

# DEEP IN THE FOREST

## TUESDAY

COLM WAS TOO FAR AWAY when the first shots rang out to return to the campsite in time to do...something. He'd been wandering the woods, giving Lorna and Chase their space because alone time was a scarce commodity when traveling cross-country with a third person.

Lorna screamed Chase's name. Colm dropped the berries he'd gathered as he bolted toward their campsite. Branches snagged his shirt and scratched his arms and face, but he didn't care. Something was wrong.

Very, very wrong.

Colm skidded to a halt at the top of the hill just as the trees began to thin, his palm landing against the rough bark of a pine tree.

Lorna was on her knees next to Chase's prone body while a person holding a gun stood over her.

"D-don't come any closer!" Lorna's voice cracked. Her eyes met Colm's for a split second—hers wide and terrified—before she raised her hands, palms out, dripping with Chase's blood, supplicating. The fear was now a vise in Colm's throat.

He couldn't just stand there. Before he could move, a gunshot ripped through the silence. Lorna fell backward, a large stain blooming across her chest, her vacant eyes no longer meeting Colm's. Colm ducked, his heart drumming against his ribs, as another shot boomed. Gunpowder and pine sap seared his nostrils.

"Don't need to," the shooter said in response to Lorna's comment not to come closer.

The voice was a male...no, a female. Colm couldn't tell because of the distance. He should have been able to, but he was still too far away to get a clear look. The bulky jacket the shooter wore made it hard to tell anything about their physique.

Colm inched closer, staying low until the killer turned his way. Colm hit the ground, face down in the dirt, staring at blue hiking boots.

The twinkling lights strung up around the van were out, thanks to the dead battery—worst possible timing. The door was locked, too. Colm had the keys in his pocket. A stupid joke he'd started weeks ago after swiping them at a diner, saying, "Now you guys can't leave me behind."

Guess the joke was on him.

Taking a deep breath, Colm crept forward, maybe fifty feet away from the person who killed his best friend, Chase, and Chase's girlfriend. No way...they weren't really dead. It couldn't be real.

The killer paced back and forth, back and forth...looking for something. "I can't find the damn shells...never mind. I'll come back for them."

After a hissed cursed and a vicious kick at the van's tire, the shooter disappeared into the night. The moment the killer disappeared, Colm darted toward the bodies. He ended up next to Chase even as he glanced over at Lorna.

Gone. Eyes dulled, sightless. Flesh shredded.

He couldn't help them now. They were dead. Colm fumbled

through the leaves and pine needles littering the ground to grab a bullet casing. Dirt embedded itself under his nails as he searched for more. Finding a second one, he slipped them both into his pocket. Then he looked back at the immovable van.

No cell service. Zero options.

Colm couldn't just leave them out here for animals to feast on. No way. He unlocked the van and grabbed his rifle before he moved back into the woods, where he'd passed some softer ground. He started digging graves by hand, making slow, miserable progress.

The faint rumble of an ATV sent a chill straight through him. Colm crouched low, gripping the rifle until his knuckles whitened. His hands, blistered and dirtied from the digging, burned against the stock. The ATV stopped near the van, and Colm inched closer, rifle raised. He watched the killer load Chase and Lorna's bodies onto the back. Colm's muscles tensed, every instinct telling him to shoot. He just needed to calm down enough...

The engine roared to life, drowning out his scream as the killer disappeared into the trees, leaving Colm in the darkness that wrapped around him like a bad dream. Eventually, he packed a bag—stainless water bottle, three plastic ones, unopened jumbo bag of trail mix, an extra hoodie, gloves, socks, underclothes, his beanie, and whatever he could grab, stuffing it all into his pack. He locked the van behind him, out of habit, and left the campsite.

He slung his backpack on, shoved a half-empty box of ammo into his pocket, and shouldered the rifle. He followed the ATV's tracks, which led him deeper into the park, and hopefully, right toward the person who'd murdered his friends.

# ONE
## WEDNESDAY

CHARLIE APPEARED in the doorway to his office where Cynthia stood, a memo in her hand. His dark eyes widened as his brown hair fell in disheveled clumps of waves across his forehead, just as it had when she'd met him in grad school. The building had been similar to this one, with its three-story red brick exterior and slightly musty, small offices that boasted a window and not much else to set it apart from any other bureaucratic edifice.

"What are you doing in here?" Charlie asked.

"What's this?" Cynthia asked, in counterpoint to his less critical question. Guilt crept into his expression.

"It says the government plans to cut our grant money by *twenty-five* percent." Cynthia flicked through some mental calculations. "That means at least one, if not two, members will be lopped off the team."

"Not necessarily." Charlie wouldn't meet her gaze.

"You and Matt discussed this already. *Without* me." When he didn't deny it, she clenched her fist around the memo. The edge of the paper dug into her skin.

Without this work, Cynthia would have *nothing* to show for decades of dedication to Charlie Bianchi and Matt Sorenson. She exited Charlie's office and headed down the hall toward Matt's lab.

"Dr. Bianchi?" Quincy, who shared a lab with Cynthia, stuck his head out the door of their lab to address her. Despite her divorce from Charlie, Cynthia never reverted to her maiden surname. She'd married Charlie before she'd published her first paper, and once Cynthia had established her academic credentials, she hadn't wanted to lose momentum. Changing her name to his had proven an idiotic choice, leaving her tied to Charlie forever.

"Give me a minute." Cynthia strode past Quincy's thin frame and hustled toward Matt's lab, annoyed by its usual jumbled messiness. Cynthia tapped her fist on the door frame. "Got a minute?"

Matt looked up from his computer screen. He scanned her expression, his lips pressing together. "No."

"Make time," Cynthia snapped.

He held up his hands. "I don't want to get into—"

"The fact that you and Charlie left me out of some important fiscal conversations?" She inhaled, steadying herself. "How long have you known?"

Matt cursed under his breath, spreading an iciness through Cynthia's veins. "Charlie told you? Look, I planned to talk to you when I got back. Next week."

"That didn't answer my question." Like Charlie, he remained mulishly silent. "You owe me, Matt," Cynthia said.

Matt narrowed his eyes. "Really, Cyn? You want to hash that out now?"

"Yes."

"I don't like that implication."

"And I don't like that you knew my then-husband was having an affair." Cynthia hesitated. "Just as you won't like it when I tell you Mindy's—"

A grimace of pain slithered across Matt's face, and Cynthia's heart cracked in sympathy. To find out that people close to you knew and hid the affair...that hurt more than the infidelity itself.

Matt squared his shoulders and faced her. "Hurting me won't change the outcome of my divorce, and it won't change the outcome of what's best for the research project."

"Actually, it will. Charlie's former student reported him for ethical violations, and the chatter in the department about you and Lavinia has grown since your divorce proceedings started." Cynthia raised her eyebrows. "The dean's stated his zero-tolerance for such relationships."

"You *know* I'm not in a relationship with Lavinia."

"She told Quincy you divorced Mindy for her."

"That's total B.S." Matt's chest heaved. "What the actual hell, Cyn?"

"I'm repeating what I've been told. Lavinia says you're in love with her, that you plan to make her a lead on this project." Cynthia crossed her arms. "Over my dead body, will you move that grad student above my name on this research. I'd go to the dean about conflict of interest and ethical violations if you try, Matt."

Matt snapped his jaw shut. "Are you blackmailing me?"

"No. I'm stating that I'm the *only one* of us who doesn't have an issue with inappropriate behavior. And I'm the only one—"

"And you'd do that? Get me kicked off *my* research project?" Matt snapped.

"It's not yours, Matt. It's *ours*."

Matt's jaw worked. "I was wrong not to include you in the initial conversation, but I never once recommended we remove you. Not then. Now, however, you better believe I take serious offense to what you just laid out. Make sure that's what you want, Cynthia."

"This isn't about *want*." If it were, so many details of her life would be different. "It's about *my* career." She raised her chin and peered down her nose. "You took my pride when you lied to me about Charlie. You took my options when you and Charlie blocked me from becoming dean." She smiled without humor when Matt's mouth fell open. "Yeah, I know about that. So do not think, for one minute, that this is even a tit-for-tat situation. I state again, *you owe me*, Matt."

"I didn't...never mind. Your statement's been noted." Matt unclenched his hands and turned away to grab his chair. "Get out."

Cynthia turned on her heel, her guts roiling and her hands clammy.

"Oh, good." Quincy beamed at her from the door of her lab, between Matt's and Charlie's. "I wanted to show you the latest migration results."

"About my two wolves?" Cynthia had been following a pair without telling Matt and Charlie.

Something about these two animals intrigued her, not just their move away from the other wolves' territory but the slow pace at which they did so. Cynthia believed something else was going on with them. The cause could be ill health, pregnancy, or injury, but she couldn't be sure without more data and eyes on the specimens.

If Charlie and Matt planned to boot her...well, she'd gather as much information about these two animals as possible. They were her research. *Hers* alone. Good thing she'd kept them to herself.

"Show me," she said, her tone harsher than intended.

Quincy glanced up at her with wide eyes. "Er...everything all right?"

Cynthia folded the memorandum and tucked it away in her pants pocket. "It will be, especially if we can prove those wolves broke away for a good reason." Cynthia might be able to get her own funding if her hypothesis proved correct. Then she wouldn't need either Matt or Charlie.

Quincy flung himself into his chair and grinned as he pointed at his screen. "You're going to *love* this."

Cynthia and Quincy huddled around her lab's main computer, reviewing the day's data. The two wolves had broken off from the former pack and traversed the terrain over a few weeks, plodding but with purpose. They'd settled into an area Cynthia knew had a warren of shallow caves carved into the rocky outcropping...an imperfect place for a den. Since settling in just last week, only the alpha male had been jaunting into the surrounding forest. He'd made concentric rings around the space.

"The behavior is congruent with a male marking his territory." Cynthia tried not to get excited. She'd been right. Oh, did that feel *good*. Redemptive.

"And our female's stayed put. Do you think that means pups?" Quincy asked.

A triumphal smile tugged at her lips. "Yes. I think that's *exactly* what our current data suggests."

"So...should we ask Dr. Sorenson to check on them?" Quincy asked.

Cynthia hesitated. Matt planned to go into the park, and he'd walk within a few miles from where the two wolves she'd been tracking had set up their home. There would be severe repercussions—like getting kicked off the project—if she didn't share this data because Jane and Matt were nearby and could gauge the wolves' health...and find out if there were indeed pups. But she'd burned any goodwill with Matt moments earlier with her threat, and Charlie looked out for himself. That man had charmed his way out of worse situations more than once. She couldn't trust either of them.

She sure as hell shouldn't be protecting them either. They'd never shown her the same consideration and they never would.

"Dr. Bianchi?"

"You know what, Quincy? Leave the follow-up to me." Cynthia shot him a smile to ease the blow.

Quincy studied her for a long moment before he nodded. Having a follower for a graduate assistant had benefits. Quincy would not push her authority.

Cynthia was *pretty* sure she could trust him, too. But pretty sure wasn't the same as sure.

"I'm going to head out for a bit." She grabbed her jacket from the back of her chair...along with one of the satellite phones the team used to communicate within the park. She tucked it under her coat and hugged it to her chest.

"Right now?" Quincy asked, eyes rounding. "But..."

"Take the rest of the day off. You did great work. And remember, I want to surprise Matt and Charlie with this." She pinned him in place with her stare. "So, I need your discretion."

Once Quincy left, she moved the folder to her personal files and changed the machine's password before shutting it down. She then put a sticky note on it, citing the need for system maintenance.

She glanced at the clock, picked up her bundle, and headed toward the exit.

# DEEP IN THE FOREST

## THURSDAY

Colm's stomach growled as he trudged along the ATV tracks, twisting around large pine trees and scaling boulders. He reached for his water bottle, only to find it nearly empty. His muscles ached from the second night spent on the hard ground, and his mind raced with images of Chase and Lorna's lifeless bodies. He should have saved them.

He kicked a rock out of his path. The rifle's weight on his shoulder was a constant reminder of his failure. Colm veered away from the tracks to a narrow stream a few hundred yards to his left. He washed his hands in the clear water of a stream for what seemed like hours. Filling his water bottle, he stood and stretched. From the corner of his eye, he saw a large, sleek mountain lion creeping toward him.

Dropping his bottle, he grabbed the Ruger and fired. The animal fled, so he didn't think he hit the mountain lion. Colm leaned against a tree. The enormity of his situation slammed into his gut. He was alone in the wilderness, chasing after a murderer, with dwindling supplies and *no actual plan.*

He'd been stupid to leave. He'd been too afraid to stay.

"Keep moving. Find the killer. Make things right," he muttered as he gripped the rifle tighter.

# TWO

AFTER HER FINAL class that Thursday, Jane Sorenson met her father at his lab at Montana State University because he needed the most recent migratory map and data. The wolves' day-of movements would help them choose the best route for the most sightings during their week-long hike into the park.

Much as Jane didn't really want to spend the first week of September hiking, she couldn't turn her father down, especially when this trip would afford her independent study credits. Plus, her father spoke to her other professors to ensure they understood the importance of Jane missing one of their classes. He'd gone to such effort, and it was a fantastic opportunity, also seeing as he sweetened the pot with a glorious fifteen-day Italian vacation he'd take her on in three months.

Jane had been dying to go to Italy for years. The history, the food, and the beautiful countryside all called to her. So, she'd agreed to this time with her father.

Early afternoon sunshine spilled through the dingy window onto her father's equipment, some of which looked like it came from NASA circa 1994. It was big, bulky, and unsophisticated next to the sleek new desktop computer that stored all his current data. The reason he had the old stuff was because it held the earliest migration patterns on the wolves, and it had been too time-consuming to move over.

While Jane sat in the office chair her mother bought him when he earned tenure, she eyed Lavinia Jones, the twenty-seven-year-old grad student who snuggled up close to her father when he entered the door.

Jane admitted Lavinia was pretty, and clearly intelligent, but her breathy voice annoyed Jane more than her sleek dark hair and soulful eyes could draw her in. Then again, Lavinia wasn't interested in Jane, though the woman had the sense to be nice to her.

"Here's some new data, Dr. Sorenson...*Matt*," she said. Lavinia was part of why her mother had served her father with papers.

"No, Lavinia, this data set isn't consistent with the rest of the information we gathered." He seemed distracted as he finished AirDropping files to his phone from his laptop. He closed the computer and tapped out a rhythm on its lid.

When Lavinia laid her hand atop his, her father frowned and stepped back. "Cynthia has a point," he mumbled.

Jane raised an eyebrow. Cynthia did, huh? Jane hadn't seen her today, though she'd popped into her lab on the way. She'd been surprised to find the room dark and empty, the machines shut off. She planned to ask her dad about that once they were alone.

Lavinia moved toward him again. "Matt, if you'd let me come with you, I could—"

"No," her dad cut in. "That's *not* a possibility. You have exams to grade and a lecture to prepare for. *That's* the reason you're here. Now, I don't know how you got it in your head that I was interested in you romantically, but it's not true." Lavinia opened her mouth, but Matt held up his hand. "Jane and I are going to check in on the wolf packs' newly established hunting grounds. Alone."

"But Dr. Bianchi said that if I had additional time with the animals, my name would be listed—"

"The answer is no." He used *that* voice, which Jane recognized for its finality. Lavinia would do well to stop pushing. She wouldn't like the result.

Lavinia seemed to have forgotten Jane existed. That felt familiar. Scott, Jane's ex-boyfriend, had done that, too. It took him weeks to realize he should break up with her rather than try to control her feelings and actions. Jane swiveled the chair again, harder, annoyed by her memories of Scott.

*The guys said you were flirting with Morris. My girlfriend doesn't flirt with other guys.*

*Don't use your knee as an excuse, Jane. You're* my *girlfriend, so you really need to come to cheer for me at my competition.*

After months of Scott's comments about who she talked to, how she dressed, and whether she was being too "bummed out" over her blown ACL and scholarship, Scott broke up with her. Good riddance, too. She hadn't realized just how much better she felt without his stifling presence in her life, but now that she was starting her senior year and looking toward a career, she knew Scott was not the man she wanted by her side.

Jane spun back in time to see Lavinia's lower lip quiver. "You'd take me off the research paper?" The woman's voice turned thin, like she couldn't fathom such a response.

Jane stilled the chair as she awaited her father's answer. For him to threaten removal from the paper Lavinia needed to cement her career would be professionally devastating.

"Yes, I'd take you off it. Even though I've treated you as I do all my grad students, let me be clear: I am not interested in any type of relationship outside of a professor-student one."

Talk about awkward. Her father's face turned as red as Lavinia's, but he stood firm. So, Jane guessed she could cross a tryst off her dad's short list of screw-ups. That realization cracked something open in Jane's chest...an aching she hadn't acknowledged as she'd listened to her mother rant about Matt's alleged relationship with the grad student.

"You...you *bastard*!" Lavinia bolted from the room. Her father rested his palms on the table's top, bowing his head.

"Mom thought you were having an affair with her," Jane said because she couldn't seem to keep her fool mouth shut.

"Ironic, considering who was having an affair, wouldn't you say?" he responded, his voice sharp but not directed toward Jane.

"You knew?" Jane asked.

"I know *now*." His eyes took on this sheen that told her he'd been devastated to learn his wife cheated. Jane nibbled at her lip, wondering if she should tell her father about her mom and Charlie.

Nope, no way. What would it solve now? Jane knew that her mother had moved on to a new man. Plus, her father and Charlie Bianchi had been friends for decades. He'd been a staple at her parents' house when she was growing up. Charlie had shown her how ants brought items back to their hills and scented the ground to return to food sources. Charlie played ping-pong with her long after her parents quit, and he'd been more than happy to motorboat her through a pond or lake while her mom sunbathed on the beach shore.

Charlie was family, and Jane didn't want to destroy what little her father had left.

But Jane took the moment to acknowledge she hadn't navigated her parents' messy divorce proceedings well because she'd been too caught up in the misery of her lost Dartmouth dream... and then the Scott fiasco she'd brought on herself.

"In Mom's defense, Lavinia is very...um..."

"Clingy." Her father sighed. "I wished your mother had talked to me, that I'd understood how much it bothered your mother. How it looked to others in the department..." He looked like he wanted to say something else. "Cynthia brought it to my attention yesterday."

"Wouldn't have changed the outcome." She rose and stretched. Even though she'd had her second surgery months ago, she still got stiff. "Mom had already decided, and you know how she gets."

His face fell, his eyes darkening. He hadn't wanted the separation, let alone a divorce, and had asked Jane's mother to consider counseling. She'd refused both options. The hardest part for Jane was that she was technically an adult. And, while twenty-two-year-old Jane Langford Sorenson had no interest in hearing about her parents' problems, her mother overshared. That proclivity worsened as Jane had gotten older, fueled by the long hours her dad worked.

"Where is Cynthia?" Jane asked, trying to change the subject.

Her father blew out a long breath. "I don't know, but she's mad at me, too."

"Wow. Cyn never gets mad. What did you do?"

Her dad's expression was pained. "It's what I didn't do, but that's my problem. You ready to show me what you remember of your mountaineering training?"

Clearly, he wanted to change the subject again. A heaviness had settled around him when the two discussed Jane's mother, but he'd finished that discussion...for now.

"Absolutely." Cyn was one of Jane's favorite people. She'd taken Jane on weekend trips into the wilderness in middle school, and Jane had loved them. She hadn't been recently. It was one more of the hobbies Jane had lost over the last few years. Even before Jane had hurt her knee, about the time she'd realized her parents' marriage was indeed broken, Jane had begun to insulate herself. Only now did she see how devastating that must have been to Cynthia, whom Jane had quit spending time with, and her father.

Her father's lids lowered. "I'll be sure to say a big thank you to Cynthia myself. When we get back, Cynthia and I have some stuff to work out."

"You're clearly upset. Anything I can do to help?" Jane asked.

"No, but thanks for the offer." He smiled. "I'll make sure that there's nothing awkward for you. Okay?"

"Yeah, that'd be good. Cyn's the best."

"She's been a better mom to you than your own."

Jane blinked as surprise swirled through her. Typically, her mother talked too much while her father kept his thoughts and feelings to himself.

She liked their new dynamic and wished they could have developed the easy rapport last year when she convalesced on his couch. That tiny spark that had flickered to life when her father suggested this trip flared a little brighter.

"I finalized my will last week," he said. "You're the primary beneficiary now."

Jane frowned. That was out of nowhere. "O-kay."

"I'm not dead yet," he said in a terrible British accent followed by an exaggerated wink.

"Good thing, I like having you around," Jane replied, deciding to ignore his silliness.

Her father clenched and unclenched his fists. "With the divorce finalized now, in case something happens to me, I didn't want you to fight your mother for financial security."

Mindy Sorenson was many things, and selfish sat high on the list.

"What does that even mean?" Jane asked.

"My father and I didn't see eye-to-eye on a lot of things, but he knew I was passionate about conservation and ecology. He set up the initial grant for our wolf study."

"I had no idea," Jane said. "That was generous."

"Very. No one else knows either, but he's paid my salary for most of the past decade through that grant. It's run its course and we'll need a new funding source."

"I know the university's increased overhead because you told me that. What does it mean for your wolves?"

Her father closed his eyes. "Inflation's way up, and the department head suggested we cut summer salaries, which is about a quarter of my income. It's...not good." He cleared his throat and offered a half smile. "But that's not important *right now*. I just wanted to make sure everything was set to rights, and the divorce was the catalyst."

Her father shot her a partial smile, distracting Jane from his emphasis on the now. She'd never asked about her parents' financial situation or needed to. She had everything she needed and more.

When Jane fell in love with Dartmouth, paying for an elite East Coast private school hadn't been an issue. She knew that was because of her dad's father, James, and his sprawling oil and gas company. But Jane couldn't stomach returning to Dartmouth for her senior year without her soccer friends. It had only been a year since the rest of her would-be teammates moved into that house together. Knowing she couldn't be part of that camaraderie had *hurt*.

It still did.

Her decision to transfer to MSU probably didn't make sense, but Jane was also coming to terms with that. Slowly.

"What are you saying?" Jane asked, not liking the deep swoop and dip in her tummy. Her father's mood remained off. Now that she thought about it, Jane realized her father had been distracted. It was very unlike him. When Jane was around, he focused on her.

"You know that trust fund your grandfather set up was *always* yours, so if you want to go to Dartmouth after this year—"

"Stop. Please. I'm graduating in May." Jane wrinkled her nose, disliking the talk about the trust fund even more than she disliked talking about Dartmouth. Her mother brought it up often—how James Sorenson skipped his son and daughter-in-law and left all his money to his granddaughter. Not that Jane could access the funds until she was twenty-five. Jane remained ambivalent about that money, especially after her mother's temper tantrums over the years and her father's estrangement from the man she'd barely known.

"You're not going to do something stupid, are you? Like take up bouldering this trip. Because my knee's not up to that kind of a scramble. Or bungee jumping?"

"No. And I'm glad you know your limits." He glanced around the lab, seeming to recalibrate. "Ready to head out?"

"Sure." Jane frowned as she remained unsettled by the conversation's turn. Her father was in his early fifties—the prime of his life. He was fit and ate well. The idea of something happening to him...

She considered telling her father that her leg hurt for a split second. Then Jane caught her father's bright smile as he beckoned her. As she sauntered toward him, the lack of direct sunlight cast a deep gloom, causing her to shiver again. The sun slid out from behind the single, thick gray cloud that puffed in the blue sky.

Just a chill from the lack of light.

"LOOK AT THAT VIEW." Jane's father pulled into an empty parking lot a good hour from the ranger station where they'd met Betty, the ranger, on duty.

Awe clung to the words and settled into her dad's expression, and with that look came a necessary flash of insight. Jane's mother had told Jane that her father cheated on her, but Mindy hadn't understood Matt. This—Yellowstone—was his *love*.

Some of Jane's worries about her future melted away as she feasted on the panorama: bristly, green-and-brown pines marched outward toward jagged, white-capped peaks that glittered under a broad dome of blue sky. An early snowfall. Granted, those were high elevations, but Jane didn't like the idea of snow this soon.

Just by looking at its majesty, Jane could understand why the National Park Service incorporated the land into the national trust.

Wilderness surrounded them, with more to come. Jane and her father were at least twenty miles from the closest town of Coulter Bay, but sixty from the *true* civilization of Jackson. Once through the eastern park entrance, they'd entered a rugged pitch of pine forest, dotted with small yellow flowers near the road. They'd crossed the Snake River as they off-roaded, by special dispensation from the park service, toward the location her father had chosen for tonight's rendezvous with a wolf pack.

The faint scent of pine leaked through the SUV's closed-in cabin. A smile winged the edges of her mouth. Pleasure bubbled up into her throat. She'd missed nature, its majesty.

"Thanks, Dad."

"What for?"

"I...needed this. I think, maybe, I've been depressed."

Her father glanced at her from the corner of his eye. "I'm a good listener, Jane. I'd love for you to talk to me."

"Dartmouth. Soccer. The first surgery failing. The long recovery that brought me home midway through my junior year. Scott—not that he was much of a loss, but having a boyfriend seemed so important, like a...a rite of passage." Jane heaved a sigh that seemed to come from her toes. "You and Mom. Mostly, realizing Mom was..." Jane didn't want to say, *manipulating me against you*, knowing those words would hurt him. But they were true. She hurried on. "Transferring to Montana State. I'm getting a great education with professors that are really engaged, but, well, it just wasn't what I'd planned." Jane paused to breathe, thankful the rush of words was out of her, no longer ripping her apart mentally and emotionally. "I think that having to pivot after two and a half years, giving up that Ivy League dream, hit me hard. I've never quit anything before."

*I also never had to evaluate choices based on my capacity before. I've never had to worry about what career I'd pursue...*

"You dealt with a lot last year. Too much. I'm proud of you for admitting it was hard and for finding a way forward. That's courage, Jane. And you, my dear, have lots of it."

Her dad placed his large, callused palm over hers, giving a slight squeeze. Warmth suffused Jane at the gesture. It was so sincere. It was so lovely to know he cared about her and wanted her to know he was there for her.

"I'm glad we're together. In Yellowstone," she murmured.

"Me, too."

"I'm sorry I didn't see that—"

"Nope, we're not going back to self-recrimination. Either of us. I've missed spending time with you, hiking and camping."

Her dad's expression was a panicky blend of anxiety, love, and grief. To counter his struggle, Jane rolled her eyes. "You just want me to fall in love with Yellowstone, like you, so I'll help out on your project."

"Well..." her dad drawled, the pain receding in his eyes. "That would be nice for me. But you said you're interested in an outdoorsy career."

"Yes," Jane said. "I miss the hours of soccer practice. I feel better when I move."

"Come on, sweetie. Chin up, let's face this adventure." He smiled. "You always were a busy thing. Since you're interested in biology and arboriculture, you need to backpack."

Jane smiled as she opened the Jeep's door. Squinting against the sun, she took in her father as he stepped out of his vehicle.

Jane's mind returned to the adoring look Lavinia had shot him yesterday. Matt Sorenson was an amazing guy...and still a catch for some lucky lady.

*Not* Lavinia, who was much closer to Jane's age than his. Still, her father exuded that charisma that made students love his lectures and women like Lavinia moon over him.

Jane wanted him to find love. Her father deserved affection and to be someone's main focus. He'd spent much too long catering to Jane's mother.

"My chin's always up," Jane quipped, her gaze dropping to the vehicle's back seat.

Her father had a pile of blankets and additional outerwear there. But the weather forecast remained clear and warm enough not to warrant packing the extra gear.

She shouldered her pack. Matt had kept Jane's backpack light: less than ten pounds. Most of that was water and snacks, though she also had an ultralight, all-weather sleeping bag, some staple camping supplies, a small first-aid kit, the extra set of Jeep keys, and her toiletries. He had the rest of their supplies in his much heftier pack.

He chuckled. "I love your enthusiasm."

"I get it from you." She stuck out her tongue, and he laughed harder—a deep belly laugh that warmed Jane's chest and made her smile back. She'd forgotten how fun her father was. She vowed never to take him for granted again.

"You get most of your best qualities from me." As soon as the words left his mouth, her father sobered. Jane knew he was thinking about her mother, wishing for a different outcome.

"I do, you're right," she blurted. "These long legs helped me to win all kinds of soccer tournaments."

Now it was Jane's turn to sigh. Her soccer career was over. Sure, she could probably play again, but never with the same competitiveness. She'd always hold back a little, fearful of another injury, and that was the difference between a good and a stellar player. She offered her father a bittersweet smile. She shouldered her bag and slid her thumbs under the straps. "How many miles are we hiking today?" Jane asked.

"The first cabin is about ten miles away. I wanted to keep today's trek light."

Jane grunted. "Ten miles might be pushing it, even with the all-clear from my doctor."

"Then we'd better get started so we have lots of daylight to rest."

He opened the tailgate. He pulled out his large, gray pack, made of the same material as the two-person tent they'd share if they couldn't make it to the Army Corps cabins, and shrugged it on.

"You're sure we don't need those blankets in the back seat?" she asked, glancing at them.

"We shouldn't. Those and the water and nonperishables under them are for emergencies—like if we get separated and you need to return to the vehicle."

"We won't," Jane said.

"I won't leave you, Jane. You know that. Still, having a plan is important. So, if we do get separated, return to the Jeep, okay? I left an Air Tag and the key in the glove box in case you need to find your way back."

"Why?"

He shrugged. "If things go terribly, like I'm mauled by a bear, you might not be able to get the key off me. This way, you have an escape route."

"But we'll be fine." It came out more of a question than she'd intended.

Her father shot her an understanding smile as he checked his pack one last time. "You betcha."

He zipped the bag closed and hefted it onto his shoulder, and he morphed from an urbane scientist and professor into a rugged outdoorsman.

*Fascinating.*

"How long have you had that pack?" Jane asked.

He turned toward her as he pulled on his ball cap: an old Huskies one because she'd asked him not to wear the Dartmouth one he'd worn for the previous two and a half years. His eyes slid into shadow just as a cloud passed over the sun, and she shivered at the sudden drop in temperature.

"About ten years. I'll need another soon."

"Why didn't you buy it when we were at REI getting my stuff?"

"My current grant covers my equipment, but I prefer to spend that money on the wolves or research. I need little."

Jane pressed her lips together, so she didn't express her thoughts aloud: that her mother, Mindy, was the opposite. But that comment wouldn't be helpful, and her parents had blown past Jane's limit for strife. If Jane hadn't let recklessness supersede her good sense, she wouldn't have destroyed her ACL's repair and spent nearly another year rehabbing it.

Today, her father could further her education on survival techniques she'd taken in middle school and learned with him on various weekend camping trips while he checked on some collar transmitter issues.

Jane glanced up for one last look at the Jeep—and saw a face staring back at her.

*Lavinia's* face.

# DEEP IN THE FOREST

Colm had discovered the hidden ATV the previous night, but the killer hadn't been there. The absence of his friends' bodies on the ATV haunted him, but he pushed aside the urge to search for them, smash the ignition, or even to hot wire the vehicle. He'd also decided against finding a ranger to tell them what had happened. Justice was his primary goal now, not escape.

Each time he closed his eyes, he saw Lorna's brand-new engagement ring, which refueled his determination to take out the sick bastard.

The solitude weighed heavily on him, a constant reminder of Lorna and Chase's brutal murder, and he'd pushed himself for so long that he'd slept deeply into the morning. The grumble of the engine woke him. Colm's mad dash to shoot the killer caused him to leave his sleeping bag and gloves behind. Angry for *that* decision, he was even more infuriated with the killer for staying far enough ahead that Colm couldn't get off a clean shot—any shot—yet again.

As dusk settled over the forest, he questioned his life choices for a fleeting moment, wondering if military training might have better prepared him for this ordeal. The fading light transformed

Colm into a mere shadow among shadows. His hunger drove him to a nearby berry bush, but the familiar taste triggered a violent reaction. He retched memories of that fateful day flooding back—Lorna's biscuits, the planned celebration, and the horrific gunshot that shattered their lives.

Shaking and weak, Colm pushed himself away from the sickness even as his resolve hardened. He would make the killer pay for the pain they had caused.

# THREE

LAVINIA'S tousled head and wide, dark eyes stared back at Jane, panic settling in her face with a silent plea for Jane to remain quiet, going so far as to touch her fingertip to her lips.

Unaware of Jane's sudden turmoil, her father grabbed the two walking sticks from the Jeep and handed Jane one. While straight and smooth, the tip ended in a long, wicked-sharp point. She brushed her thumb across the tip, testing its edge. Wincing, she stuck the appendage in her mouth to take out the sting.

He chuckled. "Everyone does that the first time. Hold it with the sharp edge up. You don't want to dull it unless you have to."

Jane released her thumb, glad to see no droplets of blood pooled there. "Why do we need pointy sticks?"

He grabbed a Band-Aid and wrapped her thumb with efficiency. Then, after depositing the trash in a small bag, he closed the tailgate and checked his pockets. He picked up his stick from the side of the vehicle and looked around.

Jane glanced into the back seat. The blankets were shifted, and Lavinia's dark hair streamed down the back seat to pool in the wheel well. She should tell her father.

"We're entering some of the most rugged terrain in the country." Jane brought her gaze back to her father. He needed to know Lavinia was in his vehicle. He'd be so mad, maybe follow through on the threat to remove her from the project...

While Jane could sympathize with Lavinia, stowing away crossed so many lines.

"Once we leave the Jeep behind, we enter the *real* Yellowstone," her father said. "I need to know you'll listen to me, Jane. I need you to follow my instructions, okay?"

"Yeah." Maybe she could just pretend she hadn't seen Lavinia. That felt like a cop out, and, well, wrong.

"I'm serious. Parts of the landscape are uncharted, and we don't even know how many apex predators dot the park. Weather can turn on a dime." He waved, encompassing the expansive, majestic view in front of them.

"Yeah, I get that, Dad. Don't worry, I'll follow your instructions. You're the one with the experience."

"Yes. If I ask you to do something, do it, even if you don't want to. Out here, we're just another part of the food chain."

"You're *not* settling my nerves," Jane admitted.

"The most remote place in the country's entirety—one of the few places a person could stand over twenty miles from a road—is *here*. That's why it'll take us four, maybe five, days to get in and hike it back out."

Jane swallowed her nervousness. Her father was a veteran Yellowstone hiker. Jane wasn't a slouch when it came to wilderness camping. They would be fine.

*It's all about the attitude, Jane.*

"I hope we see a lynx," Jane said. "I've always been fascinated by them and only seen their relative, the bobcat." Their silky coats and beautiful tufted ears belied their cunning, predatory abilities to take down snowshoe hares.

"I know, and this sector is your best bet, Janie. Did you know that the word lynx comes from the Greek root 'leukos,' which means white? The best theory I've heard is that they named the cats that because of their eye reflection when caught in the light."

"That's interesting," Jane said. Much of what her dad knew fascinated Jane in a nerdy, going-to-win-at-trivia way.

"All right, so that didn't garner your interest. What about a grizzly?" Matt asked, voice low.

"What about one?" Jane replied.

He fumbled until he got his large-gauge shotgun around his pack and in front of him. "There's one right down in that gulch. You want to see it?"

Jane swallowed hard. No, but also *yes*. She crept around her father, heart hammering. The bear's rump faced them, the brown fur shimmying to lighter edges—like frosted tips—as the bear gnawed on his meal. A small tail twitched between its haunches, its face deep in berry brambles.

All thoughts of Lavinia fled her mind as she took in the large, hairy beast. It was much, much bigger in person. Scarier and yet... more relatable. This connection was what most people missed out on.

"Fattening up for hibernation," Dad said. "He seems to be intent on it. I bet he's keyed in on something we haven't."

"Like a long winter?" Jane asked.

"Possibly. Even with our sophisticated climate models, we seem to be at a disadvantage to the bears' internal weather warning system."

Jane hummed. That tidbit of biology fascinated her, but she refused to let work overshadow the rest of her life. Jane stepped back and shoved her hands into her pockets. "I hope that grizzly stays occupied with its current food source."

"No such luck," her father murmured.

The bear whirled toward them as he spoke, enormous jaws working the berries. The juice dribbled past his lips and into the fur, staining it the same dark red as its long teeth. His nose twitched as he snuffed, seeming to home in on Jane and her father. With a grunt, the bear rose onto his back legs, taller than her father, his shaggy coat matted with leaves. He growled long and low enough to send a chill from Jane's coccyx to her nape.

Her father motioned Jane to the right with his head. His hands were steady on the barrel of the firearm and the can of bear spray he'd pulled out of one of the pockets in his cargo pants. He pointed the container at the bear but kept the firearm in his right hand. She moved quickly while monitoring her footfalls and without running, as he'd taught her. The bear watched them, head cocked, as they rounded a bend and continued their methodical pace for another quarter mile before her father pulled a handkerchief from the breast pocket of his blanketed plaid shirt and mopped his forehead. He kept his other hand on his shotgun.

"Whew. That was pretty close."

"Closer than I needed to be." Jane wrinkled her nose. "That bear *stunk*."

Her dad chuckled. They fell back into their stride and continued their hike.

"You know, back when Lewis and Clark were traversing the country for the first time, we believe there were over fifty thousand grizzlies in North America."

Jane digested that tidbit and ignored her father's eyebrow quirk. He knew she found bears interesting.

Ah.

No wonder he'd brought her into the park. The sneaky devil! He expected her to fall in love with the wolves or another animal. Clearly, her father was delusional in hoping for her to work with him in his lab.

But Jane needed to make her own choices about her career. Jane admitted that being outside, in nature, appealed to her, and she'd enjoyed her science courses—specifically dendrology. She hadn't admitted it aloud yet, but Dartmouth didn't have a strong program when it came to the study of trees. Western universities did, and Montana State had a program focused on plant pathology. Jane had loaded her semester with as many as possible, and so far, she'd enjoyed each lecture.

She just wasn't ready to announce her decision *quite* yet. She didn't think her dad would be disappointed, but she wasn't ready for her mother's constant comments.

"How many bears are there now?" Jane asked, returning to the conversation at hand.

"Less than two thousand in the lower forty-eight. Most of them are in or between Yellowstone and Glacier National Park," her father said, switching into lecturer mode, telling Jane that more than a thousand animals were roaming the greater Yellowstone region in the early part of the decade, and the bears' occupied habitat had risen by half since the seventies. Jane narrowed her eyes. She saw right through his ploy.

"Cool as that is, I'd still rather see a lynx."

"More than a wolverine? You used to be fascinated by them as a kid," her dad said, sensing her slipping interest.

Jane shook her head. "Outgrew that interest once I realized how *scary* they are."

"Any wild animal can be scary," he said. "The predators, at least, have claws and teeth and jaws made from trapping and eating prey."

They walked along the path that had widened enough to be shoulder to shoulder. Jane tipped her head back, enjoying the dapples of light that filtered through the rustling branches.

"But a lynx won't take on a bear like a wolverine will. Those suckers don't even weigh a hundred pounds—so, like an eighth of the bear's size, and they go after bears who cross into their territory."

"They go after any critter that crosses into their territory," Dad pointed out. No doubt to him, that seemed reasonable.

Jane side-stepped an enormous granite boulder. "That's *insane.*"

"Not when their young or food source is threatened."

"Too many sharp teeth and a nasty attitude, so no thanks."

He tsked. "Well, there are only seven known wolverines in the park, and in my nearly thirty years in the park, I've never seen one."

Jane released a gusty sigh. "Good."

A pine branch stuck out at head height for her dad. He ducked under it as he continued talking, and Jane let her mind drift. She'd heard this lecture about the importance of keystone species so often that she could probably recite it verbatim.

Once he came up for air, Jane jumped in. "Um...so, the wolves' territory varies based on the number of potential food sources in the area, right?"

"And geographical features, how many people are in the area...so, that got me wondering why so few wolves are down in this part of the park."

Her father turned, giving her his profile. Beyond him, Jane caught a movement. She squinted, unsure why she'd noted that particular—

Predatory but not. She tipped her head, eyes straining. Was it Lavinia? She was going to have to mention the woman after all.

"That's what we're here to check," Dad said. "The radio collars show that most of the wolves moved north, which would indicate—"

"Fewer elk, deer, moose, and other ungulates or prey species here," Jane said. "I...don't understand the fall-off in numbers, though. I mean, if this is the most pristine topography in the country, then why wouldn't it be crawling with animals?"

"Because it's also inhospitable terrain." He waved his hand over the jagged rocks that jutted from the earth, keeping the land too uneven for a meadow. "Look, if I'm boring you with this—"

"You're not. I promise. I...I thought I saw something." She jutted her chin in the direction of the thing she'd noted coming toward them. Now, though, there was nothing.

"The bear?" He peered back, pulling out his bear spray once again.

"No." She opened her mouth, then closed it. Her father had been enjoying himself. She didn't want to ruin this time. "It was nothing. Sorry, Dad."

He looked out at the horizon. "There's nothing for you to apologize for. *I'm* the one who messed up with your mother, Jane. I'm trying not to make the same mistakes again. Not with you. Our relationship is too important to me."

His intentions were good. Her father wanted to spend time with her, and he knew she enjoyed the fauna in the park. He'd set this up so they could discover one of her passions together.

"You didn't. And I'm sorry. You're important to me, too." She nudged him with her shoulder.

He still appeared sad, so she said, "I love you, Dad. You know that. And I may be wary about this trip, but I know it's going to be a grand adventure."

He softened further, his eyes filled with devotion and a little humor at her use of his lingo. "Love you, too, Jane."

"Enough mushy! Let's talk radio collars." Jane clasped her hands under her chin, batting her lashes up at him. "Please? If we're lucky, we'll get to check some, right?"

"If we're lucky."

They walked for another few hours, and her father showed her edible flora like the wild buckwheat and verbena that sprouted willy-nilly along their path as they walked. After a lunch of jerky, trail mix, and a couple of oranges, her dad gave Jane a refresher in navigation, a skill Jane hadn't used since middle school. He had smiled as Jane set their course for the afternoon.

It was late afternoon when a pop echoed through the woods, causing Jane to startle. "What was that?"

Matt pursed his lips, head tilted as the noise echoed through the woods. Worry settled with sickly surety in Jane's belly. She really didn't want to have to bring this up. Jane understood enough about academia to know that getting kicked off the research project would end Lavinia's career.

A chill crept over Jane's skin as she thought about what desperate people did. Jane had pushed too hard in rehab and then taken to the soccer pitch too soon, destroying any chance of ever playing for Dartmouth, and nearly ruining her chances of walking properly because of her myopia.

"It sounded like a gunshot." Jane focused on her dad, wanting him to tell her she was wrong.

Matt's frown intensified as he scanned their surroundings. "I hope not. No one else is in the park right now. Well, there are always a few rangers, but you know the park pretty much shuts down after Labor Day."

Jane, who scanned the terrain, swung back to face her father. "That's not exactly true..."

Surprise flooded Matt's face. "Really? What do you know?"

Jane bit her lip, almost wishing she hadn't said anything. "The blankets in the back seat. They moved. And...and...I saw Lavinia."

"What? Why didn't you say something? My God, Jane—" Anger cascaded over Matt's face, building into boiling fury. "*Lavinia* was in my car—with us?"

"Yeah," Jane said.

Her father's fury grew more fearsome. "We'll call it in to the team at the university, but I'm not circling back to check on her."

Jane's pulse fluttered as panic gnawed up her spine. "But...if she has a gun.... Dad, could Lavinia be dangerous? Would she..."

The rest of the sentence hung there between them. Bushes rustled nearby, and they both turned, craning their necks to see what was flailing through the foliage. Clearly, that gunshot had caused multiple wildlife to flee the area.

Her dad's expression hardened into stone. "This is *our* time, Jane. I'm not letting Lavinia ruin that."

More rustling. Matt pulled his rifle from his pack, checked it was loaded, and trained it on the area from where the sound emanated, slowly getting closer.

Jane opened her mouth and shut it, considering her options. "What if Lavinia's hurt?"

"I hope like hell she isn't." He peered at Jane. "You're sure?"

Jane nodded. "Yeah. I'm sure."

Matt pulled out his satellite phone as he handed Jane the rifle. He dialed a number, held the sleek device to his ear, and motioned to take back the firearm. Jane was happy to comply.

"Voice mail," he muttered. He left a message, then dialed another number. "Cynthia, I'm glad I caught you."

He listened for a moment. "What?"

His frown intensified again. "No. I haven't talked to Charlie about that. Look, we have a pressing issue. Jane says Lavinia climbed into the back seat of my Jeep and came into the park. You know I haven't had and will not have anything to do with that woman, Cynthia! Don't start with me on that right now. Look, there was a possible gunshot a moment ago. I didn't leave a firearm in the Jeep, so it's not mine."

He listened, and so did Jane, to an animal's running. Her dad narrowed his eyes and stepped closer to Jane.

"I left a message at the park service's main line, but Jane and I have to cover another few miles. Oh, and can you track the Air Tag I left in the Jeep—see if it's moved?"

Jane was impressed that her dad had used the tech. It was simple and could be synched to his normal cell phone, which he'd left back at the lab. He'd also synched the small tracking device to

Jane's phone. He was definitely savvier with the latest gadgets than her mother.

Her father listened, shaking his head. "I'm going to file an EEOC detailing her sexual harassment when I get back. She needs to be kicked out of the university, not just off the project and out of my lab."

Lavinia burst through the underbrush, panting and sweaty, too pale and wild-eyed. She held a rifle—a Henry—out to the side. "You can't do that to me!"

Jane's pulse thrummed, and fear made her lightheaded. She stepped closer to her father while he dropped the satellite phone to steady his rifle as he glared at Lavinia. "Drop your rifle *now*."

"You *can't*. Everyone will know, and I'll never find another position—"

"That's something you should have thought about before you pursued me," her father said.

Lavinia's lower lip wobbled, but she lowered the Henry, pointing it toward the dirt. Jane bent down and picked up the phone. She dusted off the thick, military-grade covering.

"Matt!" Cynthia called through the phone. "Let me talk to her."

Her dad scowled, but he offered Lavinia the phone. Jane held her breath as the other woman pressed it to her ear with shaking hands. "Y-yes?"

Lavinia raised her gaze toward Jane's dad. Tears filmed her eyes, spiking her lashes. "I *need* this position. I *need* the authorship. It's all I've ever wanted. Dr. Bianchi—"

Lavinia listened. She lowered her head, a flush burning up her neck and over her cheeks in a tidal wave of contrition.

"Okay."

Lavinia handed the phone back to Jane's father. "I'll wait here for a ranger to collect me." She wiped her nose on her sleeve. Jane cringed but guessed it didn't really matter. Just...

*gross*. "I have a satellite phone, too, so I'll be able to call for help."

"Good." Her father stared at Lavinia's rifle for a moment. "Don't point that weapon at us, understand?"

"Yes, Dr. Sorenson."

"And you'll give up this romantic nonsense between us?" he asked.

The grad student gave a short, sharp nod as her face crumpled.

Jane's adrenaline eased as she watched the older woman sniffle. While Jane's pulse still thrummed in her throat, she grabbed her dad's wrist and squeezed. "Give me a minute." She tipped her head toward Lavinia.

Her father pursed his lips but backed away—just not that far. He wasn't going to let anything happen to Jane. She rounded toward the older woman. "Don't make this worse."

"How can it be worse?" Lavinia asked. Tears spilled down her cheeks, landing on her hiking boots.

"I'll talk to Dad." Jane kept her voice low and steady, though she didn't feel anywhere near as confident. "But you can't keep bugging him. He said no. Think about when you say no—you mean it, right?"

"Yes."

"Respect his right to that, too." Jane pointed to the rifle. "You know how to use it?"

"Yes."

"Good. We saw a grizzly. I don't want you to get hurt."

"I know. I did, too."

Understanding dawned. "You shot it."

"No," Lavinia said. "I shot *at* it when it lunged at me. It ran away. I know about poaching in the park, and I wasn't going to jail for a bear I didn't want to kill."

"Okay," Jane offered, like an olive branch.

Lavinia raised her gaze to Jane's. "I'm sorry. About your dad. I shouldn't have pushed him."

"No, you shouldn't have."

Lavinia opened her mouth, pursed her lips, and shook her head.

"What?" Jane asked.

Lavinia's gaze seemed far away, and she took a moment to answer Jane...as if she were thinking. "Office politics."

Jane snorted at the non-answer.

Her dad returned from the other side of the clearing, "Let's go, Jane."

Lavinia headed to a large, flat-topped boulder. She settled on it. After a brief hesitation, Jane followed her father back down the trail.

"Do you think she'll be okay?" she asked, panting a little from the effort of catching up.

"With the ranger? Of course. She'll feel better once she's back at the university and has had a chance to get past her embarrassment. Cynthia said she'd check in with her early next week. Talk to Lavinia about moving to her lab. That way, Lavinia will keep her spot on the research project, but I won't have to deal with her directly."

"That might be a good idea. What else did Cynthia say?" Jane asked.

Matt waved his hand. "Nothing important."

Jane fell into step beside him. "I'm sorry I didn't say anything back at the Jeep."

"We would have had to take Lavinia back to the ranger station ourselves. At least this way, we're not starting over. Let's just enjoy the hike and the good weather."

Jane understood that her father was finished talking about his graduate student. She peered up at the sliver of blue sky. "You think that'll change?"

"This is Yellowstone, Janie. The only maxim that applies is to be ready for anything."

"Is that why you like backpacking in here? Is it an adrenaline rush?"

Her dad walked, and she followed. He pushed on for a good half mile before he answered.

"I think you might be on to something there. I wasn't ever one to sky dive or bungee jump but coming out here...being as close to the land as our ancestors, living off it like they did...turning off the electronics, going back to my senses, my wits...I like that."

"I can understand why," Jane said. "I mean, so much of our world is artificial. What time you have to be at work, or me at class. When to eat, when I go to bed, wake up...that's all decided by the activities I planned, not by anything concrete, not really. We're all tied into the clock, completing tasks that have no value outside getting me closer to a degree and you a paycheck."

"That's one reason..." He trailed off, then cleared his throat. "My point was that I like it out here. I like having this...complete autonomy over my life, my decisions."

Jane's father stopped at the edge of a meadow. On the other side, a lake—deep, based on the shocking blue color—reflected the sky and puffy white clouds off the water.

"Whoa." Jane breathed out the word almost as a prayer.

"Yeah. Whoa. This is one of my favorite spots."

Jane let her gaze drift over the terrain, feeling off balance by the inverted images in the water, the sun's brightness after the forest's shadows.

*Nothing could have prepared me.*

She had no idea how true those words would become.

# DEEP IN THE FOREST

The earthy scent of sweat hit his nose. Never had he been so glad to smell that.

It meant he was near people.

He hesitated some distance back in the trees when he heard the anger in the man's voice. Colm moved close enough to see three people: an angry older dude, a crying woman, and a younger woman.

Two had rifles, which had Colm's finger twitching on the trigger of the Ruger American Predator. It had a twenty-two-inch barrel. Lightweight. Deadly accurate from a distance. Perfect for this scenario, but he couldn't shoot yet. He had to be sure it was the killer. He craned his neck to see their footwear.

Not blue. He settled back against a rock, unwilling to shoot someone unless he was sure. Exhaustion pulled him under, and he woke with a start, springing upward, whipping his rifle forward as an ATV engine rumbled closer.

Blinking his bleary eyes, he noted the older of the two women who'd been fighting with the older guy sat on a rock, crying.

As he considered going down there, asking to use her phone, the ATV broke into view.

If the killer was following Colm, if the killer had figured out Colm was a witness to Chase and Lorna's death...

Colm stumbled backward into some berries. Those damn berries...that scent that had haunted his short bursts of sleep drifted across the breeze, tickling his nose. He'd hate that smell until he died because the scent triggered memories of his friends' deaths, his fear, and his impotence.

Screams.

Gunshots.

Helplessness.

No! *No way*. He'd sworn retribution for his friends. Colm slid behind a tree, closed his left eye, and squinted with his right, lining up the shot like his dad had shown him ages ago the one time they'd gone hunting. Colm hadn't liked it, so they never went again.

Colm took a deep breath. Then another. *Focus on the shirt. Aim for the chest—that's your best shot.* From where he was, he could make out the back side of the dull brown National Park Service shirt.

He lowered his gun. No way he'd shoot a ranger. Still, that ATV was the same as the one he'd been following. He'd swear it.

Which meant...which meant...the ranger killed his friends, or Colm was wrong and this wasn't the same ATV.

Colm shifted, trying to get a better angle—to see if the boots were blue. Then, he'd know.

"I'm so glad to see you." The woman's voice carried high and thin through the still air. "You got here way sooner than I thought. I've been waiting a couple of hours."

The ranger made a motioning gesture toward Lavinia but didn't say a word.

She sped forward, only to stumble to a stop about three feet from the vehicle. Colm gnashed his teeth as she blocked his view of the ranger.

"Wait." Her voice shook. "What are you doing?"

Colm's finger shook on the trigger, and bile spurted up into his throat. If this wasn't the right person, Colm would be as much of a murderer as his friends' killer. But this could be his last shot at justice for Chase and Lorna. He bit down on his lip until he tasted blood.

The ranger moved. Colm caught a glint of something in the ranger's hand.

The park ranger said something, but because that person faced away from Colm and still wore a helmet, the words and voice were distorted.

"What? No! You set me up with Matt—Dr. Sorenson. You messed with my head, with my job!" Lavinia's voice cracked with disbelief, but then she lifted her rifle.

The barking pop never reached Colm's ears as the woman collapsed to the forest floor because the pistol's end was capped in a slim black cylinder—a silencer.

*The park ranger shot her.*

Colm had been right. He should have trusted his instincts. Different clothes, but the same person: Chase and Lorna's killer. The killer strode forward and picked up the woman's rifle. He caught sight of the blue hiking boots.

Colm brought his rifle back up, sighted down the barrel, and breathed in once. His finger settled on the trigger. Breathe in. He pulled the trigger, and...click.

He hadn't reloaded the damn thing after the mountain lion. He didn't remember shooting the rifle four times. He fumbled with the box of ammunition, trying to pull out a bullet so he could single-feed it into the rifle.

He was too slow, and the ranger sped off on the ATV, leaving Lavinia in a pool of blood on the forest floor. Colm crept forward, his body shaking, until he reached Lavinia. Her eyes were wide open, empty—just like Lorna's had been. She was dead.

Colm staggered back, his foot catching on a branch, sending him sprawling. His gaze snagged on a scrap of plaid that fluttered on the bark of the tree where the ranger—killer—had fallen back moments before.

When he finally got up, he went to the scrap of fabric. It wasn't much, but he pulled out his pocketknife and cut it in half. He tucked one piece into his pocket, leaving the other under a heart-shaped rock near Lavinia's body.

The killer was going after the older man and a younger woman who'd spoken to the dead woman—Lavinia—earlier.

*He must warn them.*

# FOUR
## FRIDAY

JANE and her father hiked another mile, maybe two, before they reached the Army Corps cabin, which had stood up well against time and the environs. However, it was still a tiny wooden box in the woods filled with dust, spiders, and other critters who liked warm, safe places to hide.

Exhausted from the physical activity, Jane had slept hard even before her father turned the lights out at nine. As she awakened, Jane glanced outside from the single-paned window, where the skyline blushed with the faintest streaks of pink and yellow, fingering its way into the velvety black of night.

"So, what's the plan for today?" Jane asked as she packed up her things and felt her muscles loosen in that familiar, well-used manner that made her crave more exertion. She smiled, excited for the day.

"We're going to go look for the new wolf pack Cynthia discovered."

"Really?" Jane's eyes widened. "A new pack. Isn't that unusual?"

"Yeah. Cynthia's been keeping up with the two wolves for months." He pinched his lips together, which told Jane that something was still off between Cynthia and him. "She told me they'd broken away during the late spring and set up base near here. I told her we'd check on them."

Jane frowned. "You seem weird. About Cynthia."

Her father grimaced. "A professional disagreement. We'll work it out. *Especially* if Cyn's right about these wolves. And she probably is."

Jane picked up her mug of Irish Breakfast tea and sipped it, enjoying the heat as it slid down her throat. She would have liked to add oat milk and honey but could tolerate a few days without her typical pleasures. She knew when she had that first oat milk latte, it would taste better than most of the ones she'd consumed the previous year.

There was something important to changing up her routine, to realizing just how good Jane's life was. She hoped she'd remember that lesson from this trip.

She shoved her feet forward, admiring the scuff marks decorating her newish hiking boots. Because Jane had gotten these before she tore her ACL the first time, she hadn't worn them much. She was too busy juggling soccer, college, and Scott.

Boy, dating Scott had been a mistake. She'd met him at the orthopedist's office. He'd invited her to coffee, then dinner, and well, Jane had liked him. Liked that he already knew fun people at MSU and knew the best professors. He'd made her first semester at MSU much easier...until he hadn't.

Enough of those thoughts for now. Jane wiggled her toes in her wool socks, ready to find that joy in the outdoors she and her dad had shared when she was younger and life had been straightforward, easy. In some ways, he had tried to resurrect the joyous moments of her early elementary years when they'd camped and fished together, when Jane had run through meadows of wildflowers straight into his arms. He had sat her down at the fire pit and taught her how to make a fire, clean dishes with fine-grain sand, pluck a duck, or check for predators by scat droppings.

"So?" she prompted. "You only brought me into the park to observe the wolves?"

He cleared his throat. "No. I mean, yes. I always want to observe the animals. They fascinate me."

"How do you collar a wild animal?" Jane pointed her finger at him and said, "Don't you dare say carefully."

"We consider the size, sex, and age of each animal and adjust their collar to their neck size. Just like people, wolves vary in size and shape: some of our pack animals are thinner, lankier, stockier, or more muscular than others."

"It's a personalized process?" Jane asked.

Her father nodded. "Not unlike backpacking and wilderness training, I suppose."

She waved him off. "I'm not great at this survivalist stuff."

"Yet you agreed to come with me. And I'd say your skills are growing. You're up from a..." He paused, waiting.

Jane's lips quirked upward just a little, aware of the game he liked to play. "A three."

"At least a four!"

She chuckled. "*Now*, I'm a four."

"I'd say a six-and-a-half, closing in on a seven. You know a lot more than a city slicker."

Jane's smile grew along with the warmth in her chest. Her dad was such a good guy. "That's because I have you here to help me work through what I don't know."

His expression turned somber. "That's what a parent should do, sweetie. My job is to make sure you're as capable as possible in any situation."

"Thanks, Dad."

He kissed the crown of her head. "No thanks needed. This has been a treat for me, getting to spend time with you."

She hugged him. "Me, too."

They talked about the project as they finished breakfast. "It's all fascinating. I can't believe how much adding a predator improved the park's biodiversity," Jane said as she rinsed out her mug and slipped it back into her pack. Her father frowned, no doubt planning to carry it again, but the mug weighed next to nothing.

"Goes to show how little we still understand the world, doesn't it?" he responded. "We're learning, albeit slower than I'd like. I hate the idea of leaving you with these huge issues: climate change, biodiversity, extinctions..."

"Luckily for you, my generation's pretty savvy about all those things. And once we wrest power away from the old people who don't want to give it up, we'll be making some changes." Jane smirked.

Her father laughed. "Pretty sure that's why you'll need to wrest it away."

"Probably."

Jane rolled up the sleeping bag she'd laid under the one she had in her pack, the muscles in her forearms bunching as she scrunched it enough to settle it into its mouse-proof bag. She retied it to the string hanging from the ceiling and glanced around. Their chores were complete once they removed the ashes from the wood stove and laid a new fire.

"What else do we need to do?" Jane asked.

Her father had pulled out his satellite phone. Reception out here remained nonexistent, thanks to the mountainous terrain and lack of cellular towers. That's why her father brought his compact sat phone—to do his daily check-ins with the team back in Bozeman. He'd told her it had a nine-day battery, so they'd be covered the whole time they were in the park.

After another moment of intense concentration, he returned the phone to his pack.

"Sorry. Did I interrupt your call?"

He shook his head. "Nah. I couldn't get through."

"I thought those always worked." Jane frowned, not liking the breach of one of her security blankets.

"Usually. Almost always, so I'm not sure..." Matt frowned. He tipped his head back and eyed the sky, almost as if he expected rain clouds. But the sky was clear—a shimmery, bright blue.

He'd dropped the phone yesterday. If the device didn't work, then she didn't want to leave this spot. Now, she worried about being stuck and having no way to call for help.

"Should we stay here?" she asked.

"Nope. The weather's good, and I want to follow those wolves."

Jane swallowed her trepidation and finished her chores. The faster they left, the faster they'd get to the next cabin...just in case something went wrong.

"I think it's really nice that we're leaving the cabin even better than we found it," Jane said.

"It's not so much about nice, but you're right. The next visitor could be in a bad way. We want to make sure they only need to strike a match to the tinder to have instant heat. You felt how quickly the temperature dropped last night. Well, it's worse when the snow comes. The heat differential can be life-threatening. That's why I split more wood while you were tidying up in here. Always leave more than you take."

"An excellent motto for the world in general." Jane tried to fill the gap before her father could start thinking about his ex-wife again.

But she was too late. His smile wavered, but the warmth in his eyes told Jane he was honest when he said, "Now, let's go find you some wolves to photograph."

"I thought we were checking their radio collars."

"That, too. But nothing can beat a selfie with an apex predator. Am I right?"

Jane slid on her pack. Her father followed suit and locked the door, double-checking the padlock. He pocketed the key.

"Want to be in charge of finding the next cabin? I'll even let you boss me around when we get there."

Jane snorted. "Just because I'm interested in hiking and even the wolves, though not as much as the bears, doesn't mean I'm going to volunteer for your project next summer."

He tipped his head back and breathed in the cool morning air. Golden sunlight filtered down through the tall, swaying pines, sprinkling him with patches of its warmth.

"Doesn't mean you *won't*, either."

She smiled. His plan to coax his daughter toward a career as a wilderness biologist, or at least a park ranger, made sense. He'd understood long before she did that Jane would be happier—much more content—when she was closer to nature.

On the flip side, Jane also had a lot of her mother in her: soft beds and sturdy locks, flushing toilets, and hot coffee all made the world a *much* more pleasant place. Over time, Jane would figure out how to merge the two sides of herself.

He bumped her shoulder. "You've had a rough go."

Jane knew he'd been stuck on thoughts of her mother. Well, maybe he just needed to talk it out. Maybe Jane did, too. "So did you."

He squinted up at the vast blue sky. "I made mistakes. That's different. You...you were a kid. Kids should never pay the price for their parents' issues."

Jane considered that and discarded the argument for the more prescient one. "You trusted her."

He nodded. "And I love her still, even knowing what I do. But she's not wrong when she says I was gone too much. "I wish..." he began. Instead of continuing, he walked away. "Daylight's burning." He picked up his pace.

Okay, then. Hiking it was. Sharing would come in time.

They passed a stream and a beaver dam that her father said wasn't in use. She glanced over at one of the pines as they passed it. The circumference was more comprehensive than her hips, and forty feet tall. Jane realized she needed patience to accomplish much during this slow, perpetual life. Life thrummed under that bark each day, expanding the tree and pushing out new needles. Jane had to be like the tree—majestic, patient, and ready to stand tall at whatever came next.

The woods, the quiet, crept up on her. It was a religious experience.

Her lips curved again. "You were correct. There's something meditative, soothing to the soul, about the solitude, the quiet."

"Agreed."

They moved along the trail at a good clip. Her father held up his hand a few minutes later, so Jane stopped. He pointed. A herd of elk lazed in the last of the browning grass in the small meadow —about forty of them tucked in close together. A bull rose to his feet, antlers spearing toward the sky as he sniffed the wind.

"We don't want to disturb them," he murmured.

He tipped his head to the right, and they diverged from the narrow track to drift between the trees. Jane followed, still filled with the same awe she'd felt since they exited the Jeep yesterday.

*Definitely* a religious experience.

"I wish we'd done this sooner." Jane's tone softened with regret. He shot her a smile over his shoulder. He'd pulled out his compass, cupping it in his left hand as he walked.

"You had soccer."

"And Scott. And Mom's silly ideas about wilderness rolling through my head." Jane paused. "What did you wish before?"

Her father remained silent for a long time as he and Jane

watched the elk. "I like to think that I would have been mature enough to work out a better solution than the one we all ended up in the last couple of years, especially since everything fell apart about the time your injury happened."

He paused again, his throat working as he attempted to move past the emotion that caused his expression to fall. "You needed us —me—and I was so wrapped up in feeling betrayed, I failed you. I hate that I failed you. And myself."

He hadn't wanted her to hear that, but he'd said it out loud and into the woods. Because that was *his* truth, and it needed to be told. Jane inhaled the rich, piney scent but said nothing. Sometimes acknowledging those realities made the difference. Jane had just made that rather important discovery when she had to admit she could no longer play soccer at the elite level needed to receive her scholarship.

"I'm glad I came back to Montana, Dad. I think...I think everything that happened was for the best."

Dad turned toward her, smiling. "I'm so glad, Janie. So glad. You know, for what it's worth, I just want you to be happy. Whatever that is for a career, wherever that is for school."

"I wish Mom felt that way, too," Jane said. Her father hugged her and kissed the top of her head.

"That may be asking too much of your mother."

"But it's not wrong," Jane said.

Her dad shifted away, walking toward a break in the trees and a faint, narrow path. "You know what?"

The woods remained quiet—maybe even expectant. As if the woods themselves held their breath.

# DEEP IN THE FOREST

Faint vocalizations drifted toward Colm: a bass, masculine tone, and a softer, higher, feminine voice.

*Finally.*

He'd found them, but the thick underbrush slowed his progress. The only plus was that Colm had been able to keep the blasted ATV within hearing distance. He'd gotten ahead of it by cutting up a steep rock face, but that left him panting and thirsty.

Colm moved closer, planning to ask them for water and tell them about the killer. Then they'd all head out of the park together. As he moved toward them, light caught on the barrel of a rifle across the clearing.

He hadn't gotten in front of the killer.

Colm opened his mouth to yell but fell into a crouch instead. If he yelled, he'd lose his chance to avenge Lorna and Chase. Not gonna happen again.

He raised his Ruger. This time, he wouldn't hesitate to shoot.

# FIVE

"WHAT DO YOU MEAN, you've lost contact?" Cynthia Bianchi asked her research assistant, scrambling around her desk toward Quincy's workstation.

Quincy, a second-year grad student who'd joined their program from Purdue, was conscientious, studious, and right now, wilting and self-conscious under Cynthia's glare.

"He's not answering his device," Quincy stuttered. "It's like there's a block. *Nothing* is going through."

Cynthia scowled. "That doesn't make sense."

"I know. That's why I told you."

"Pull up the weather," Cynthia said, a foreboding feeling prickling along her scalp.

Quincy fumbled his way to the correct website. He and Cynthia stared at the screen, disbelieving.

"Oh, that's bad," Quincy said. "Oh, that's *really* bad."

"Catastrophic," Cynthia breathed. "We have to let Matt know."

"The storm's moving in, and fast." Quincy pointed at the twenty-four-hour clock, and they watched again as the vast mass thundered south and consolidated over the exact area where Matt and Jane were hiking.

Unaware. Unprepared.

"The forecast showed a potential for rain later in the week... but see? That system's charging down from the Arctic." Looking up, Quincy's face pinched as annoyance flashed in his eyes. "Could the weather system block our transmission?"

Worry slammed into Cynthia, trying to burst open her skull and rip through her guts. On top of this new danger for Jane and Matt, Cynthia hadn't heard from Lavinia again after the young woman let her know a ranger had found her, but then, Lavinia was flighty as well as lovesick. Cynthia was too worried about Matt and Jane's well-being to focus on Lavinia's supposed heartbreak.

"They're too far in to hike it out before the storm hits. He won't have time to get Jane out of there without ATVs." Cynthia rose from her hunch over the monitor, squinting against the pain in her head. She began to pace.

"What do we do?" Quincy asked.

"Try the phone again while I think."

On the plus side, the park service knew about Matt's trek into the park with Jane. The team always cleared their itinerary with the local rangers. But...she shook her head. Matt would need to bring their physical exertion down to Jane's level, which meant he was less capable because he would be focused on his daughter. If they got caught between cabins, they'd have to wait out the storm in the small tent Matt carried. It was doable, but the scenario was dangerous. More dangerous than Cynthia was comfortable with. She wanted Jane at her dad's house, far from hungry predators and other weather events that accompanied heightened winds and large, unexpected blizzards.

She stopped pacing, raised her eyebrows, and looked at him askance. Quincy shook his head.

"Sat's not going through, cell is unavailable. Okay, call the park service," Cynthia said. "And the Cody, Wyoming, search and rescue team. They're hours closer to Jane and Matt than we are."

"But...what do I tell them?" Quincy asked.

"That we have an incoming weather emergency and need an extraction, stat." Jane was in good shape before her surgery, but she'd spent months rehabilitating...and lolling on the couch as she struggled to come to terms with her new reality.

Quincy spoke into the phone, all trepidation missing from his tone. He worked his way up the ranger service personnel phone tree, repeating the details each time.

"Um...we have another problem," Quincy said.

"What?"

"Two kids—siblings—went missing outside the park this morning. Cody and the park service mobilized their resources to find the kids."

"Shit," Cynthia exclaimed. She tipped her head back and stared at the ugly, institutional ceiling. "Okay...we'll have to go in ourselves."

"How?"

"I'll call Mindy, ask to borrow her ATV."

"Y-you're going in?" Quincy stuttered.

"I'm not leaving Jane and Matt out there unaware and unprotected."

Her phone rang. She glanced at the screen and winced. "Hello?"

"Dr. Bianchi. This is Detective Tara Fremont—"

"Wow! That was so fast. I have their last coordinates—"

"What are you talking about?" Detective Fremont asked.

"Matt Sorenson and his daughter, Jane, are in the park. There's a storm coming in, blocking our signal. Search and rescue are combing the woods for some missing kids."

"That's unfortunate, but also outside my jurisdiction," Detective Fremont said.

"They could die," Cynthia cried. Tears filled her eyes.

"That's a possibility," Detective Fremont said. "And a terrible one—"

Cynthia's guts pressed painfully into her spine. She didn't have a choice. She closed her eyes. "I don't have time for your call, Detective."

"I'm looking into Arthur Ford, who died in the hunting on Mindy Warner Sorenson's family ranch."

Quincy shot her a concerned glance. Cynthia offered him a faint smile, and he went back to his phone call.

Cynthia licked her lips. "I...ah...don't know anything about that. I told the other detective so. I mean, I was there, but Mindy, Charlie, and Matt are the hunters—better with firearms than I am."

"You know what I think, Cynthia? I think you're protecting someone. But you've piqued my interest in *that* case and this one, too. I'll be in touch."

CYNTHIA STARED OFF INTO SPACE, dazed and slightly nauseous from the details she'd revealed to the detective.

Fremont's parting words, "*you've piqued my interest,*" swirled through her head. Matt had been upset that Charlie hadn't been hired at the university. Mindy was conniving enough to have talked one of her father's ranch hands into committing murder, especially if they were hunting. Accidents happened, especially when there were guns involved. Cynthia had wanted to believe that scenario—that was the one floated by Mindy at the time, and

Cynthia certainly hadn't said anything then to challenge the idea because *murderer...*

Cynthia shook her head. That seemed extreme.

For now, she needed to focus on getting Matt and Jane out of Yellowstone before the storm rolled in.

"What did the park service say?" she asked Quincy.

"That all their personnel are out looking for the kids. But she —the ranger's name was Betty—promised to leave a note in their next planned cabin stop, telling them to stay put there and ride out the storm. I asked her what we should do if they didn't make it to the cabin, and she said hope they find shelter." Quincy looked up at Cynthia with that youthful hopefulness Cynthia couldn't bring herself to quash. "Which they'll do—right?"

"Matt's smart and he's a great outdoorsman," Cynthia hedged. "Good work, Quincy. Really good. Thanks."

He went back to his application, but Cynthia remained restless. As she considered the distance between cabins and how quickly the weather was moving in, her lips pressed in a tight, grim line. The odds of survival lowered with each degree drop in temperature and each extra inch of snow.

Cursing herself for being all types of a fool, she dialed Charlie's number. He didn't answer. Of course he didn't. She sent a text: *You need to return to the office now. We have an emergency.*

"This better be good, Cyn," Charlie said when he called back. Of course, he took his sweet time. Charlie preferred mind games to simple communication. That drove her bonkers.

"Matt didn't check in this morning. None of his devices are online."

"Not good," Charlie said. "But it's not a biggie, either. Matt's a trekker. He's been deep in that backcountry multiple times. So has Jane. Well, she's gone on a couple of expeditions. That means she's not a novice. They'll be fine."

"I wouldn't normally worry, but there's a storm building,

Charlie." She swallowed. "It's supposed to move right over the Washakie Wilderness. And the current projections are three to five feet."

"*Definitely* not good." Charlie's breathing changed. He must be running. Each harsh exhalation exploded into the phone. He muttered the curse again, then again.

The call dropped. Cynthia glared at her phone.

"What?" Quincy yipped.

"*Where is he*? I need Charlie here now to help me coordinate this situation."

She shoved her phone into her pocket and paced, frustration at Charlie's lack of work ethic snapping through her. How Matt would keep him on and not Cynthia irritated Cynthia to no end.

Charlie called her back a couple of minutes later.

"Where are you?"

"I told you, I'm golfing with potential donors to save the grant. All hush-hush, back room...not a finished thing until we sign a contract. I'm working on different angles here. I'll try to be there in an hour."

"*Try*?"

"I'm going to call S and R."

She explained about the missing kid, and Charlie finally understood her fears.

"But that storm...with Jane's recent injury..."

"I know, Charlie. *I know*. That's why I called you." Charlie might be an asshole, but he was nearly as accomplished a backpacker and Yellowstone tracker as Matt. Better than Cynthia, though she hated to admit it. "I'm going to talk to Mindy." Matt's ex-wife lived with her head in pretty martini-flavored sand and wouldn't believe anything could happen to her daughter. "I'll cajole her into letting us use her ATV once we're in the park."

"Get out of the way," Charlie yelled, his breathing ragged and harsh into the phone. "I don't care that I'm messing up your game. I'm dealing with life and death here, asshole."

Yeah, her ex was a pearl of gentlemanliness. Charlie might be rough around the edges—and in the middle—but loyalty mattered to him. And his closest friend was in jeopardy.

He didn't say what Cynthia had been thinking ever since Quincy mentioned the lack of check-in—without a way to communicate with Matt, he and Jane were walking straight into serious—deadly—danger.

"You're not going into the park—or to talk to Mindy—without me," Charlie panted.

"Then you'd better do more than try to get back here in an hour because I'm heading to Mindy's now."

# SIX

JANE TUCKED her phone back into her pocket, giddy from the close contact with the wolves. They'd found the animals right where Cynthia's coordinates suggested. Three tiny pups—barely beyond the weird guinea pig stage of infancy—romped in the sunshine inches from the den's opening.

"What—"

Her father placed his finger to his lips and pointed toward the den. Yellow eyes and sharp teeth flashed against the gloom. With painstaking slowness, the female wolf, dark fur brindled with white around her ear tips, ruff, and tail tip, lurched from the den's shadowy interior.

Jane bit back a gasp. A mass of half-healed gouges and wounds covered her left hip. She limped and whined, and the movement appeared painful, but the gleam in her eye and the flashing teeth made it obvious she would protect her pups.

Her dad grunted, his expression showing his displeasure. He guided Jane back from the small glen that housed the wolves' family. There was a sharp rise of rock and dirt to the left, and the canids had dug out a den behind a narrow opening. It was safe and warm, something the wolves would appreciate in the coming weeks. Probably sooner rather than later, seeing as they were already a week into September.

"Those pups are too young." Her father's brows pulled low. "And she must have birthed them here. The alpha's hunting for her and the pups, maybe to the detriment of his own nutrition. These guys may need some help to make it through the winter." He bit his lip and stared, unseeing, at the trees. "We'll need to get the young ones collared."

"You don't think she'll survive?"

Pride shone from Dad's features. "She already did. Those wounds are deep, and they must have torn into her muscle."

"What do you think got her?" Jane asked.

Her father shot her a side-eye. "Wolverine. No doubt this was its territory, and the little guy didn't want to give it up."

Wolverines were vicious critters. "But if she's convalescing..." Jane led.

"She might heal enough to be a functional member of the pack. It's clear her alpha is doing what he can to ensure her survival."

"Hers? Or his babies?" Jane asked.

"That's a brilliant question, and one I cannot answer at this point. But she's a couple of weeks away from weaning. Then, the wolves of the pack will have to make the tough choice whether to continue to feed the female alpha as they search for food during winter..."

Jane swallowed with difficulty. "Or let her starve."

"Yes. But I doubt the alpha will do that. They seem pretty ensconced together. As long as he can find enough to feed them all, he will."

"I hope you're right," Jane said. They continued to walk along the narrow trail. Jane smiled up at him. "I have to admit...getting that close, seeing the pups was a treat!"

He laughed as he turned toward the faint path that led back toward the route he and Jane had plotted out for today's adventure.

"What's that smell?" Jane asked, wrinkling her nose. It was too sweet, with faint hints of vanilla. The powdery sugar undertone irritated Jane's sinuses.

"Mmm?" her dad asked. "Oh, that's a berry. It's called..."

A staccato pop broke the silence. Birds shrieked and shot into the air. Her father faltered as he grunted, pivoting away from her. He whipped his rifle from his back and brought it up, sighting. Before he could pull the trigger, there was another pop—a gunshot—that caused her father to stagger and gurgle.

Bright red soaked the front of her dad's fleece, blooming larger and larger like a rose spreading its petals.

Lavinia...gunshots yesterday, now, here. Every hair on Jane's body rose as the sharp scents of gunpowder and blood clogged her nostrils. She screamed, falling backward on her butt. Terror shadowed the world that dripped in her father's blood.

"D-daddy—"

HER DAD STAGGERED, his breath wheezy. He brought the rifle up and fired, his jaw clamped. "Henry...barrel needs to cool...you *gotta* go, baby girl," he wheezed through a rattling throat and shattered chest. "Please, Jane," he gasped. "Go. Can't lose you. *Run...*"

With one last searing look at her father, she watched him stagger, turn, and raise his arms, desperate to give Jane time, to do everything he could to save her. Another bullet caught his shoulder and spun him toward Jane.

Her dad's eyes were pleading, desperate. "Run, Jane. *Please.*"

He faltered as he stumbled forward between Jane and the

bullets. He dropped to the pine needle-strewn forest floor as blood sprayed from his multiple wounds. His eyes were sightless, his body limp.

Jane ran.

# DEEP IN THE FOREST

The sharp staccato ping filled the air, sending birds into flight, cawing and screaming. Once again, the killer had fired first—and accurately.

The gray-and-blue plaid covering the older man's chest blossomed with blood, and he stumbled. Colm's gaze sought the woman: her eyes wide, her mouth opened in a scream, face bleached of color.

"Daddy!" she cried. The other words were lost to the ringing of his ears.

She whimpered it again, just as Colm had when he'd dropped to his knees in front of his best friend. He missed Chase. He hated this, hated watching the woman suffer. No more.

Colm raised his Ruger and sighted down the barrel. He pulled the trigger, aiming for the tiny bit of white he could make out from the shadows.

"Die, you monster," Colm muttered. "*Die.*"

"Run," the older guy yelled. "Jane...*please.*"

When she bolted, the woman didn't bother to glance in Colm's direction. Colm wondered if she'd registered two different weapons. Probably not. She was in a full-blown panic as she sped into the dense copse of pines like a rabbit sprinting from a coyote.

Colm's muscles bunched as they fought the urge to jump and chase her. Instinct did *not* rule him. Colm had waited for this chance. He could manage another few minutes to avenge his friends.

A glimpse of color, too far away now for Colm to hit.

Dammit.

New choice: *follow Jane or stay to shoot the shooter?*

One choice, one blink...

# SEVEN

JANE CRASHED THROUGH THE UNDERBRUSH, unwilling to relive the last moments with her father yet unable to think of anything else. She slammed into a tree, the rough bark tugging at her fleece before she righted herself and sped onward.

"No, no, no..." she moaned.

Her heart pattered faster than the running should force it to work. That must be adrenaline. It poured through her, allowing Jane to dart between rocks and gallop over stones and fallen branches with more agility and speed than she'd usually expend. The rustling of nearby underbrush propelled Jane forward, fear and determination battling within her.

"Lavinia will kill me, too," Jane panted. "But I have to go back. I promised my father."

*Keep running, Jane. Don't stop. You promised.*

"I can't let Lavinia gun me down. No, no, go back. Save my dad..."

Her head twisted and revolved, conflicts clashing. So, Jane did what Cynthia taught her and emptied her mind.

After a deep breath, Jane shifted her running stance, extending her legs—the long ones she'd inherited from her father

—and lifted her chest. Her eyes drifted from left to right, taking in the blurred terrain as she pelted over it. She sped farther and farther from her father, from Lavinia.

"Run, Janie," she said. "Like your dad told you. *Run.*"

Her muscle memory kicked in. She lifted her knees a little more to accommodate the thicker-soled boots.

Minutes, maybe an hour later, Jane's toe caught on a tree root. She stumbled, wincing at the tug in her ankle. She ran at a breakneck speed, which was dangerous. Shadows created cool pockets of air that brushed against her perspiring skin. Her breath ripped and dragged out of her lungs. She never trained for races like this.

Jane bit back the sob that tried to press up into her throat. No time to cry. It would use energy she couldn't lose. She must continue to move forward toward safety.

"Wherever *that* is," she muttered.

She didn't know how to go back. She didn't know where she was. Jane needed a plan so that she didn't continue to flail around in a panic.

"What would my dad do?"

*Look for the animal tracks. They choose those particular routes for a reason, Janie.*

She clamped her lips tight at the memory of her father peering at her after he pointed to a faint trail. Right. Elk and deer created narrow paths and stuck to them. They were the most likely to be cleared of hazards. Now Jane just had to find one, but she didn't want to do so. Instead, her arms slid down to dangle at her sides, and her feet slowed to a shuffle as the realization hit her hard: many killers roamed this terrain—bears, badgers, wolves, mountain lions, *and* the shooter.

# ELSEWHERE IN THE FOREST

Cursing, hands trembling, the hunter examined the wound. “Impossible. I don’t make mistakes.”

Meticulous in planning and flawless in execution...yet the hunter’s biceps now bled in the woods like some amateur.

“It’s just a minor setback. I’m still in control. I’m always in control.”

Peeling off the blood-stained ranger shirt, the hunter winced as the fabric clung to the wound. A rookie mistake, getting shot. But even legends had off days, didn’t they? And Matt was quite good with a rifle.

Just another reason to hate him.

The shirt was buried deep, soil packed tight until no trace remained. That kind of care had always been instinctive. Fresh clothes, steady breaths. The plan shifted and reformed, sharper now. This was still the hunter’s game—one bad moment didn’t change that.

Though the thought of Jane still alive was an affront, a blemish on a perfect record. The hunter’s phone vibrated, a reminder to head toward the rendezvous point. Hesitating, torn between pursuing Jane, the sad little prey, and sticking to the plan. Indecision was unfamiliar territory—unwelcome, too.

The bear's sudden appearance created a complication. The animal must have been drawn to the blood, but how dare it interfere with this hunt? Storming forward, rifle leveled, ready to shoot...the grizzly thundered closer, teeth bared as the rifle clicked. Empty chamber.

Retreating to the waiting ATV was prudent. His ego was bruised, but his resolve remained unbroken.

"The game's not over until I say it is. I always win. *Always.*"

# EIGHT

AS JANE RAN, trying to ignore the growing stitch in her side, she remembered that Wyoming's southern border lay along the forty-first parallel, the same equatorial line as Italy. Whenever Jane thought about Italy, she pictured sultry summer days. Bikini weather where she could sink into the warm sand of the Adriatic Sea while drinking Bellinis or Prosecco—something extraordinary and lovely and so utterly European.

None of those fantasies equated with her perspiring face or the hair now clinging to her wet scalp. Jane's T-shirt stuck to her soaked torso underneath her jacket that she'd unzipped most of the way down—but not all the way, so that it didn't catch stray branches or vegetation.

Jane didn't know how well Lavinia could track through the wilderness. Jane could minimize her signs, but she had to assume Lavinia would be able to follow her trail. Which meant she needed to...do something.

What?

"What can I do?" Her legs trembled with each step as she pounded her feet, pushing forward. "I don't know where I am."

Worse still, she was without a sat phone. She didn't even have the sharply pointed stick to ward off predators because she'd dropped hers next to her father's body.

Her breath broke as anxiety rooted deep and spread faster than a virus.

"Okay...okay...calm down. *Think...*"

There! The sun peeked through the patches of trees, still just about overhead. Her watch showed nine twelve a.m. So...she must be heading...north.

*Wrong way, Jane. Stop, get your bearings...*

Jane bit at her thumbnail. Okay. She had a compass, but she didn't have a big enough opening to get her bearings and maybe find a landmark, which hampered her ability to follow the path she and her father had charted. But she didn't *need* to follow that path now, anyway. Finding more wolves was low on Jane's to-do list. Getting out of the park alive was at the top.

Lavinia would *expect* Jane to stay on the trail. If so, moving at a diagonal—or in the opposite direction—was smarter.

"But heading in the direction Dad and I plotted leads to the closest exit to the park," Jane muttered. "I need to get to it, where park services expect me. I have to find a group to make sure I'm safe. Hide from any single person..." Jane shuddered. "Oh, how I've fallen to the bottom of the food chain."

Much as she sought to find a break in the trees, she worried that might be even stupider, might give Lavinia another shot at her. She kept moving, though her pace had slowed to a walk. Still, she forced one foot in front of the other, refusing to stop. Standing still meant a greater likelihood of being caught by Lavinia...or a wild animal.

Jane took a deep breath. Dad. Focus on him. "What would he tell me now?"

Something like: *The only way out of this situation was through it.*

"Okay, through, it is." Jane found that her voice grounded her.

Branches rustled, and the wind whistled, causing Jane to shiver. The forest closed in, pressing against her, full of eyes, teeth, claws, and blood.

That deep crack Jane would forever associate with a rifle firing ripped through the silence. Four, five, maybe six bullets in rapid succession. With a terrified squeak that pushed the last of the air from her lungs, Jane dropped to the ground, uncaring about the pine needles and rocks that poked into her cheek, neck, chest, belly, and legs.

Nothing above her exploded.

No bullet slammed into the earth. Lavinia must be too far away, but she'd heard Jane talking.

"I'm a fool," Jane whispered. With a grimace, she muttered, "*Stop talking.*"

Jane didn't catch another whiff of gunpowder from the latest shots, and she hadn't heard anyone move past her, making Jane certain the shooter hadn't gotten downwind of her position. She lay still, face against a lichen-covered rock, heart pounding faster than when she sprinted.

After minutes or hours— it was impossible to know—Jane rose from the ground, biting her lip to keep from groaning as her sore muscles screamed their protest.

She needed water, something to eat, and time to recover from the exertion. That meant finding somewhere to hide...and the forest floor wasn't the best place.

The idea of a cave concerned her because bears and wolves might live there. But remaining in the open terrified her more.

Jane glanced upward. There wasn't any reason to stop Jane from taking advantage of the higher ground.

She searched for a moment until she found a tree with branches low enough for her to grab onto. The rough bark dug into the tender skin of her palms, but Jane ignored the bite and levered herself upward, using her feet to scrabble against the tree trunk.

While she had completed all the workouts the coach forced upon the student athletes, she'd believed, like many of her friends, that upper body strength wasn't necessary. A few half-tried pushups were about the best they did. Today, Jane realized why her coach pushed the women on the team to do just one more. Hauling her entire body weight plus the pack up a tree exhausted her. Jane stopped, panting, aching, wanting desperately to quit. That wasn't an option, and she wasn't going to give up or give in.

She shook her arms, trying to find the energy to keep moving upward. If Lavinia was in the area, Jane needed to head higher into the flimsy protection of the thicker evergreen needles.

She gripped the next branch and gritted her teeth when she landed hard on her belly, knocking the air from her diaphragm. She gagged and gasped, but she wriggled onto the branch. Looking up, she almost choked. Jane gnashed her teeth instead. There wasn't another branch for ten, maybe fifteen feet. Nope. Definitely not going to work.

Jane huddled against her current trunk, mulling over her options. Branches snapped below her, and Jane froze, heart pounding even harder.

*Lavinia had found her*.

Jane squeezed her eyes shut, and she folded herself into a tiny ball with her knees touching her forehead. She waited for the gunshot that would rip through her sinew and bone and blow her out of the tree. Would she be able to run?

"How many bullets does Lavinia have?" Jane tried to count the shots she'd heard. A full magazine, maybe more.

Another stealthy shuffle that parted the underbrush. Yet...no shots. Jane opened one eye. Perhaps she could jump on Lavinia, take her to the ground. Shoot her.

Because now, the choice was to kill or be killed.

The shadowy figure shifted, coming nearer...

Ever nearer...

Jane clamped her lips behind her teeth and shoved down the scream that clawed at her throat. Something significant shifted the flora below. Something *too* significant to be Lavinia.

Antlers appeared. Then, a long, brown snout.

Jane released her fists, then her breath. "Moose. *Just a moose.*"

The large, lumbering animal shambled into the space below her tree as Jane's head went hazy with relief. She hiccupped before sucking in more air, her lungs stuttering.

Her dad said moose were underrated animals that deserved more love and interest from the public.

*Daddy.* He'd told her to go, begged her to. She hated herself for obeying. She wanted another chance to make a different decision. To stay with him. To fall with him. But she'd promised to obey his commands, and she had. Now, all she wanted was her father back.

"Another chance. I...I'd do better, Dad. I'd save you."

Except...she couldn't. Her father was gone.

Dead.

Tears threatened, and a sob built, pressing hard against her chest into her throat.

"Not now...not now...cry later. Once you survive this."

She would tell *everyone* what happened to her father, and she'd get justice. That was the only thing that mattered now. Survival, then justice.

Jane clung to the tree, letting the rough bark abrade her cheek as she calmed.

The moose glanced up, its jaw churning as it chewed its bite. Unconcerned by Jane's presence, it went back to grazing.

More in control of her emotions, Jane eased one hand from the tree's trunk and wiped her face. Before she could talk herself out of it, she scooted outward on her branch and caught the other limb in her hands. She pulled herself upright and stepped as far across as she could, gingerly setting the ball of her foot down. Firming her hands, she leaped onto the branch, mouth opening in a silent scream as it wobbled beneath her.

Hands tensed, Jane eased forward, gripping and sliding until she got to the tree limb. Above, now, she could make out the blue sky. She squinted against the sun and pulled herself up again.

Once more, Jane found a crook in the branch that allowed for a decent reclining chair-like pose. The branch's base widened enough for her to settle her butt comfortably, and the trunk was solid against her back.

Jane removed her pack and resettled it against her front. She didn't love her twenty-plus feet from the ground. If she fell, she'd break her leg or arm, and that would leave her at Lavinia's mercy. Or any predator's.

"Drink, eat, stay in top physical condition." Coach's rules, and good ones that both her father and Cynthia also told Jane, though in different words. Jane pulled the straw from the pack to her flexible water bladder and drank in greedy pulls.

Thirst quenched and throat no longer achy, Jane grabbed a piece of beef jerky. She'd made a face when her dad tossed it in her pack yesterday.

"Really, Dad?" Jane had sighed out then, wrinkling her nose.

"It's full of protein and will help you with your stamina. You'll thank me for it later."

*You were right, Dad. I am thankful.*

The moose eventually ambled off. A squirrel darted along a branch nearby, chattering and scolding. When it saw Jane, it paused before turning and darting back into its hole.

It had found safety. Jane wished she could do so as easily.

She checked the watch on her wrist. Though simple and basic, the watch was new, as was the battery.

The face read two fifty-seven. Jane had been here a long time, then. The sun headed toward the mountain peak, meaning that the direction must be west. Jane should head south toward Flagg Ranch Information Station. It would be easier to walk that way than try to cross Yellowstone Lake.

Okay. So...not a brilliant plan, but at least Jane had a goal. Right now, that was enough.

A story she'd skimmed came back to her now: every person had a homing device deep in their brain. It was called the entorhinal region, and it told the mind which direction the person faced and which direction they would need to head in the future to reach their destination.

Jane had never tested her entorhinal region before. She really hoped hers worked.

She let her head fall back against the tree and stared up at the too-bright sun in the vast openness of the western sky.

Okay...what had her father told her about the cabins?

"The Army spaced them a day's journey apart—sixteen miles. Nowadays, most have fallen apart, but the ones that are still standing and repaired are used as visitor contractor stations."

She was likely closer to the cabin she and her father planned to stay in tonight than the one from yesterday. Going back to the previous cabin seemed foolhardy because the killer would expect her to do that—Jane theorized, anyway. She needed to be random. So, she'd get near the next cabin tonight but not stay in it. Then, she could follow the markings to the next one and reevaluate her plan for that evening.

She just had to hope Lavinia didn't find her before she could extricate herself.

# NINE

SIXTEEN MILES PROVED *NOT* doable when darkness came with abrupt efficiency and the precipitous drop in temperatures nipped at the inside of her nose, heralding the bitter hint of snow. All around Jane, lodgepole pines rose, tall and seeming to go on forever, blocking her view of the stars and the land's geography.

By her best estimate, Jane had managed another six, maybe seven, miles toward her goal.

She pushed on even as the temperature continued dropping, and she wondered if she'd find *any shelter* that would protect her from the elements. She plodded along and passed another tree... and another...and another.

All wasn't lost. She wouldn't despair. Her father had outfitted her with a sleeping bag, wool socks, and a layer of outerwear—bright orange and other colors, designed for comfort and warmth, not stealth.

"You just had to pick the cutest one," Jane grumbled. "Stupid, so stupid. What are you going to do now?"

Perhaps she should have considered circling back to her father. Jane knew that when someone checked in on their last known location, they'd find his body. He had a GPS device and a sat phone, which might still be on. And if it were, that meant a signal for the search and rescue teams. But...circling back and hunkering down there also meant a higher possibility of running into Lavinia.

Jane couldn't do it. The mere thought of heading back in that direction, finding and facing her father's murderer, caused her skin to break out in a thick, oily sweat and her lungs to seize.

Logically, Jane understood that Lavinia could have gotten in front of her, but that scenario remained unlikely. Jane wasn't in top physical shape these days, but she was still above average. Lavinia wasn't an athlete—she had bemoaned the feel of sweat in Jane's presence—so Jane couldn't see how she'd best Jane at running.

Okay. She needed to find a place to sleep tonight because being out when she couldn't see as well as the predators wasn't smart. Since the cabin was too far, Jane would have to settle for a cave. She and her father hadn't discussed caves on this trip, and if they'd talked about them before, she couldn't remember.

The tears she'd pushed back threatened once more, along with a writhing ball of emotion pressing against her sternum. She blinked them back with the ruthlessness she'd learned while playing elite soccer.

Tears were for *after*.

Full dark had settled over the forest, blanketing her in a thick pitch punctuated by shifting Mammalia and small, sharp eyes that followed her between the trees. Plumes of frosted breath dissipated before her face, bathing her exposed skin in a cold shower with each step, causing her body heat to plummet.

Her shivering increased, and her teeth clacked. She slipped her arms from her pack and pulled out the bright orange jacket. As quickly as possible, she turned it inside out so the gray interior was exposed, then shoved her arms into the waterproof outer material, which caught on her fleece. She clenched her jaw as she struggled into the coat, fumbling with the inside zipper. At least the orange no longer showed a beacon for binoculars or a rifle scope. She tugged on her gray knit cap, thankful she'd gone with sentimentality there, bringing the one Cynthia had made her.

Jane re-shouldered her pack and tucked her hands inside her jacket sleeves, balling them into fists. She hurried forward over tree roots, cursing her poor night vision. She groaned with relief when she found a split between two rocks. The opening proved almost too narrow for her to fit. Good. That meant other animals would also struggle to get inside.

Trepidation skittered along her nape as she tugged out her phone from her pocket.

She held her breath, her stiff fingers clumsy, as she turned on the flashlight and shined it into the crevice. The floor was relatively free of debris, though bits of pine needles and other foliage littered the floor. The space remained tight, but it was deep enough for her to lie down.

God. That sounded *wonderful*. She could rest...maybe sleep.

Jane squeezed into the space, too cold and wrung out on fear... or pondering how she'd get out in the morning to worry more about the possibility of a critter coming in after her. She tugged off her pack and powered down her phone, wanting to conserve the battery for when she might get near enough to civilization to send out a text...a call...*something*.

After much maneuvering in the narrow space, she righted her coat, so the lining was against her fleece pullover. She pulled her sleeping bag from her pack, and with a few contortions, lots of grunting, and a couple of curses, she slipped inside the thin but heavenly-warm mummy-shaped material.

She ate a piece of jerky, drank as much water as her stomach allowed, and then placed the pack under her head. Though lumpy and too hard to be a good pillow, it was better than nothing.

In some ways, being out here, alone and without any connectivity to the rest of the world, reminded Jane of her high school and early college years. But being alone in Yellowstone was lonelier. At least in high school, Jane could have walked into another room and spoken to her parents. More often, she'd video-called a friend. Now, she just had her own thoughts to keep her company, and those kept trying to circle back to her father's murder—the one thing Jane didn't want to remember.

Sleep must have slammed into her exhausted mind because, seconds later, Jane sat up with a colossal wheeze, her heart thrumming as grunts and snuffles lingered outside her makeshift bedroom.

# DEEP IN THE FOREST

Colm had been right to follow her because Jane moved with purpose and seemed to know where she was going.

He'd been lost, both physically and mentally, for days, so this new development felt good. Jane would get him out of here...if he could catch up to her. He considered calling out to her, but he wasn't sure if the killer followed them. No reason to give away their location.

Without the element of surprise, Colm wasn't sure he could beat the killer if there was a rematch. He hadn't won that round. Not really.

His stomach still ached from pulling the trigger. He'd thought vengeance would make him feel better.

Wrong.

That was the reason he'd followed Jane. Deep down, his subconscious had chosen life rather than death. He didn't want to be like the killer.

Colm stopped for a minute. He fumbled for his water bottle, took the final slug. Water was a top priority.

When he lowered the bottle, Jane had vanished. Panic blasted over his skin.

Okay...okay...think....

He was a computer programmer, and logic told him to create ever-widening circles to find Jane...or at least an idea of her direction.

Tracking proved more consuming than Colm had ever believed it would be. So was living off the land. Colm's van had amenities like a stove and a shower. Fresh water wasn't something he'd ever take for granted again.

Aw, man. Water. He was thirsty, and his body wouldn't be able to go too much longer without fluid. He stopped at a narrow trickle between two moss-covered rocks. Colm ripped at the greenery, wincing as his fingernails caught on the rock. He tipped his head back and squeezed, nearly moaning in delight as cool liquid hit his tongue and trickled down his throat.

That was so, *so good.*

Cool trick. Thank goodness for hours in front of the television. He dropped the moss and took off again, agitation making him move more quickly. When he walked past another one of the berry bushes, he grabbed a handful and shoved the fruits into his mouth, thankful for the calories and a bit of juice that trickled down his throat.

He kept going, but he was so tired. He needed sleep. But he couldn't rest until he found Jane again.

Colm cradled the Ruger American in the crook of his arm. As much as he appreciated the rifle, he wished he still had a sleeping bag. And gloves. He really missed his gloves.

He glanced up at the clear sky, wondering if it was going to snow. It had that hint he knew well from Philly, but he couldn't see a reason for concern...yet.

It was too dark to continue through the woods. He needed to find a safe, preferably warm place. He pulled off his pack and added his clean shirt and sweatshirt to his top half. After some debate, he pulled off his hiking boots and added his second layer of socks, pulling the material as high as it would go. Now, his extremities were better insulated if the temperature continued to plunge. Not great, but doable.

He hoped.

Still no sign of Jane. He climbed into the tree and stared at the bright, endless array of stars that glittered across the night sky.

The sheer number stole his breath. He'd never seen anything like this in Philadelphia. He stared at the entire Milky Way. This was what he, Chase, and Lorna had wanted.

Reality slammed back into Colm's chest as something hooted and something much bigger snorted below him.

Could be he'd made a mistake following Jane. Nah. They shared something—she just didn't know what yet.

He understood her shock and fear.

He'd find her. He had to. Because without Jane, one thing was clear: he'd end up like his friends.

Dead and forgotten.

# TEN

## SUNDAY

DAWN HADN'T FILTERED DOWN to their location, but the forest had lightened to the point Jane could make out the bear's angry, beady black eyes. Saliva dripped from her inches-long incisors.

Jane's father had said five hundred thousand black bears were roaming around North America. He also mentioned that they moved in response to the seasonal availability of food and had excellent memories, particularly regarding food sources. Who didn't remember their favorite restaurant?

Unluckily for Jane, the sow outside her hidey-hole was a female black bear, who was probably pregnant and choleric that Jane had dared to sleep in her territory.

Growling low, the bear rose on her hind feet to tower over Jane, who had sat up and pulled her legs tighter into her body, trying to stay as far away from the sow as possible. She stuffed her sleeping bag into her backpack with quick movements. She glanced at her hiking boots, glad to see them tied.

The sow roared again, conveying clear "don't mess with me" vibes. Jane's heart pounded against her rib cage as she tried to remember what to do in this situation.

*Don't run.* Her father's words slid into her mind, a comforting blanket even as she shivered with fear. *Don't play dead, especially around a hungry bear. Act as big as you can, as loud as you can. Make yourself seem like more work and effort than the bear is willing to put in for a meal.*

The bear swiped a claw-tipped paw into the cavern entrance. She wished she had bear spray. She desperately wished she had a gun.

Wait, no, she didn't.

She *never* wanted to see a firearm again.

Hysteria bubbled up, and Jane let it out. Her cackling proved sharp, grating, even to her ears. Jane lifted her left arm over her head and pulled her pack off her right arm as she laughed. She dropped her left arm to pick up the backpack and waved it while lifting her right hand above her head. Using her legs, she pushed off the ground and used her back to guide herself upward along the cave wall.

The bear grunted, cocking her head. Her mouth closed with a soft, slow movement, not unlike the hinged drawers in Jane's mother's kitchen. The memory of those stupid drawers. The safety of what they represented—enough food, a soft bed—all caused the laugh to catch in her throat and turn into a snuffling, wet screech. The need to survive bloomed solid and harsh, cracking in her chest with the same mighty fury as the storm.

"I will *not* die," Jane hollered.

The bear opened its mouth and roared back. Jane cringed as the noise blasted her ears. But deep in her gut, that hard place she'd encountered as she stared into the dripping jaws of death caused her to raise her pack, wave her arms, and yell back.

"No, Yogi. I'm going to survive this hell! To get out of here."

Jane had to. She *had* to make it out. She was the only one who could tell her father's story.

The bear dropped onto all fours, her head waving back and

forth as she decided how to handle Jane's unusual responses. Jane's arms ached, but she kept them raised.

"Run away. Go. Shoo."

The bear shifted its head to the left, then right, like a pendulum. The first rays of morning light sifted through the pine needles, but Jane's breath still puffed from her lips.

Jane waggled her arms and grunted, snarled, sobbed, and cursed. Anything to keep ahead of the crushing fear that swamped her chest.

"I miss my dad!" By now, Jane's voice shrilled. At least the screaming had an effect.

"Leave. Me. Alone." Jane waved her pack.

She lost her grip, and the backpack tumbled out of her hand. Jane gasped, dropping forward on instinct. The bear grunted, made a curious sound, and then snuffled again. Fueled by anger and fear, Jane picked up handfuls of rocks and threw them. The bear growled with more caution.

"I'm not food," Jane shrieked.

The bear grumbled and then turned, deciding the berries weren't worth the effort and noise. Jane lay on the ground of the narrow cave, gasping for breath as the sow plodded away.

Jane's gasps turned to sobs, but she gritted her teeth and forced herself upright and the tears back down. The bear hadn't left because of Jane. There were elk nearby. The giant animal became a blur of black fur as she pelted after the prettified ungulate. In the blink of an eye, and the bear made contact.

Such a stupid cliché, yet so damn true.

Jane grabbed her pack and shimmied out of her sleeping spot. She couldn't stay here—the spot wasn't safe, not after her screams. Lavinia would be able to pinpoint her location. She stepped around a giant fir and deeper into the woods. And ran.

*Out here, we're just another part of the food chain.*

The elk's squeals drifted over Jane's harsh breathing, but she kept pumping her arms and legs. She'd been too close to death once again.

Within moments, her breathing grew labored and her legs leaden. She needed to stop, to shoulder her pack to keep it from getting caught on a tree limb or ripped, but instead, Jane darted forward.

"Keep moving," she whispered under her ragged breaths. "Keep going. Don't stop. *Don't stop.*"

# ELEVEN

*DISLIKE* WAS TOO tame for what Cynthia felt for Mindy Warner, formerly but sometimes still Sorenson...when Matt's surname benefited her. Charlie's distaste for Matt's ex-wife used to be even more profound, and he'd told Cynthia once that Mindy would ruin Matt.

Cynthia's lips twisted. Of course, that was before Cynthia became aware of Charlie and Mindy's affair. So, it was quite possible that Charlie cultivated his dislike of Mindy to mirror Cynthia's, using it as a cover to keep Cynthia from looking more closely at their illicit relationship.

Well, that was in the past. Needed to stay in the past because Matt and Jane were in danger.

Cynthia and Charlie met Mindy in her driveway at eight a.m. Sunday morning, as she hauled a bag of groceries from the back of her monstrous Escalade, which cost more than most people's annual salary. Mindy's was the highest-end model she'd bought herself as a divorce present. Like most vehicles in Bozeman, dust coated the metallic black paint, and mud from the tires splashed up onto the undercarriage, speckling the sides.

"What do you want?" Mindy sniped. She settled her sack against her trim hip and glared.

"We need to talk to you about Matt and Jane," Cynthia said.

Mindy rolled her eyes and headed through her garage toward the door that led into the mudroom. Cynthia barreled forward, using her momentum to keep the door from shutting them out of Mindy's house. While Matt's bungalow was cozy, Mindy insisted she needed the space and luxury of a much larger home. Mindy's parents owned an enormous cattle ranch near Havre, Montana, and it was the location where a Montana State professor had died during a hunting accident...the cold case that Detective Fremont had called about the day before.

Mindy shoved the bags on the counter, then rubbed her biceps. She grimaced and dropped her hands back to her sides.

"There's a blizzard blowing in," Cynthia said. "And Matt's not answering his sat phone."

"What's wrong with your arm?" Charlie asked.

"I hurt it in Pilates yesterday," Mindy said as she set squash in a neat row—four bright yellow gourds against the dark stone beneath. Cynthia blinked back the image of blanket-wrapped shrouds.

"We're worried," Cynthia said.

"They'll ride out the storm in one of those cabins." Mindy pulled out apples next. "My guess is *that* experience will cure Jane of this backpacking foolishness. Maybe she'll realize her father's a fanatic and move back home—where she belongs."

"We'd like to borrow the ATV," Charlie said.

His nostrils pinched, and his upper lip turned white while Mindy's pretty sky-blue eyes held that...*thing*...that made her look guileless. But Cynthia knew the serpent within waited to strike.

"Too bad. It's not here."

Matt had used that ATV for years to take Jane deep into the woods. Mindy had insisted on it in the divorce settlement. To get rid of it or to try to erase Matt's connection to his daughter, no doubt. This petty vindictiveness was why Cynthia couldn't stand Mindy. That and the bewildering hold she had over the two most important men in Cynthia's life.

"Anyway, you don't really want to involve me. You're *Matt's* friends." The implication was that they weren't *her* friends.

Wise woman. Cynthia had seen Mindy for what she was: an ambitious woman looking for the easiest score. Matt's connection to James Sorenson's oil and gas company had been enough for Mindy to latch onto him as soon as they met. Only later did Mindy learn Matt refused to have anything to do with his father's money.

"And we're concerned about his and Jane's well-being," Cynthia said slowly, as if talking to a toddler during a meltdown.

"I don't know what you think I can do. I mean, they're in Yellowstone. It's not like I can just drive up there and ask Janie to step into the school's office. Especially without that stupid ATV." Mindy folded the sack and laid it next to her fruits and vegetables while she shot Charlie a poisonous glare.

"That's not what I'm asking you to do," Cynthia growled.

"How about this?" Charlie cut in. "What if you explain the weather concern to the local police, along with Jane's recent surgery?"

Mindy bounced her attention from one to the other, then back, her slender brown brows tugging a little toward her nose. Maybe she was *finally* picking up on her family's danger.

"This is such a waste of time," Mindy said. "Matt's an outdoorsman. He knows how to handle the weather."

"You're forgetting those tiny cabins are sixteen to twenty miles apart," Charlie argued. "That's a challenging day hike in good conditions."

Mindy threw up her hands with a grunt of exasperation. "*Fine*. I'll call the police."

Charlie and Cynthia stood inside the doorway while Mindy moved deeper into the living space.

"What did Matt see in her?" Cynthia asked, but she wondered, *what did you see in her?*

"You know, at one point, Matt thought I was using you," Charlie said.

Cynthia raised her eyebrows. "You were. Until you decided to use the bartender at the off-campus bar. Or when you chose to have an affair with *her*." Cynthia tipped her head toward Mindy.

Charlie shot her an angry look. "That's all ancient history. I don't know why you insist on bringing it up."

Cynthia was about to turn fifty and had spent the last decade alone. As she'd aged, she'd mellowed, thanks to her fears of loneliness and a look through her own mirrored funhouse of mistakes. Booting him from her bed and house hadn't cut him cleanly out of her life...and she missed him. And *that* was why she communicated with him via her grad students most of the time.

Mindy had pulled out her phone and plopped her butt on her couch. She kicked out her leg, letting it swing in a lazy arc as she spoke into the phone.

"Well, I'm not worried, but Matt's two colleagues are. They seem to think my ex-husband will jeopardize my daughter's safety."

"Are you kidding me right now?" Charlie plowed across the room, intent on snatching the phone from Mindy's hand, but Cynthia moved even faster.

"That is not what we meant or what we said," Cynthia said into the phone, and directed a harsh scowl at Mindy. "Matt would *never* jeopardize Jane's safety. We wanted to call Jane, too, in case she could pick up the call. She's on a different carrier than her father. Neither Charlie nor I has her new number and can't give it to the park service to track via GPS."

Charlie glared at Mindy, who smirked at him, her Cowboy-boot-shod foot swinging back and forth. She had the kind of expression on her face that Cynthia loathed. Mindy seemed to be saying *I used you. I took you to my bed because doing so hurt Matt.*

Or maybe Cynthia was projecting, but that didn't change the fact that Mindy only cared about and for herself.

"Give us Jane's number," Charlie snapped as Cynthia said her goodbyes.

"Why?" Mindy asked. "We both know there's no reception there, not even on her fancy new phone and new network."

There it was—the dig that Matt didn't offer Jane the same level of luxury that Mindy did. Mindy adored the projection of being a better provider. She liked the control she exerted when she'd given Jane a brand-new device the week she left on this trip, conveniently turning off the other phone to which Cynthia had access.

"Just...humor us," Charlie said. "The sooner you do that, the sooner we leave."

Mindy rolled her eyes as she reached forward and snatched her phone from Cynthia. One of her nails gouged into Cynthia's palm, and Cynthia was sure the other woman dug it in on purpose.

"I'll just leave *my* daughter a message and ask her if she minds me sharing her contact information with you."

"I've had her number for years," Cynthia said.

"Mmm. Not this one. And Janie wasn't quick to share it, was she? Seems to say something about how close she thinks you are."

That dig struck deep in Cynthia's heart, and Mindy grinned cheekily as she pressed a button and lifted the phone to her ear. After about thirty seconds, her blue eyes dimmed a little as her brows puckered. She gasped, her eyes wide and mouth dropped open as she listened. Her fingers shook too hard to end the call, and she flopped back against the seat cushions.

"What is it?" Cynthia asked.

"That can't be right," Mindy breathed. Her eyes were wide, her skin so pale that her veins stood out against the stark whiteness.

Charlie snatched her phone from her and redialed the number, then pressed the speaker option. The phone rang and rang, but once it hit voicemail, Charlie gripped Cynthia's biceps and stared, horrified, as Jane's trembling voice poured from the sleek device.

"Dead...followed..." Crackles followed dead air. "...looks like snow....trying to get....use phone's GPS...." crackling, huffs, as if Jane was running. "Half the battery left." Jane sniffled.

"Repeat. Dad's dead."

# TWELVE

A GRAND AND TERRIBLE IRONY: water surrounded Jane, and yet since she'd drunk the last of her clean, safe water last night, she was *thirsty*. Her throat ached with the soreness of too little saliva, but she continued to move. Keep going, never stay in one place too long... don't get comfortable.

As she stared at the small accumulation of snow against tree trunks, Jane swallowed the spittle that pooled in her mouth, enjoying the rush of fluid. Liquid burbled *right there*. She just needed to scoop it up and...no. That wasn't smart, and Jane *had* to be innovative.

Both the mountaineering training and Cynthia reinforced over and over again that Jane must boil any form of liquid and that germs and microorganisms weren't killed in frozen forms of water, just frozen. Those drink-anywhere straws remained tucked away in her father's pack, which lay on the ground next to his body...or with Lavinia, if she'd been smart enough to raid her father's stash.

She also couldn't continue to keep up her current pace without hydrating.

*Think, Jane. What are your options?*

She had the flexible water skin in her backpack. And she vaguely remembered something about using dark-colored rocks for warmth if a fire wasn't available. Well, that option proved better than *nothing*. When Jane found another thicker patch of snow, she took out her water pouch and crouched in front of it. Unsure about the cleanliness of her hands or gloves, Jane opted for the gloves, which seemed more sanitary than her bare skin.

Jane did her best to keep the waterproof covering on her chilled fingers and pushed the snow toward the mouth of her water bladder. She had to cap it and move to another location, where she shoved clean snow into the water bag before finding a third, then fourth, pile of snow.

She wasn't sure she'd filled the bladder, but Jane's gloves were soaked. So, she hunted for a dark rock in the exposed sun. Jane found it, set the water bladder and gloves on it, and retreated into the nearby forest shadows. She unzipped her outer jacket and shoved her cold, wet fingers into her armpits, trying to warm the sensitized skin.

Jane stepped back and splashed into a puddle, causing the faint scent of sulfur to grow stronger. Jane crouched to touch the water seeping from the crack in the rock.

It warmed her skin...no, it was *hot*.

Jane wanted to jig, but she settled for a bit of shimmy. Of course, Jane knew hot springs were the most common hydrological feature in the park. She'd spent enough time at Old Faithful as a child to find the geyser mundane. But this...this slow seep of snow must have percolated downward through layers of crack-riddled rock and met with the hot brine heated by the magma that sat under most of the park.

Much as Jane wanted to drop to her knees, she resisted. Wet pants would reduce her ability to maintain heat. Jane ran her palms through the water, sucking in a breath at the intense heat.

She brought her palms to her face and scrubbed her neck, cheeks, and forehead, repeating the process twice to get her face as clean as possible. Jane lifted her shirt and washed the hot water into her armpits.

Not as good as an actual bath, but she was cleaner... and *warmer*. Her hands' heat on her pebbled skin felt miraculous. She adjusted her clothes and bent to her hiking boots, where she considered putting on a new pair of socks.

A rustle of the nearby shrubs changed Jane's mind. She whirled, heart pounding as she sought out her father's killer.

"I'll shoot," Jane snarled. "And when I shoot, I aim to kill."

She didn't have a gun, didn't have anything but bravado and deep-seated anger. Nothing moved. Jane waited another few breaths. Maybe she was paranoid, and the wind had shifted the vegetation. Jane bit her lip to keep the giggles from bursting forth. Of course, she was paranoid. She'd watched her father get shot right in front of her.

She refused to take the chance of remaining on the outcropping. It was exposed with less vegetation surrounding it, which meant it got more direct sun. Clouds diffused its light into a bright, if eerie, twilight as the snow stuttered, seeming to stop—for now. But darker clouds roiled over the ridges, promising additional snow and rougher conditions.

Jane darted forward and grabbed her water pack and gloves before skidding around the rock and down the other side of the outcropping into the dubious safety of the Ponderosa pines.

Bullets didn't shatter the silence or her body, so after sprinting over the terrain, Jane slowed her pace again.

Jane drank the cold water as quickly as possible, which sloshed in her belly as she moved at a good clip. She had fluid, and she was clean...ish. She hadn't heard Lavinia trailing her since the day her father died. Perhaps the woman had given up hope of finding her.

Perhaps Jane's luck had finally turned.

CYNTHIA SAT NEXT to Charlie on the hard wooden seats of the local police precinct, still numbed and shell-shocked by Jane's message. Smart of Jane. She'd known that her updated message would upload whenever the phone connected to the 5G network, which it had done at some point in the last two and a half days.

Cynthia based the timeline on her last conversation with Matt...about her pups. How unimportant that seemed now that Jane's voice rang inside her head: *Dad's dead.*

Matt had a physical just a couple of weeks ago, and the doctor stated Matt was in prime health. Granted, she knew the story of athletes dropping dead from heart attacks and strokes, but she just couldn't imagine that happening to Matt. A predator attack seemed the most likely, but Matt shot well, and he carried a Sig Sauer rifle, a reliable choice.

Mindy was nearby, on another uncomfortable chair. She shook her head, tears streaming down her cheeks, as she sobbed, "No. No. *Not Janie.* No."

The officers who'd taken Mindy's statement walked toward them. Tara Fremont had a no-nonsense look and a ground-eating stride that Cynthia appreciated.

"Do either of you have anything to add to Mrs. Sorenson's account?" Detective Fremont asked. Her gaze homed in on Cynthia, and a flash of cold followed the intensity of heat Detective Fremont's stare burned into her.

If Jane's message was true, then Matt was dead. Like their former department chair, Arthur Ford. Cynthia's gaze rose to Detective Fremont's face. The other woman studied Cynthia's hand snuggled against Charlie's, but her face remained impassive.

"No," Cynthia said.

"Well, we'll be looking into this case as it dovetails into another I'm working on," Tara Fremont said. "I think you'll find that we're very thorough, Dr. Bianchi."

"You're looking into Matt, right?" Charlie asked. His voice was raspy, as if his throat was too clogged for normalcy.

Detective Fremont glanced at her partner, Detective Horton, who pressed his lips together in a tight line.

"We will follow up as soon as possible. We'll take in a skeletal crew to process the crime scene, but with the rangers and all of Cody and the surrounding staff searching for those kids, we don't have many resources, let alone personnel at our disposal."

Horror shattered the numbness that had encased Cynthia. These people couldn't leave Jane out there. Her chance at survival shrank with each passing hour.

"So..." Charlie choked up as if he couldn't say the words: *Jane might die, too.*

Cynthia's shoulders folded forward. She'd been too late to sound the alarm. Impotence and worry churned in her belly and chest, creating a noxious stew of regret and what-ifs that she was too afraid to speak.

"We've called up our local members, but they've lent our chopper for the kids' search. Those little ones don't have even the skills Jane has, and they're priority one. So, the best we can do is send in all available crew members the minute the storm passes," Detective Horton said with an apologetic look.

"You can't simply leave Jane alone out there!" Mindy shrieked. "Drive up to the gates and demand the rangers get their snowmobiles the minute the snow's deep enough and—"

"And put them at risk, too?" Detective Fremont shot back, her expression shuttering with disgust.

"She's not skilled enough in survival techniques to withstand the dropping temperatures," Cynthia said, her voice cracking.

Jane had basic survival skills, but this storm was massive and fast-moving.

"Does she have that? Matt's gear?" Mindy asked.

Cynthia sought out Detective Horton's gaze. He dropped his lids and studied the battered desk between them. Probably not.

And with no resources and no volunteers to search for her, Jane was on her own. Cynthia wasn't sure *she* could withstand a blizzard of the magnitude Jane would face, even if she was outfitted correctly. That didn't mean Cynthia wouldn't try.

Because she planned to go into the park and steal a snowmobile if necessary. No way would she leave Jane there. Jane was like her daughter, too. *She'd* been the one to take Jane on the mountaineering weekend all those years ago because Mindy didn't "do dirt."

Jane called Cynthia when her ex-boyfriend Scott told her she *had* to go to his competition with him, when she'd wanted nothing more than to study and wallow about the implosion of her parents' relationship. Jane called again when a boy in her bio-ethics course had asked her out, and Jane wasn't sure she aspired to date or believed in marriage anymore.

"We understand." Detective Fremont and her partner exchanged glances. "We'll be out there as soon as possible."

"Well...go talk to the boy, at least," Mindy said.

Cynthia noted Mindy hadn't offered to traverse the dangerous terrain to find her child.

"What boy?" the partner, Horton, asked.

Cynthia eyed the door, not interested in Mindy's chittering. She fantasized about striding toward it, climbing into her Subaru, and driving until she found Jane. She clicked through the checklist of items she needed to add to her hiking pack. She kept it stocked, which meant a few more layers and dry socks. An extra set of thermals would be smart.

"Scott. Jane's ex-boyfriend. He's on a shooting team."

Cynthia turned back to the discussion. “Why are you talking about shooting, Mindy?”

Detective Fremont narrowed her eyes. “I’d like to know that, too.”

# THIRTEEN
## MONDAY

WALKING along the edge of the hot springs, Jane paused a few times, a prickle of awareness from being watched on her nape. But she could never find any indication of another person.

Jane rejoiced when she found one of the shallow caves that pockmarked the area. The earth emitted warmth, similar to radiant floor heating. She settled in and waited, but no one followed her. She released a long breath that pushed out some of her anxiety. She was alone and, for the moment, safe.

After applying her deodorant and brushing her teeth, Jane could almost pretend she was on a camping trip. She settled into her sleeping bag with her pack for a pillow. Toasty-warm and clean, she slept hard and deep.

Jane awakened just as the first rays of light dribbled over the spiky pines. As she emerged from her shelter, where a fine layer of icy crust settled on Jane's jacket and hat, it gave her a good idea that the temperature drop wasn't a fluke. Her nose stung as the sensitive tissues struggled against the biting cold. Blizzard-bloated clouds churned over the mountain peaks to the north.

The plunging temperatures forced her to leave the jacket facing outward. She covered the bright orange fleece with dirt, hoping to make herself less obvious as she walked through the woods. Genuine fear settled as the temperature dropped and the sun rose. She couldn't find enough cover, even in the woods. Huddling in her sleeping bag might keep her from losing her fingers and toes...but it might not. Unsure how to handle this new predicament, Jane plodded forward, following the narrow, overgrown track that meandered through the woodlands. Still, she kept her pace as fast as she could manage, increasing to a jog as she moved downhill, her breathing coming a little too rapidly for comfort.

She turned her head and stifled a scream with her hand clamped to her own mouth as she fell.

Eyes stared back at her, unblinking. She'd been right. Someone *was* following her. Jane's fingers flailed to grasp her backpack as she scooted on her butt, ineffectually moving her feet, desperate to get away from her father's killer, to *not die*.

Wait. *Those eyes*. They were low to the ground, reflective. Not human. They were too round, too small.

She let out her breath in a faint hiss as she stared at the creature's eyes before her gaze slid over the rest of its face, tracing the white markings to the deeper shadows that must house its black nose.

"Oh. *Wow*."

She'd never seen a badger, but the telltale markings pointed toward that animal. Her father had explained to her that badgers were solitary creatures that rarely showed up on camera in the park.

To Jane's knowledge, her father had never seen one either. They tended to congregate in the open savannah-like Lamar Valley and dug burrows to hunt for ground squirrels. She didn't know why one would be in the woods, but it must have been looking for a meal.

She inhaled as the residual panic receded—a bit—and she

wondered if she'd ever return to her once-normal state of relative carefree young womanhood.

The animal still hadn't run away. She frowned, disturbed. Such stillness was unusual for the species.

She studied it, aware that it studied her in return. As her breathing regulated, she heard a faint whimper. Her heart rate increased, and she inched closer to the beast. Again, it didn't run away. Though it flinched back.

Its leg was caught in a trap.

A theory formed in Jane's mind—one she didn't like. This trap was illegal. The person who'd set it wouldn't like Jane messing with it. That didn't deter her, though. As she moved closer again, within about fifteen feet now, the badger bared its teeth, making clear to Jane its displeasure with what it perceived as her aggression. She spoke low, her voice shaky with fear, but she refused to abandon a trapped animal.

As she inched a little closer, the badger lunged toward her this time ending with a deep howl of distress, and Jane knew she'd been right.

There—she could make out a black casing much larger than the badger's right front paw, which bled freely from the deep wound.

Glancing around, Jane tried to find something she could use to leverage open the sharp tines digging into the badger's flesh. She didn't have all the tools to make this unexpected camping trip doable, but she had a screwdriver attachment to her Swiss Army knife. The knife and screwdriver were too small, so Jane had to risk getting near the badger to free it.

She met the badger's eyes, noting the fierceness in them as they glared at her. She wondered how long the little guy had been trapped. From the look of its foot and the free flow of blood, she didn't think long. Overall, that was a good sign. The furry mammal hadn't tired enough not to fight when she invaded its space.

Taking a deep, steadying breath, she inched closer once more. The badger lunged and snarled, and Jane fell back onto her butt. Hard.

"I'm trying to help you!" she gasped. The animal hissed and snarled again. She pressed her lips together to keep from snarling back.

Animals were her dad's wheelhouse. Jane decided she preferred plants. An arboreal species would never bite her, let alone *maim* her, if she messed up its treatment. The badger frightened her, but that didn't mean she'd leave the poor creature there. She swallowed hard and did her best to view the trap from all angles from a good ten feet away. The pin was on the far side, closest to the tree, and at the most challenging angle.

"Of course," she said. "Of course, that asshole set it up like that."

So...if Lavinia wasn't her father's killer, then would a poacher resort to *murder*? She considered the loss of liberty and the sum that was higher than many people could afford to pay.

"People have murdered for less. But my dad's life was worth way more than five years of some criminal's."

That theory didn't settle quite right because Jane was now miles from the location where her father died. She found it hard to believe a poacher would have been able to set traps for tens of square miles in the park without a park ranger noticing.

That meant Jane now had two potential killers to offer the police.

"This whole situation is complicated," Jane said. "And it sucks."

The badger's head shifted as if it were listening to her words.

The stick she found had an extended, narrowed tip, but it was not thin enough for the trap's catch hole. Jane whittled it down while monitoring the badger. The creature nibbled and licked its trapped ankle but hadn't reached the point of chewing off its foot. She worried she couldn't save the animal's foot. All she could do was her best, but that might not be great.

Once the tip was thin enough, about an inch past the point where it would need to fit into the lock mechanism, she put away her Swiss Army knife. With a deep breath, she looked into the creature's eyes.

"I want to help you."

Jane inched closer on her butt, still startled and fighting down the fear each time it snarled at her. Was it her imagination, or was the badger's snarling less intense? No way to be sure, so she assumed she was correct. When she was within proper distance, she levered her stick forward, struggling to get the tip through the metal into the mechanism. Sweat bloomed, and she strained to listen.

"I really want to meet another hiker. Gah—I wish there was someone else here, but it'd probably be the poacher, and he'd kill me. *Everything* in this place seems to want me dead." Jane clamped her jaw to keep it from quivering. Her dad had told her that, inside the park, she was part of the food chain.

Just before she snapped the branch in the trap, the badger pounced with a strangled scream and shredded the wood to a pulp.

"Well, isn't that just great? You could be thoughtful, you know."

Anger kept her going this time. Jane whittled her next stick faster. She hadn't moved away from the badger the entire time. Maybe that's why the animal didn't snap when she inserted the stick into the mechanism—first try this time, thank you very much.

Jane had to wiggle it a bit, but the badger appeared more intrigued than frightened or angry. After another moment, the mechanism unlatched.

The badger leaped forward, a snarl rippling across its muzzle, its teeth inches from her nose. Jane held her breath, her entire body tensed. She'd dropped the stick at the badger's side, though. Jane didn't remember doing so.

The badger settled back on its hind legs and whined. Much to Jane's shock, it lay down and offered her its paw.

"Oh, now we're friends?" Jane asked. She chuckled, but it felt rusty and cut off too soon. Adrenaline slowly faded from her system, leaving her hands as shaky as her breath.

The beast cocked its head at Jane, but it didn't offer a response. She shook her head. "Actually, you are the closest thing I have to a friend out here."

# DEEP IN THE FOREST

Colm couldn't believe Jane had left her cave so early. He must've dozed off at some point, but his tight, rumbling stomach woke him. When she said she'd shoot him if he got too close, Colm hung back. Didn't want to test if she actually had a gun.

He really wanted to talk to her, but how the hell could he start that conversation out here? So, Colm just waited, trying to come up with a plan. Watched what she did and cleaned up a bit. Man, washing his face and hands felt amazing. Never thought he'd get so hyped about being clean. Filled up his water bottle with some snow before finding another cave in this Swiss cheese mountain. Those damn berries again barely took the edge off, and his stomach wouldn't shut up about it.

Now Colm squatted nearby, watching Jane with that badger, trying to ignore his growling stomach.

He didn't want to spook the badger and have it go psycho on her.

"My mom would've loved this," he murmured, his voice cracking. "She always had a way with animals, just like Jane."

He'd lost both his parents last year in a car wreck during their big road trip. That was partly why he'd hit the road himself. He'd been stuck in a funk and couldn't find joy in anything. When Chase mentioned driving to the redwoods—where his folks were headed—Colm felt a tiny spark of interest.

Not anymore, which was why he wanted to tell Jane they weren't so different. Get her to help him like she helped that wild animal.

She was pretty. He hadn't really looked at her before, thanks to all the running and shooting and surviving. But she was. Pretty. Her hands were slender, delicate even.

She'd braided her long, blonde-brown hair. Her gray beanie sat on her eyebrows and covered her ears. Even from here, he could make out the blue of her eyes. Navy blue was his favorite color.

When he spotted movement behind Jane, Colm's breath hitched.

"Oh no, no, no," he whispered, panic creeping into his voice. He raised the rifle, his hands shaking. "Come on, Colm. Steady. You can do this."

As he sighted Jane through the scope, Colm's voice became a mix of determination and desperation. "Please, Jane. Just move. I don't want to...I can't..." His words trailed off, replaced by the sound of his ragged breathing.

# FOURTEEN

"WHY DON'T you tell us why you brought up Scott?" Detective Tara Fremont suggested. Now that she'd gotten Horton's cooperation, Tara had called Mindy back in this morning to ask more questions about Matt and Jane, as well as Arthur Ford and Mindy's relationship with Charlie Bianchi.

"Well, you heard what Jane said...that Matt's dead," Mindy said. "So, I just assumed you'd want to know about Jane's ex-boyfriend because he liked to shoot stuff."

Tara watched without sympathy as Mindy pressed a tissue to her nose. "Now my baby's alone in the wilderness. Alone and scared."

Okay, Tara wasn't going to get more out of Mindy about Scott now, so she tossed out a softball question about Jane and Matt's current schedule.

Mindy shrugged. "I didn't bother to memorize it. Cynthia takes care of those details. I just know that Janie's supposed to be home Monday evening by eleven o'clock. I planned to take her out for shrimp pasta."

"Jane left for Yellowstone on Friday morning?" Detective

Fremont asked, her voice pleasant. She wanted to ease into the conversation, find some common ground to get the suspect to talk.

"Around 6:30, or some ungodly hour. She texted me to let me know because she and her father met at the university on Thursday, then headed out to some motel in Cody for the night so they could get an early start. I'm sure that was so Matt could introduce Jane to his newest 'research assistant.'"

Mindy let the venom of that euphemism drip from her tongue. It was clear to Tara that Mindy hated those young women who surrounded her ex-husband. Most likely, that was because the women were twenty years younger than her, and Mindy couldn't compete with their youth any longer.

"Did that happen often?" Detective Horton asked. He was impatient with this line of questioning, wanting to move it along. Tara bit her tongue to keep from asking him to *shut up*.

Horton faltered when he caught sight of Tara's narrowed eyes, and stuttered out, "Jane going to the university. Also, Dr. Sorenson introducing Jane to his students."

Luckily, Mindy thought Horton's stumble was because he couldn't keep his head around her, and she sat up a little taller, preening.

Gross. Tara had never been even the slightest bit empathetic toward self-absorbed people. Their world was tiny and boring—revolving around them. But Tara had begun to form another opinion of Mindy, and it was even less flattering.

"No, to the first, because Jane was away at Dartmouth for two and a half years. And she didn't show much interest in what Matt did until she returned to Bozeman and moved in with him. Why she did that, I'll never understand. She has a much bigger room at my house. Clearly, Matt's brainwashed her into thinking his work is more interesting than mine. As if real estate could ever be boring. Anyway, I make way more than Matt does."

Poor Jane, having to live with this woman.

"All right," Detective Horton said. "Tell me about the research assistants."

They'd prove a waste of time, just as Jane's ex-boyfriend, Scott, would. But it was their job to follow the leads and not make assumptions. Well, not too many assumptions, anyway. Though Tara was pretty sure Mindy was more involved in Matt's death than she wanted to share.

That comment about a shooter. Oh yes, Mindy knew things.

Tara and Horton would suss out the truth. Hopefully soon, because Jane's life hung in the balance.

"They're invariably female, and Matt worked longer hours when they were." Mindy raised her eyebrows. "Two plus two always equals four, as my daddy likes to say. He's the one who told me to lawyer up."

Tara wasn't sure if Mindy meant against Matt or them. Working through a lawyer would impede their investigation.

"That must have been difficult," Tara murmured, trying hard to look sympathetic. "Why don't you tell me about the hunting trips on your parents' ranch?"

"Daddy made good money on those," Mindy said with a shrug. "All that land, all those animals. Smart business decision."

"Did you ever suggest any people for him to invite? Back when you and Matt were married. For...I don't know...personal reasons?"

Mindy's brows scrunched together before she remembered herself and smoothed out the frown. "A few times. There was a group of professors who liked to study the flora. Or is it fauna? I never remember."

"Flora is plants," Horton began. Tara kicked his shin.

"That's so nice of your dad to allow mere professors onto his ranch. I mean, I'm sure they couldn't pay as well as big game hunters."

Mindy waved her hand. "Daddy's not just about money. He liked to help Matt and me when he could."

Tara clucked. "So sad what happened to that one professor."

"The old guy who died? Yeah. Matt liked him. That was the last time he came up to Daddy's ranch."

"Oh?" Tara asked. "Did other faculty return?"

"Charlie and Cynthia did for the next five, six years, maybe. Then, they got the big grant to study wolves in the park." She glanced up at Tara, a calculating look in her eyes. "Not that that ended all that well. Janie must be so frightened. I should never have let her go." Mindy sniffled.

Mindy had changed the subject—brought it back around to her daughter. No doubt because she didn't want to talk about Arthur Ford's death.

Mindy offered a tiny sob as her fingers clutched the tissue, squeezing it with an intensity that caused it to stick to her palm. "He's c-clearly not the responsible adult he likes to portray himself as. I mean, what type of man introduces his daughter to his mistress? Or takes a barely healed child into the wilderness?"

"But you agreed to the trip?" Tara asked.

Mindy's gaze snapped up, and the venom there told Tara that Mindy had never navigated the woman-friend social situation well.

"Let's go over the entire time frame and the voicemail once again," Detective Horton said.

"Why? You *know* what happened. The only thing that matters now is where my daughter is and when she will get home." Mindy bit her lip and sent Detective Horton a beseeching look. "But you're sure...you're sure Matt's dead?"

"Yes, we're sure," Tara answered.

"H-how?"

"We tracked the GPS unit's data that Cynthia Bianchi provided. It's been stationary for a few hours. A body has been discovered, and we'll get a team in there to analyze the crime scene."

Tara watched as Mindy finally put together that she spoke to detectives—the people who *solved* crimes. Not the ones who went looking for them. And Mindy had been the one to bring up Scott's shooting ability *before* the detectives knew anything about Matt's death.

"Oh, I get it. You asshats wanted to pin Matt's death on me. That's *laughable*."

Tara was still following the money trail, but she knew Matt had much less wealth after Mindy divorced him. She knew Matt's father had left a large trust for Jane. If something happened to her daughter, Mindy must be the beneficiary. So, yeah, she considered Mindy to have a motive to remove both her ex-husband and her daughter from her life.

# FIFTEEN

WHILE JANE TENDED THE BADGER, snow thickened in the air, and the shrieks of wind penetrated her consciousness like a blade through flesh. The Ponderosa pines and elevated rock formation she'd slept in last night remained a buffer, but not enough of one to shield her from the frigid squall.

She tucked under the tape around the badger's paw, shivering as tingles crept across her skin, and lifted her hands. "All done!"

The animal sniffed at the gauze and gave it an experimental lick, which ended in a universal head shake and grimace of disgust. Jane couldn't help but giggle at the badger's reaction.

"Well, you needed an antibiotic cream to keep out an infection," Jane chided. "The trap has been exposed to the elements. It has to be covered in bacteria."

The badger eyed her, content to lay nearby...almost close enough to share body heat. Jane swiped her palms against a cloth, noting its filth, before taking a long sip of her water through the attached straw.

The badger edged closer, snuffling.

Maybe it was thirsty? Jane couldn't spare the water. Anyway, with snow on the ground, the badger would be better adapted to munch that into liquid than Jane.

"Are you hungry?" She rummaged through her pack, noting she'd eaten over half of her jerky. Worry settled in her stomach, below the angry grumble of her body's needs. She wasn't sure how far she'd run yesterday, but her tight hamstrings and calves caused her to think it was a substantial distance...farther away from her father's Jeep and those rations, water, and blankets, which seemed like a worse decision with each snowflake that fell.

Jane couldn't go back and make a different decision now. She'd done the best she could with the data at hand. Her only choice was to move forward and solve the next issue, then the next.

Jane tugged out the smallest piece of jerky and laid it in her palm, offering it to the badger.

"All right, buddy. Eat up. That's all I can share."

The animal's velvety nose touched the skin of her fingertips, causing them to tingle. The rougher brush of its whiskers sent many sensations through Jane's hand and arm and caused a tightness in her scalp.

*I'm touching a badger.*

Its teeth and moist tongue darted out, pulling the meat from her hand...and leaving Jane with a sliced palm as one of the animal's incisors broke the tender skin. She hissed, closing her hand into a fist against the sting.

"Not careful enough."

The badger looked at her before darting off, its prize between its teeth.

"You're welcome." She opened her palm and noted the blood pooling there. With a long sigh, she used her good hand to clean up her palm, consuming most of her small stash of antibiotic cream and band-aids.

After tossing a handful of trail mix into her mouth, Jane cleaned up her mess, tucking the waste into the pocket of her jeans. Tidying the outdoor space was inherent—a habit her father had taught her years ago, reinforced during her mountaineering day—but, as importantly, Jane didn't want to leave any trace for Lavinia or the poacher to find.

The badger had hightailed from the clearing, and Jane missed the minimal companionship it had offered. She hoped her new friend stayed out of trouble...and kept the paw.

She rose, dusted off her butt, and pulled out her phone. After a long hesitation, during which she stared down at the device—her lifeline to the outer world—Jane powered it up as she walked. Less than a quarter of the battery remained. While she walked through the woods, hoping someone could pinpoint her location, she updated her voicemail for a second time. Because she couldn't be sure a text or call would go through, her only link to the outside world would be a brief connection to a cell tower long enough to make the update.

Perhaps her efforts were futile, but Jane needed to try.

She persevered past the commentary about her father's death, forcing her voice to remain steady as she documented, to the best of her ability, where she was and what direction she planned to head. Perhaps the search and rescue team had caught her phone's GPS signal while it was powered on. If not, her mother and some of her friends might hear that message, which they could relay to the National Park Service and appropriate authorities. By now, Jane assumed people must be searching for Matt and her. They'd missed two of their daily check-ins. Cynthia, at least, would be worried.

When she and her dad missed their park checkout tomorrow, more authorities would get involved. *If* the snowstorm didn't make a rescue impossible.

Snowstorms at this time of year might be uncommon, but they

weren't unheard of. And the weather out here moved in quickly, with deadly results. Many visitors to the park didn't understand that closures weren't to keep people *out* as much as they were to keep people *safe*.

She wished she were tucked into her bedroom at her father's house with a mug of cocoa. He'd made such an effort this past year while Jane had to convalesce after her second surgery. Once aware of his misplaced focus, her father spent all his free time with Jane. They'd watched movies, and he'd brought her more ice, helped her walk—anything she'd needed when he was home. And Jane hadn't told him how thankful she was for his time or support.

This was why there was that saying about hindsight. It was trite, but that didn't make it less true. Now, Jane had to live forever with the realization she hadn't tried as hard with her father as she should have. She was so angry with Lavinia for cutting her time with him short.

A rustle in the canopy dissuaded her from her loneliness. Every muscle in her body vibrated with the need to flee as unsettling sounds drifted toward her. They were so very human.

Grunts. A curse. Definitely a person.

*Lavinia.*

She must have followed Jane this far. Or...*the trap*? Someone had to have set it, and Jane had already wondered about that.

"Jane? Can you hear me?"

Jane froze. Even her lungs stilled.

"Jane! I'm coming your way. I *really* need to talk to you. Please. Just hear me out."

Not Lavinia. The voice was too male. He knew her name. Fear pumped through her body, energizing her muscles, giving her speed.

"Jane!"

Her father had told her to run. She would run to the park's

edge, possibly even all the way home, before she stopped to talk to a random man—probably her father's killer.

"Please, Jane, just—wait!"

She didn't. She bolted.

That was how she ended up in the middle of a bison stampede.

# SIXTEEN

COLM COULDN'T WAIT ANY LONGER. THANKFULLY, the threat he'd noted had been some kind of big bird. He didn't know what kind. Didn't care either. It spooked him, though.

The snow was piling up. He was too cold and hungry to continue alone. Plus, he'd just watched Jane's body bow under the grief and exhaustion, so he knew she was close to her limit, too.

They needed to work together.

Okay, so he'd just...reach out. Like talking to a woman at one of the frat parties at Penn State. Fear slicked his belly, but Colm forced himself to call out to her.

She snapped to attention, eyes darting around, searching for him. Before he could reassure her, Jane bolted.

Colm groaned at the oily slick in his belly, morphing into an anchor of terror when Jane ran straight toward a bison herd.

Colm's breath came in ragged gasps as he moved. "Okay, Colm. You've got this. Save Jane from certain death by angry fur tanks. She'll be thankful then."

As he picked up speed, chasing after Jane, Colm's voice became a mix of determination and desperation. "Jane! For the love of all that's holy, stop running...those bison will turn you into a human pancake!"

JANE SPED past the tree line, toward the great plain. Her mind hadn't caught up with her body's need to flee.

One of these days, Jane would look before she leaped. Or in this case, ran. Granted, it would be fantastic to make a decision that didn't have dire consequences, as in life and death.

The voice...that voice...

Not Lavinia's. But...but Lavinia had shot her father. *Lavinia* followed Jane. There was no other option.

Except...the trap. Poacher...

A guy calling her name.

Jane cursed. From an early age, when she witnessed a bison rip into a desperately hungry coyote, she'd understood the might and fury of these beasts. Honestly, she'd rather deal with a grumpy female bear.

And fair point to Jane, she *wanted* to give the animals a wide berth, but a sudden glint of metal flashed through the brush, coupled with the man yelling her name yet again, caused a visceral reaction.

*Run.*

Her muscles quivered with the need even as her rational brain wrestled for control.

She was surrounded by enemies: the guy calling for her, the weather, and possibly...she hoped it was *only* possible...the bison. Her body shook, but she no longer knew if it was from cold or fear.

If she stood out here, and the man was close by, he'd see her. If she stood out here, and by some miracle, the man didn't see her, she'd freeze and die from exposure.

Jane trudged onward, finding brief—and cold—comfort as the snow fell thicker and heavier than before, whiting out not just her visibility but his, too. A fresh blanket would erase her tracks within minutes, but the dropping temperatures and wet nature of the snow posed a real and present danger of exposure. If Jane remembered correctly, the wet snow meant the temperature would be in the upper twenties, which was too cold, but not as life-threatening as below-zero would be.

Especially now that she'd left the densest part of the forest and moved onto the plain where the bison grazed. She should have realized immediately that the man had been pushing her this way. Whenever she tried to correct her course to remain in the woods, he called out to her...moving her closer to the forest's edge...

To open ground where he'd have a straight shot at her heart.

She blew into her gloves again, and the heat from her breath brought sharp pricks to her fingertips and hands.

So far, so good...if she could only feel her feet. She stumbled and then splayed out on the ground. With a groan, she sat up and huddled against a large boulder.

Her knee ached from overuse and new damage to the tendons. She tried, again, to heave herself upward. If she couldn't keep moving, the snow would cover her. The longer she sat, the colder her muscles grew. Already, she felt the lethargy seeping into her limbs.

She had to get up. She tensed, holding her breath. Someone or some animal crept past.

"Come out. Jane. *Please.*" His voice rang out through the forest, bouncing off trees and reverberating through the silent wood. "I won't hurt you. I promise I won't. Swear it even. Just... *please*...I—I...I need to talk to you. I know your dad died."

Jane flinched, biting her lip, hating his voice. She hated the fear he engendered more.

Images of her dad collapsing, the blood streaming across his chest, flitted through her mind. Until now, she'd focused on running—getting away.

But that was impossible. The man would continue to track her. He'd already followed her this far.

She shoved her gloved hand into her mouth and bit down hard. She stifled the sob, but her muscles contracted, shivering as fear took hold. She was trapped.

And the man following her must be the poacher. He must also be the murderer, *not* Lavinia, as Jane had assumed before. This man was a god out here—the hunter, like Artemis. Unstoppable, all-powerful. Killer of innocent beasts.

Killer of Matt Sorenson. He'd kill Jane, too.

The snow continued to fall, thicker than before. The mass of precipitation swirled around them in a sheet. This intensity of snow qualified as a blizzard. She huddled back into the drift even as she tried to force her limbs upward, to move...to run. She wished she'd never agreed to join her father.

He walked past her, his teeth chattering, and Jane cowered, squeezing her eyes shut as the accumulating snow fell atop her. Cloaking her.

His footfalls were heavy and his breathing thicker as the snow collected on the tops of his boots. She wasn't the only one underprepared for the weather—and he'd spent at least the past night out in the elements, meaning the freezing temperatures.

The fact that they were still both alive was miraculous.

He moved closer.

*Go the other way!*

Her muscles tensed as he took another step...maybe fifteen feet from her...twelve...

Without conscious thought, Jane darted from the snow drift and ran faster than a jackrabbit. Snow blinded her, and his shouts echoed in her ears, though she couldn't understand what he said over her heart pounding.

She pumped her arms and legs, no longer lethargic, as the adrenaline kicked in. Her back tensed as she waited for the bite of the bullet...

"Stop!"

Too late.

Jane skidded to a halt within mere inches of a brown, woolly hide.

# SEVENTEEN

BECAUSE OF THEIR search and rescue status and their exact coordinates for Matt's last check-in, the park ranger manning the park's entrance let them through the barricade. Well, that and because Charlie worked his charm on the woman. As he did with all women. That was why he didn't have female grad students. Matt and Cynthia split the women between them, though that might have to end now that Lavinia had been so into Matt.

Everything was a mess.

Cynthia's worries over Jane made it difficult for her to find Charlie's behavior as irritating as she usually would. She flexed her toes inside her double-layered socks and tried to even out her heart rate as Charlie sped over the ruts and potholes, heading deeper into the wilderness. They'd be able to drive to within three, maybe four miles of Matt's last signal, meaning they would normally be able to pinpoint the spot within an hour of their arrival...except that the snow was falling too hard for ease of travel.

One more hour, and they'd know if Matt was truly dead and if Jane was missing.

Cynthia urged Charlie on even as she closed her eyes, fiddling with the edge of the memo she'd shoved into her pocket. The memo that had caused Cynthia to go in and yell at Matt last week...to have him leave angry, possibly distracted. She couldn't stomach his death on her conscience, but neither could she continue to withhold information from Detective Fremont about Arthur Ford.

"She's alive," Cynthia murmured.

For now. Cynthia watched the clouds roll over the mountains, and the snow fall in thickening sheets. Worry settled heavier on her chest because Jane was right in the teeth of the storm.

She shoved the memo deeper into her pocket. It meant nothing. Cynthia and Matt had a professional disagreement. Most colleagues did at some point. No one would blame her.

"If we're lucky, then maybe both Matt and Jane are alive," Charlie replied.

"Of course I want that, too."

"But you think Jane told the truth in her message," Charlie said, his voice flat.

"Yes, I do. Jane's never been prone to hysteria." *So* unlike her mother. "That said, she sounded scared on that message, which tells me we're walking into something pretty traumatizing. And her ACL repair might not hold up. You know how daunting the terrain can be."

Granted, terror made people—and animals—react in strange ways. They'd seen it often in their research. Otherwise, stoic wolves or even the wolves' prey would never make wild choices that could only get them hurt...or killed.

Jane might have a good head on her shoulders for a twenty-two-year-old, but she was still young. Untried in life-and-death situations. Or rather, had been.

Charlie's lashes drooped for a moment before he clenched his jaw. "I can't believe this about Matt."

"I understand. It's shocking," Cynthia murmured.

Charlie blew out a breath. "We'll see what we see."

Silence pounded against Cynthia's skull, but she held onto the door handle as the truck sped over the bumpy terrain. Two park rangers rattled behind them, towing the four-wheelers that would speed up the next step—getting them close to Matt's pre-designated walk.

Cynthia glanced up at the heavy clouds that sat, sullen, spitting snow down on the peaks, the moisture worsening with every breath. This was close to blizzard conditions, just as Cynthia had feared. She squeezed her hands tighter as her heart thrummed against her ribs.

The storm would be a monster that none of them could fully prepare for.

*Stay safe, Jane.*

AN HOUR and a half after they parked the car at the ranger housing and hopped on the park service's ATVs, they found Matt's corpse amidst the tall pines and granite boulders so common in that part of the wilderness. Charlie's sharp bellow scared birds into the air with staccato caws and an irritated flutter of wings.

Cynthia noted Detective Horton from the corner of her eye as tears filled her eyes. Charlie stumbled forward through the maze of meticulously set ropes that formed a grid. Ignoring the shouts of alarm and two forensic techs who'd been photographing the scene, he dropped to his knees onto the mat of loam and pine needles next to his best friend. His mouth opened, and his chest heaved as he reached forward to touch Matt. He gripped his friend's blood-crusted shirt, clutching Matt.

Detective Horton stepped forward into the chaos Charlie had

created. His boots sinking into the thickening mud-snow slush. Soon, the snow would be too deep to see the ground.

"You need to stand up and step away from that body exactly the way you came in. *Right now*, Dr. Bianchi." Fury poured from the words and shone from Horton's eyes.

At least the police and technicians had gotten to Matt before any large animal did. But smaller ones had been at his fingers and earlobes already. That hadn't taken long, but then again, death was part of the cycle, especially here in Yellowstone. Nothing was wasted. Not even a human's remains.

"You need to let go, Charlie," Cynthia said, her tone sharp.

Charlie drew back onto his heels as Detective Horton stepped with care into the tangled ropes and stakes and dragged Charlie back.

"Would have been much better if you hadn't done that," Detective Horton said. He muttered a few choice curses as he continued to push Charlie away. "I got him. Go ahead and finish your work," Horton called over his shoulder to the forensics team.

Charlie raised his hands and stepped farther away. His eyes were rimmed in red, and his face was nearly slack with grief. "I won't go near him again. I'm sorry." Tears traced his cheeks, and he wiped them away. "Sorry. I wasn't thinking."

"Where's your partner?" Cynthia asked as she kept an eye on Charlie. He seemed better in control of himself.

"Following up on Jane's ex-boyfriend, Scott." He grimaced. "And Mindy's alibi, which should prove the more useful of the two items. You two need to get out of here. This is my crime scene."

"We'll go. Soon," Cynthia said. She needed to know which direction Jane had run.

A tech walked up to the police officer. "We found ATV tracks," she said. "They're beyond the casings. The number is consistent with the body's wounds, minus the ones that dug into the dirt and tree."

"Good work," Horton said. "Thanks for the update. I want to know everything we can about both the bullets and the ATV."

"I'll tag it priority," the tech said before hurrying off.

Detective Horton watched, impassive, as two technicians hefted Matt and settled him into a thick, black bag. Then he walked over to the rest of the tech crew, conferring on who knew what. One ranger—a middle-aged woman named Betty—sidled closer to Cynthia.

"Wow, Charlie's upset." Since Betty stated the obvious, Cynthia didn't answer. "It's different from a dead moose or bear," Betty continued. "You know? Brings the world, mortality, into focus."

Cynthia nodded. She leaned against the rough bark of the pine and tipped her head up to peek at the sky. The typical deep blue only found out in the wilds, the reason why Matt loved to hike this area so much, was obscured by the boiling mass of clouds.

Precipitation gathered on the ground, covering the shadowed places in more than half an inch of the powder. They'd been just in time to find Matt.

"Any idea where Jane might have gone?" Cynthia asked.

"Yeah." Betty's tone dripped with disappointment at Cynthia's lack of tracking skills. She pointed toward the broken vegetation and disturbed pine needles veering deeper into the park.

*Oh, Jane. Why'd you pick* that *way?*

Because, just as Cynthia feared, the young woman had been terrified, and that had been the most straightforward direction, no doubt.

What most people failed to understand was that the amygdala's fight-or-flight response, when called forth, proved impossible to resist.

Jane had acted on pure instinct and terror. And now she would pay the consequences of that decision. Cynthia glanced around at the woods, eyeing the formidable terrain beyond.

Jane's likelihood of survival had risen by running from the threat but plummeted the deeper she moved into the park's heart.

"This has been a crazy week," Betty said. "First, that girl you called us about called back to say she caught a ride out of the park and now this."

"Girl? Do you mean Lavinia?"

Betty nodded slowly. "That sounds right. She said she was heading out of the west side with a group of students. Would have been nice if she'd let me know *before* I closed down the guard station, but no real issue, I guess."

"She called you to tell you that?" Cynthia pressed.

"Yeah."

"But how'd she get your number?"

Betty blinked once, slowly. "From you?"

Cynthia shook her head. "Not from me. Are you sure she left the park?"

"Ben said an SUV pulled out a few hours later. They were from MSU..." Betty trailed off and swallowed. "No, that's not...I *assumed* that. The timing was right." She tilted her head, concern filtering into her expression. "You don't think..."

"I don't know what to think, exactly," Cynthia said. "Lavinia should have been picked up by an ATV. That's what we discussed."

"I'm sure she's fine. Just give her a call when you get back," Betty said with a dismissive wave.

Cynthia didn't respond to that because she was too busy connecting dots she'd hoped weren't related. "The SUV. Was it big? Do you know? Black? New?"

Betty shrugged. "I can ask Ben."

"Do. Please."

Betty wandered off while Cynthia continued to stare at the scene in front of her. She didn't like where her mind returned each time.

"Ben said yeah to all that," Betty said, breaking Cynthia's fevered reverie. "You know who it was? You should tell the detective." She tipped her head toward the forensics team and Detective Horton, who huddled at the edge of the clearing.

Betty's face grew animated. "They're talking about the blood splatter on the foliage and our guy's fall. They're saying his daughter couldn't have shot him."

"That was never a possibility," Cynthia said, her voice low, though rage simmered in her belly.

Betty shrugged, her eyes bright with excitement—not unlike a magpie that planned to steal its neighbor's prey. "You *know* it is. The police will look at all angles. Including the daughter as a suspect. Makes the most sense, seeing as how she was the only one out here."

Cynthia pushed off the tree. "Well, we know that Lavinia was here, too. With a rifle."

"Oh." Betty blinked, deflating as Cynthia poked holes in her theory.

With her own heartfelt sigh, Cynthia headed toward the law enforcement group. "Detective Horton, I'm concerned that our grad student, Lavinia, is still unaccounted for—"

"Oh? Where is she?" Horton asked, his sharp gaze locked on Cynthia's face.

"She's *still missing,* too. And...and Mindy's car was covered in mud, which is weird because Mindy doesn't do mud. I just had Betty check, and she said the ranger on the West side of the park noted a big black SUV heading out of the park not long after Lavinia was supposed to be picked up. I don't like where this is pointing—at what I'm thinking."

Detective Horton rocked back on his heels. He'd changed into hiking boots, fleece-lined jeans, and a thick, cable-knit sweater under his North Face coat. A colorful, knitted beanie coddled his egg-shaped skull. He'd dressed for hours outside.

"And what are you thinking?" he asked.

Closing her eyes, Cynthia inhaled. "I think Mindy's involved not just in Matt's death, but with our missing grad student."

Horton rubbed his reddened chin with his gloved fingers. "That's an interesting angle, and one we'll follow up on. Now, how about you head back home so I can actually do my job?"

Cynthia opened her mouth to say something, but Detective Horton was back to talking to his people. She caught Charlie's eye as he helped the other ranger—Ben, Cynthia thought his name was—roll Matt's body bag from the back of one of the park service's ATVs.

"Jane went that way," Cynthia pointed.

Charlie's gaze drifted over her shoulder. "I'm going to help Ben settle Matt, and then we can head out."

*Toward Jane*, Cynthia begged Charlie with her eyes.

# EIGHTEEN

TARA FREMONT'S bitterness raced up through her chest. *This professor had clearly loved his daughter. He was one of the good ones—way better than my POS ex, who refuses to give me a penny more than necessary for our kid's necessities.*

Tara wished she could shut her ears against Mindy's whining. She'd opted to stay at the station that morning, continue interviewing Mindy Sorenson née Warner, and then visit Jane's ex-boyfriend, Scott. Tara Fremont did *not* like the outdoors. As a native of Montana, this brought her nearly as much shame as her unlucky love life. The lack of enjoyment in wilderness pursuits was why Tara remained single at forty, working too many hours with only Horton for company, especially now that her daughter spent her weekdays with Tara's ex.

"Jane didn't circle back to the car?" Mindy asked.

"No, she didn't," Tara said. "Or if she did, she didn't find it."

Mindy's brow furled. "But...*why*? She could have driven it out of there...been home...with me...safe..."

"A ranger located the Jeep *before* we found Dr. Sorenson," Tara explained again. "It hasn't been touched." And we're not moving it because Cynthia said Jane has the keys to it. If, by chance, the young woman was able to circle back around, the Jeep would be her best option out of the park.

Mindy waved her hand. "Whatever. Focus. *Jane.* Do you know where she is?"

"We don't know why, exactly, but Jane took off deeper into the wilderness—at least from what we can tell from the scene."

"Jane's usually smart," Mindy said.

"So, we found ATV tracks near where the killer shot Matt. We have video on some traffic cameras of your ATV loaded in a trailer behind your Escalade last weekend. Where did you take it?"

Mindy's poker face was good, but it wasn't great. "Out. Some of the land I show is pretty remote."

"You left the ATV in a remote location?" Tara pressed.

Mindy shrugged. "It wasn't where I parked it when I came back for it. It may have been stolen. I don't know. But Jane hasn't been using it, so I didn't think it mattered all that much."

"All right. Tell me about Arthur Ford."

"Who's that?"

"The man who was shot and killed on your father's ranch."

Mindy visibly relaxed. Foolish woman. Tara hadn't finished her questions. She'd changed tactics to get Mindy to talk, and the woman did, though it took her a moment to come up with the person Tara had mentioned. "Poor old guy. He probably shouldn't have been out there."

"He was using one of your rifles, wasn't he?"

Mindy frowned. "I own a couple. My daddy bought them for me because I liked to go riding."

Tara knew about them from the gun registry. She also knew that Mindy hadn't taken a gun safety course in fifteen years. "I heard you were a great sharpshooter," she said with a smile, widening her eyes.

"Oh. Yeah. I liked to shoot. Mostly bottles or squirrels. Daddy took me big game hunting once, but I didn't like how the animals smelled."

"The scent of blood bothers you?" Tara asked. "I get that—"

"No, I'm not squeamish." Mindy wrinkled her nose. "The bighorn stunk. Like BO but animal version."

"Gotcha. So that was it? One and done with the rifles? You lent them out to Arthur and others who came to the ranch."

"We have a nice selection of long guns. Arthur must have liked that one."

Tara made a production of lifting the paper and glancing at the words. "Oh! My mistake! It was *your* Henry rifle that was used to shoot Arthur."

Mindy blinked. "I...didn't know that."

"That's okay," Tara said. "We're going next to talk to Dr. Sorenson's colleagues again—now that we have more information that puts you in contact with Professor Ford at his time of death." Tara's sixth sense had pinged the moment Cynthia Bianchi called in about Arthur Ford's case. But when Tara read the notes, she'd agreed wholeheartedly with the former lead detective's view that Matt, Mindy, Charlie, and Cynthia all had the opportunity to kill the man. He hadn't wanted to label Ford's death accidental, but Mindy's rich daddy leaned on the department to do so. Now, Tara was positive one of those four had killed Arthur Ford, and she was pretty sure it was Mindy. "Here's the list of people I had there. They include both Cynthia and Charlie Bianchi as well as Matt. Does that sound right?"

"I can't remember," Mindy said, her response terse. "What I want to know is what you're doing to find my Janie."

"Everything possible, I promise. Detective Horton went out to the park and found Matt's body."

Mindy smiled. "Oh. I...wondered where he was."

"Do you have anyone jealous of you?" Tara asked, doggedly plowing through the list of questions she needed to answer if she was to collect a list of suspects. "Who'd want to hurt you? Maybe your lover—"

Mindy touched her pearls with jittery fingertips. "Jordan would never..."

"Jordan?" Tara asked, her brows drawing low.

Mindy hadn't mentioned a man before now. Getting information from this woman proved more trouble than a root canal. Maybe she should have volunteered to head out into the blizzard... nope! Not for Tara. She'd been trapped in one as a child, and her throat closed at the mere thought of snow piling around her.

She hoped Jane came through this experience better than Tara had.

Mindy licked her lips. "Jordan Shaw. He's my...well, as silly as it sounds for a woman my age, I guess you'd call him my boyfriend. He's an accountant at the firm Loughton and Shaw. I'm sure you've heard of it."

Tara pulled out her notebook and wrote Jordan's name and his place of work.

"Thanks," she said. "We'll talk to him."

Mindy licked her lips. "He's a busy man. Why haven't you checked in with Scott? His breakup with my Janie was awful. Bitter. Hateful."

"He's my next stop. But right now, I'd like to know if you can tell us anything that might give us a better idea of who killed your ex-husband," Tara said, her tone gentling as she brought up the point she'd been circling around for far too long —the one she feared would send Mindy into full hysterics. "That same person will continue to hunt for Jane," Tara added.

As expected, Mindy dissolved into a pile of wet eyes and harsh sobs. Tara sat stone-faced through the ordeal. Once Mindy wound down, Tara leaned forward. "You see why we're worried—checking every single angle, no matter how seemingly unrelated. I want to bring Jane home to you as quickly as possible. So, help me out, Mindy. Why are you so focused on Scott?"

"Well... I heard her—Janie—talking to her father. She told him that Scott wouldn't leave her alone."

*Stalker.*

"You know something else, huh?" Tara prompted. She eased closer to Mindy. She gave the woman a conspiratorial wink. "We're both mothers. We don't take their word for everything, do we?"

"Too right. I checked her phone. Janie had deleted a bunch of texts from Scott. She blocked him, too. So...I did additional digging."

Tara grinned. She'd only recently learned that some text messages could be recovered. They had to be from the past month, possibly up to forty days. "So...you did what? Gave yourself screenshots of those messages and then re-deleted them?"

Mindy smiled smugly, but she didn't say that's what she did aloud.

Tara gave a good-for-you nod. "*Of course* you did. You scoped her social media accounts, didn't you?"

Total invasion of privacy, Tara thought as Mindy nodded, enthusiastic to have an audience who understood her.

"He's taking classes at Montana State, where Matt teaches—taught—just like Jane. He's in a fraternity." She rattled off the name.

Tara stood after she'd closed her notebook. "Thank you for your time, Ms. Sorenson. We'll be in touch soon."

"Should I set up a TV interview? Go on those morning shows and plead with people to help find Janie? That'd get more people motivated to find my daughter."

"Not at this point," Tara said.

Mindy blinked at Tara, her wide eyes filling with tears. "Well...what am I supposed to do?"

"How about you call Jordan?" Tara suggested. "I'm sure your boyfriend will want to be here to support you during your time of need."

Tara left the room with a heartfelt sigh of thanks. She walked to the parking garage, and Tara opened her door, slamming it shut behind her. With a deep breath, she rolled out into the thickening snow.

# NINETEEN

JANE QUIVERED AS SHE STARED, eyes wide, the wind and snow pummeling against the exposed organs, but she couldn't blink...couldn't look away.

The bison turned toward her, its massive head dotted with water, ice, and snow droplets. Its eyes were dark and wide, and its nostrils were flaring, mucus forming a wet barrier on its snout. The animal's short horns glinted in the watery gray light. Its dark eyes gleamed, intent on Jane. They weren't angry *yet*.

That was a good thing. Great.

Jane held still, heart hammering, skin tingling as fear reared up. In this scenario, Jane thought the armed man might be less dangerous than the bison.

"I'm not dead yet," she muttered in a terrible approximation of a British accent. "You always made that joke, Dad. I thought it was *so stupid*. Now, I'd give anything to hear you say it. To be somewhere safe with you."

No time to think about him now. Jane remained an easy target for the shooter behind her, and she had a goal. The shifting snow and winds created swirls of snowflakes that continued to change their patterns and looked like large animals encroaching ever closer. And she had to force her muscles to relax—no easy feat.

"Jane, are you okay? Come back. Please, *please*," he begged... almost as if he feared for her.

"Ridiculous," she muttered to herself. "You're being *ridiculous*." The guy had shot—murdered—her father.

Jane couldn't trust him. Never would.

The bison's wedge shape emphasized their awkward tapered bodies as they huddled in a shaggy group, impervious to the increasing pelting of sleet.

They docilely faced the snow, some lying down behind the protection of their neighbors' flank, especially now that she was within distance for them to strike. She shuffled her cold, wet feet forward yet again, ignoring the quivering in her thighs and the impulse to turn tail. She must go ahead. So, she did.

Three additional large, bushy heads with hot, dark eyes swiveled in her direction. They stood still and followed her every move in those glossy, black depths—like marbles—reflecting her image back to her. Her lungs tried to seize as panic clawed through her, but she stepped forward. *This* death, at least, would be of *her* choosing—not his. For the past few days, Jane had done nothing *but* react. Now, with this choice, she was taking charge.

Being gored would hurt, and Jane had enough sense to fear the pain. But she could not—*would not*—let the gunman kill her. Not if there was a slight chance that she could survive and bring him to justice. To make sure he paid for her father's death.

Now, inches separated her from the nearest animal. They all seemed to inhale harder, dragging in her scent. Their wet noses flared before they exhaled giant puffs of frost. One snorted just as Jane set down her foot, and she flinched, muscles coiled, ready for the strike. But all the bison did was turn its head away, clearly disinterested in her...realizing Jane wasn't a threat.

"Step away from the herd, Jane," the guy said. "Christ. They're even bigger up close."

She chanced a glance behind her. The man stood thirty yards away and was backlit by the watery sun that kept trying to break through the low, thickening clouds. His short hair held bits of leaf while pine needles clung to his shoulders. His rangy build reminded Jane of many of the young men in her classes. His rifle was on his shoulder, ready.

Jane's attention shifted back toward the animal in front of her. Which was the more significant threat to her safety?

Bison, her father had explained, were curious creatures, but they were also proud and untrusting. Putting her faith in any of the wildlife not to harm her was like trusting the man, her father's probable killer.

She moved in close enough for the faintest heat to touch her gloved and wet palm, and Jane bit her cheek to keep from crying out at the sensation. It felt delicious and painful.

She drew even nearer, aware that for her to be safest, both from the gunman and the elements, she needed to be between the beasts.

"Don't," he said again. "I won't hurt you. I need your help to get out of here. I just...I want to get out. That's all. That's why I called out to you. Swear to God."

Jane's caustic laugh exploded from her throat. A few of the bison shifted as they grunted. An energy swirled between the animals, causing the herd to spring to alertness.

"You killed my father."

The bison shifted again.

"*No.* I didn't. I swear. Look, it took me days to gather the courage to talk to you. You have more skills out here than I do. Work with me. Please. Let's help each other."

He seemed sincere...but she couldn't believe him. Jane inched forward. She could dive between the musky bodies and disappear into their shaggy shelter.

"Jane, I was hunting—"

"We're humans," Jane's voice shrilled through the air. Two bison rose and shook off a thick cloud of dirt.

"I've been hunting the murderer who shot *my* best friends." He raised his left hand from the rifle and held it up. "Swear to God and on my life. I got close the day your dad died. Then, well, I had to choose. And I chose to come after you when you ran."

Jane's mind stuttered. That sounded plausible. But it was highly improbable. "I don't believe you."

"I get that—I do, but I can prove it to you."

"How?" Jane asked.

Exhaustion and fear slammed into her, sending her reeling. Talking to him kept some of that fear at bay, but she was within touching—goring—distance of two-thousand-pound creatures known for their volatility.

"My friends, Chase and Lorna, were with me. Doing the Van Life thing. My...my name's C-Colm. We'd spent two weeks d-driving out from Philadelphia. We'd just set up camp here. I w-was p-picking berries."

His teeth chattered because of his inadequate clothing. He needed another layer or two, plus a thick, downy coat. Why did he tell her his name? He was humanizing himself to get closer to her.

"I heard the shots. Couldn't d-do anything. Th-they were d-dead. G-gone."

His voice held grief and anger and resentment—all emotions that bubbled inside Jane, unmoored and ready to explode.

"The shooter wore a d-dark sweatshirt, hood up. Plaid shirt. Rifle's stock was w-walnut." He swallowed. "Followed that asshole."

"You're telling me you *saw* the killer?" Jane asked, against her better judgment. The massive bison near her feet snorted, huffing.

No way, this was some sort of setup. What was this guy playing at?

With a whoosh, she blew out a breath. "Do you know Lavinia?"

The man...Colm...shivered as the snow fell around them, clearly uncomfortable with Jane so close to the bison, but she didn't want to leave the meadow or the dubious safety the herd provided her. Colm must have realized firing his rifle would start a stampede.

Jane inched closer to the shaggy animals.

"A woman? Dark hair. Tall. Willowy. Annoyingly breathy voice."

"The k-killer wore bulky clothes. Not p-positive it was a man."

"You didn't shoot my dad?" Jane asked against her better judgment. *He* had followed Jane. Every word from his mouth had to be a lie.

Yet Jane wanted to believe him. In fact, all her instincts screamed at her to do so.

Maybe that was why she missed the bison's graceful rise to its feet. She didn't, however, miss it pawing the ground...and ducking its head, eyes focused on her.

# TWENTY

CYNTHIA BALLED her icy fingers into fists, seeking warmth against the smooth lining of her gloves as she waited for Charlie to respond to her unspoken request to search for Jane. He wanted to be the one to take Matt home, she knew—and understood. No one else would offer the same care to his lifelong friend.

But Jane was much closer now than she'd be if they drove back to Bozeman, where they'd get sidelined by the storm that had already pounded the mountains on the northern flank of the park. The clouds were pouring over the Rockies, and even in the last hour, the temperature drop had been substantial.

Cynthia breathed in and out, devising a way to cheat Yellowstone and her majesty of just one young woman...

Then, she remembered she'd asked for something similar when she'd wanted her wolves to escape Yellowstone's death grip that came each winter. She'd gotten that boon in a park that had gained a reputation for its challenges, especially when snow fell.

Getting two boons, her career *and* Jane, seemed unlikely.

A series of emotions flitted across Charlie's face, ending with his lips pressed together and his eyes narrowed with determination. He gave a slight dip of his head, acknowledging her plea. He would do the near impossible: leave Matt. Charlie would help Cynthia look for Jane.

The thick, silent wall of white scuttled Cynthia and Charlie's attempts to track Jane. They holed up in the tiny Army cabin that should have been the last one used by Jane and Matt the previous Friday. They'd hoped to find Jane curled up in one of the narrow cots.

No such luck.

They parked the NPS's snowmobile and attached trailer that they'd "borrowed" in the doorway. Only a certain number of vehicles were allowed in the park each winter—a newish rule instituted by the park service once they realized how much pollution the snowmobiles emitted. She and Charlie should feel bad for taking the vehicle, but Cynthia didn't. Not if she could save Jane.

With difficulty, Cynthia unlatched the lock with the key she'd talked Betty into giving to her. The ranger hadn't liked the idea, but she'd heard Cynthia giving Detective Horton another suspect. Cynthia used the woman's chagrin against her, stating that she and Charlie had to save the *innocent* girl's life. Betty had folded faster than a lawn chair and handed over the key.

Now inside, Cynthia busied herself with setting up the woodstove, trying not to convulse from the cold that had set in miles before. She'd been the one to push for this trip, and she had to buck up—

"You don't always have to be the strong one, Cyn. It's okay to lean sometimes."

Charlie placed his hands on her shoulders, making her aware she'd taken on his bad habit of mumbling thoughts aloud. She turned and pressed her nose into his chest, thankful he'd unzipped his jacket enough for her to get the warmth of his wool sweater. Her shoulders heaved as she lost herself to the fear and guilt that had ravaged her from the moment she'd seen the storm.

Charlie held her, his cheek coming to rest atop her crown as she sobbed, clutching at him like a tow raft back to safety in a tumultuous sea. Slowly, her tears eased, and she pulled back, head bowed sheepishly.

"You know," Charlie said, "that's the first time I've ever seen you cry. Wasn't sure you had it in you."

"Oh, I cry. Often. Just not around you." Cynthia peeked at him as she busied herself going through their pack. They should consume something hot...

"Why ever not? I was your husband."

She dropped the pack and glared. "You were the *reason* I cried."

He gawked. She fisted her hands, then turned away. "Well, then, anyway..."

Silence fell between them, thicker than the drifts piling ever higher outside the door. When Cynthia peeked at him from beneath her lowered lashes, she watched Charlie's jaw snap shut.

"I never knew..." Charlie said. "You didn't seem to care...just went on with your career..."

She turned back toward him fully. "You mean after the miscarriage?"

He flinched, his face draining of color. But what else was there but the truth in this small space? They were in some of the most rugged country in the world searching for Jane, knowing her survival was a long shot. Cynthia's typical defenses were gone. She'd just sobbed all over him, after all.

"I always assumed that's when you started cheating with

Mindy. You spent so much time at her family's ranch." She said it conversationally, but the pang of embarrassment and loss ripped at her sensitive heart.

"I...don't know what to say." Charlie came over and pulled out the rations she'd been looking for moments before.

She watched dully as he melted snow on top of the stove, adding bits of wood to boost the sad flames that had done little to warm the space. At least they gave off some light.

"Tell me when it began, Charlie," she demanded. "Tell me why. I *deserve* that." She'd never asked him before...just sued for divorce and tiptoed from the home they'd shared...the one with the half-done nursery she couldn't bear to look at ever again.

His back straightened, and his shoulders nearly touched his ears before he slumped. Turning to face her, she noted the tension around his mouth, the sadness in his eyes.

"Everything turned around when Art died, and I was offered the professorship. You got pregnant. We were working toward tenure."

"And then I lost the baby."

"After you got out of the hospital, you were...gone. Slipped away somewhere I couldn't get to you."

Her fist banged on the table loudly, causing Charlie to jump. "No. No. You left me the night after—"

"That night, I went to Matt, asking for his advice. We ended up at the pub, drunk, me crying in the corner because I knew how much that baby meant to you—how hard you'd taken the rest of the news."

Cynthia sucked in a breath. The end of her dreams of motherhood were all wrapped up in one paltry word: *complications*. "There were complications, Mrs. Bianchi."

She detested that word. She'd hated Charlie for leaving her. She was hissing out some of that emotion now because she was too full of worry for Jane, too anxious about Matt's death to carry that old, heavy anchor any longer.

"I knew you were at the bar. Cordelia Huxley told me—"

"The bitch," Charlie snarled.

Cynthia blinked at him as the niggle of worry she'd felt built in her chest. This wasn't the Charlie she'd lived with, the Charlie she thought she knew.

"Well, yeah, she could be, but she was also a very smart and dedicated researcher, and the students loved her courses."

Color flooded Charlie's face and flashed in his eyes. "Damn, I'm glad she didn't get tenure. She was a manipulative piece of work."

Cynthia swallowed the rubble churning in her throat. "She told me you—"

"What?" Charlie said with a sigh.

"She said, then, that you seduced her."

"Of course she did." Charlie sneered, and Cynthia tipped her head.

"You really didn't like her."

"No, I didn't."

Cynthia's heart did its best imitation of a hummingbird's wings. "She also said *you* were the one who shot Art Ford."

"And you believed her?" Charlie scoffed.

"N-no, of course not." Cynthia licked her lips.

She didn't tell Charlie that she'd gone to Tara Fremont with what she'd remembered from that weekend. How she'd awakened, and Charlie wasn't there. She'd gone downstairs to the kitchen, hoping some chamomile tea would relax her. She'd overheard part of a conversation—how Mindy would give Charlie her Henry, and he could fix the little problem that was keeping them apart.

Charlie's eyes were fathomless as the flames flickered upward, inching into them. "Cordelia was a liar. So is Mindy." He bit his lip, hesitated. "You know that, right?"

Cynthia nodded.

"I'm pretty sure *she* killed Art." Charlie's expression crumbled as he lowered his head and sniffed. "And...and...I bet she's the one who shot Matt, too. She always hated him for not taking his dad's money."

# TWENTY-ONE

THE BISON'S shoulder slammed into Jane's midsection with the force of a Mack truck.

Colm had been right—they were fur tanks. Dazed, Jane stared at the hulking dark lumps of the bison. She landed on her back, then her head slammed into the earth, cushioned by the few inches of snow.

She gasped, then grunted, the sky swimming in and out of focus for a shuddering moment as she tumbled head over butt, again and again...like a rag doll descending a steep hill. The earth rumbled. Jane tensed but still couldn't manage a breath.

The bison herd charged.

The scream that had been knocked out of her midsection rose in her throat and poured out her mouth as the thousand pounds of furious bison sped toward her. She covered her pounding head—or was it the earth?—with her shaking hands, knowing it wasn't enough. Still, she curled tight, small, with the only hope she had left: they'd miss her.

Jane closed her eyes, ignoring the tears slipping down her cheeks.

All the running, the hiding, the hope that she outsmarted him —all for *nothing*. She was still going to die. Here, in this meadow.

The beast's musky smell permeated her nose, cloying up her throat. She tensed, preparing for the sharp pain of hooves, the impossibly heavy weight of their mass born on her one-hundred-fifteen-pound frame.

Still, when the impact occurred, she screamed as much from surprise as fear. A glancing blow meant the snow beneath Jane absorbed most of the impact. But that didn't stop the weight of two thousand-plus pounds just above her knee—her *bad* knee. A moment later, the pain stole her breath.

The crack of a rifle caused her to flinch. The second shot and harsh bellow caused her to peek out from behind her arms. Colm raced forward, toward the bison...*toward* Jane.

Arms out, yelling and shrieking, eyes dark and wild, he sprinted into the avalanche of bison as the mass careened ever closer.

Still running, Colm lowered the rifle and fired into the herd. This shot, perhaps the others before, caused a mild resetting of the leading herd's trajectory.

*Away* from Jane.

"Move!" Colm bellowed, and Jane obeyed, scrambling back from the onslaught of hooves and horns and imminent death.

He raised the rifle again and fired another shot. The typical echo from the firearm's kickback muffled into the cold, dense air hanging around them, but it had the desired effect on the bison. They whipped away from the noise, veering deeper into the valley and away from the lip of the rocky forest where Jane huddled.

One bison straggler thundered up behind Colm, head lowered, nostrils flaring, and slammed into his back, sending him reeling, tumbling, much as Jane had done mere moments before.

*He had saved her.*

Nothing made sense, and the pain in her shoulders and knee

caused additional fogginess, making it difficult for Jane to focus. The world dimmed, then flared too bright.

Perhaps she'd suffered a concussion. She'd heard her friends talking about the symptoms before, and this...weirdness in her consciousness seemed to match.

Biting her lip against the gut-churning throb in her knee, Jane scrambled closer to Colm. He'd talked to her, pleaded with her. *He'd saved her life* with the same rifle that may have taken her father's.

Finally, Jane had crawled close enough to see that he still breathed. Then, she noted the cracked, pink lips under the multiple days of dark scruff. His dark brows were tugged tight over his nose—a straight, quite attractive nose, really.

"Oh," she sighed.

He wasn't much older than she was. And he looked rough, like he'd been out here for days.

"Oh, no..."

If he'd been telling the truth, then Jane's savior now bled on the thickening carpet of snow falling faster and thicker around them.

# TWENTY-TWO

THE SNOW, which Jane had cursed moments before, was now her best defense against the pain in her knee, shoulder, and back as well as Colm's injuries. First, she needed to wrap his wound to prevent additional blood loss. From her untrained eye, it looked as if he'd already gushed out most of his volume.

"Don't die. I'm sorry. I'm *so sorry*. I should have listened to you."

Admitting that felt good. Some of the terror from the past few days eased, though plenty—too much—remained.

She heaved a choked breath and shifted so she could sit next to him. She cried out, clenching her teeth as she got her first look at her knee. The area had already swollen, and the tissues were so tender that even the slightest movement shot agony up into her jaw and down into her toes.

"Worse than the surgery," she muttered even as she buried the aching joint in the snow. "Now, to tend your wound."

Her hands shook, her nervous system not quite ready to relinquish her trepidation of the man in front of her. She'd been running for so long...Jane shook her head. Two days—she'd spent two *days* playing hide-and-seek with this man. Except he said he wasn't the bad guy.

Her head hurt too much to iron out all the details. For now, she'd think of him as *Colm*, her savior.

Even still, she grabbed his rifle and brought it to her lap, giving her the advantage.

"It's empty," Colm whispered. "Used all my bullets..."

Jane frowned. "Why?"

"To save you. Couldn't let you die, too. So much death...just... *couldn't*."

"Thank you."

His lashes fluttered, and his eyes opened. His face might be youthful beneath the ravages of a week's worth of nature's fury, but shadows of despair filled his eyes...a pain and longing for peace Jane had never seen before but had heard about in books and television. In fiction, it was always the look in the eyes of war veterans.

He *had* been waging one this week. Against the person who'd murdered his friends. *Allegedly* murdered...

That train of thought halted when his face softened, and he brought his hand up. His fingers trembled as he touched her face. "You are so strong. You k-k-kept me g-going. I w-wanted to quit, but you d-d-didn't."

"I wish I'd known you were there. I could have used a friendly face," Jane said.

"S-saw you with the b-badger," Colm said.

Jane pulled back, taking his hand and laying it gently at his side. She wasn't sure how she felt about his intrusion at that moment. It had been private. Intimate.

He studied her and seemed to realize her discomfort. He continued to stammer through his words, his teeth clacking together like a motor revved too high. "Why couldn't we have gotten stuck near a Taco Bell? That would have been plenty of adventure, and I'd destroy a Crunchwrap Supreme right n-now."

"Y-you're hungry?" Jane asked.

"Been eating berries for the last couple of days. I hate them." He shifted, groaned. "That *hurts.*"

"I'm sure it does. I'm going to field dress it." She didn't have the right supplies, maybe not even enough of the ones she had left. Her father had been the one with the larger first-aid kit. She wished, once again, she'd insisted on more items of her own.

"Can you roll onto your side? I have some gauze and ointment."

"Sure." Colm's face paled, and he sucked in a breath before he managed to turn. Sweat beaded his brow, but he remained silent.

"That had to hurt, and I'm sorry. I can't walk...I think my leg's broken." Not to mention her shoulders and head. Jane inhaled. "But we're alive."

"For now," Colm said.

Jane looked down and gasped. A bloody mess of torn flesh pushed through his padded flannel and gray undershirt, revealing his back just below his ribs. But it was below his ribs, at the top of his hip, one of the few areas that didn't cause significant organ trauma.

His vertebrae rose prominently from his back—no wonder he'd said he was hungry.

"You're the real life of the party. A sunshine kind of guy."

"Haven't had anything to smile about in a while."

Jane removed her pack and pulled out her meager first-aid supplies, her gloves making her hands clumsy. Four pieces of gauze, half a tube of ointment.

She shouldn't have wasted the bandages on that badger.

"Okay. First, I need to clean this out," Jane said, struggling to remember the details from the first-aid badge she'd received in middle school.

"Just do it. I d-d-don't n-need a play-by-play."

She shifted his clothing upward enough to create space for her to work, but not enough to put extensive skin at risk of exposure.

She picked up a large handful of snow and rubbed it against the torn flesh. He went rigid and hissed through his teeth as Jane massaged the snow into the damaged skin. With a muttered apology, Jane grabbed another handful, doing her best to remove any dirt or germs from his skin that may have been left by the bison's horn and bits of cloth.

"Good news is it isn't too deep."

"Feels like it," Colm grunted. His teeth had stopped chattering, so he must be clenching his jaw.

She probed the area longer, then sighed with relief. "The bleeding has slowed. We need to watch for infection, but I'll use the cream, which should help, along with the cold. Did you know that bacteria don't grow much in cold weather like this?"

"Who told you that?" Colm asked.

"My dad. He was a biology professor." She pressed her lips together to keep her chin from quivering. Jane decided not to add that he'd also said wounds needed oxygenated blood to heal and that might have inhibited the female wolf's recovery. Based on her wounds, her father had thought she'd been injured in late spring—a time of large snowfall.

"Tell me about the killer," Jane said.

Colm sucked in a breath. But Jane wasn't sure if that was because of her request or because she'd shoved another mound of snow against his wound. Once it melted, she pulled it away, not wanting it to moisten his clothes more than necessary.

His eyes met Jane's, and in them she saw the same horror she felt each time her mind spun back to her father's bloodied torso.

"My friends..."

Jane bit her lip. "They were shot. You said earlier."

"Yeah." Colm breathed it out, like releasing a weight much too heavy for him to carry. Colm was taller than Jane and probably had an additional forty to fifty pounds when he was at his optimal weight. She could tell he typically did some exercise because of his well-defined back and abdominals.

"When?" Jane asked.

Colm's eyes filled with tears, and his mouth compressed. "A couple of days before I watched that woman and your father get shot."

"That's so many people," Jane whispered.

"I...I winged the shooter. I think," Colm said. "I'm not the best shot—never really needed to be. Never wanted to be either, until now." His expression shifted to one of retribution and a fierceness Jane understood all too well.

"Hmm."

Colm opened his eyes and met her gaze. The pain in his had to be mirrored in her own. "I'm sorry I didn't kill him."

"I'm not," Jane replied with such speed that she surprised herself. They both blinked. After a moment of thought, she continued slowly, "That means you won't have blood on your hands. Justice isn't for us to decide, Colm."

"Then who should decide?" he asked. "Our lives are dramatically different than they were before. The piece of shit who killed my friends and your dad—"

"Your friends," Jane cut in. "Tell me about them."

She tried to redirect the conversation away from vengeance. Neither she nor Colm could do anything for their loved ones right now. Even knowing what she did about the killer's history, she wasn't sure she'd ever be able to shoot a person in cold blood.

Hell of a time to realize that. Jane had considered herself analytical...stone cold after she had to pull the plug on Dartmouth.

But she wasn't—not even close.

She closed her eyes against their dryness. The fatigue and

tension of the last few days had created a headache Jane hadn't acknowledged until now. Sure, her temples throbbed, but she wasn't alone.

Somehow, she'd get them out of here.

"Chase and I worked for a car parts manufacturer, writing code and algorithms for parts. It was mind-numbing, but the pay was good. Chase hatched a plan to head west—see the redwoods and the Pacific. Once we'd saved up enough, we split the cost of a camper van. Seemed like a fun adventure before we had to go back to the real world, you know?"

He shrugged, and Jane froze as a rush of thoughts slammed into her. That slightly lost feeling...the need for meaning, searching, struggling to connect with something. Yes, that was all familiar. Those were all feelings Jane had pushed away, avoided for the past couple of years. It was easy to simply put one foot in front of the other and never bother to look up.

Her father had brought her here to see the beauty in the world. He'd wanted Jane to *live* again, not just go through the motions of life.

"Traveling around was Chase's dream. His parents never left their town in central Pennsylvania. He went to Penn State, less than an hour from his hometown. We met there. He met Lorna, his girlfriend, there. She'd finished her degree this past August. Chase and I lived together in Philly, but it was crowded. Loud. Chase hated it. He said...he said he was a farm boy at heart."

"So, the three of you left Philadelphia and...what?"

Without another option, Jane exposed her T-shirt and used the inside to pat his skin dry. His shivering had increased because of his skin's exposure to the snow, but Jane couldn't rule out shock. While her muscles, specifically her leg and head, still ached, tending to Colm's needs settled her nerves. Tending to Colm distracted her from the throbbing in her skull. Instead, her battered mind turned to the only questions that mattered: how to fix him and how to get them out of here.

"Lorna's coming was last-minute," he said. "She was struggling to find a job, so Chase asked if she could join us. I knew I'd be the third wheel, but I'd fallen in love with the idea of van life."

"I can see how that would be appealing." Jane uncapped the antibiotic ointment before she tugged off her glove with her teeth. She shoved her fingers into the snow and did her best to clean her skin of germs, breathing through her nose at the unpleasant chill in her fingers.

"So, yeah. We'd come across the middle of the country. It's much more open—all these big skies and stuff—compared to Philly. And the people. They're friendly. They stopped to talk to you instead of rushing off to an appointment or grabbing their phones and ignoring us, just because they could."

"That sounds about right. Here...well, at least in Bozeman, where I live, people are friendly like that."

"Lorna liked Wyoming. That surprised Chase and me. Lorna's a townie, and she liked the city okay, but there's something magical about the vast expanse of sky, especially when the stars came out. Lorna and I had gotten into astronomy. I found a small telescope, and she and I had been studying Venus. It's a really pretty planet, so bright and white..." He cleared his throat. "Chase didn't have the patience for it."

He lapsed into silence. Jane rubbed the cream into and around his lacerations with careful strokes. His skin began to warm again, and there was something beautiful about touching another person.

"I was out, collecting berries and firewood, but really just giving the two of them some time together," Colm said. "They were really in love. I was sure they'd be that couple still holding hands in their nineties."

His voice thickened, and he heaved a breath, unsettling the

bandage Jane had just pressed to his skin. "I'll have to tell their parents they're gone. I can't...it's going to be so hard..."

Jane inched even closer. She clasped his hand. There were no words of sympathy she could offer. They both knew firsthand the trauma and grief that spiraled out from the deaths. They stared off across the snow, lost in their own thoughts.

Colm's shivering increased, and Jane roused herself.

"I'm going to rip some strips off my shirt to hold this better in place and give you a bit of protection from the snow. It's the best I can do."

"You did great, Jane. Thank you," Colm said, shooting a small smile over his shoulder.

They were quiet for another long moment as she worked.

"I miss them," Colm mumbled.

"I know," Jane said, her throat tight.

# TWENTY-THREE

THE SNOW HAD THICKENED from a light drift to a full-on blizzard. It fell in that soft, straight-down pattern that told Jane they were in for many inches...possibly feet. She glanced up, squinting against the snow falling in her eyes at the thick, black blanket of clouds cutting out the sun's potential light.

The two of them, Jane and Colm, might as well be alone in the world. But they weren't. A wolf howled in the distance, answered by one of its packmates, reinforcing Jane's concern about being out in the open.

Yet, with Colm's injury and her inability to drag him anywhere, they were stuck.

And that wasn't smart or safe. Yet, it was the reality. Jane rearranged his clothing, her muscles heavy, not just with fatigue but with sadness for Colm and what he'd experienced.

Watching her father die would haunt Jane forever. To have witnessed multiple deaths...Jane shook her head. Colm had no one to talk to. No one to turn to. For a week, the man had mourned his friends even as he worried where his next meal would come from or if a bullet would strike his back.

Jane studied him again, shocked by his strength. He'd kept going despite the horrors.

"I..." Jane bit her lip. It was dry from too much sun exposure and not enough water.

Colm met her gaze. His expression was taut from the pain, but his eyes were calmer than they'd been when she'd first looked into them.

"I'm so glad you're with me," she whispered. "I'm sorry about your injury—"

"It happened. I'll deal."

Guilt wracked her, but Jane nodded. They didn't really have a choice. "I have some pain pills. And jerky."

"Really?" Colm perked up. "It's not a burger, but that sounds *so good*."

Jane snuffled as she laughed. It felt amazing to laugh. A bit more of the stress of the last few days eased. Jane tugged her backpack closer. She gave Colm the pills and the biggest piece of jerky, which he attacked with enthusiasm.

"So good," he muttered. "Best thing I've eaten."

"No, it's not, but I sure am glad my dad made me take it."

The wave of grief washed over her as she drew out her sleeping bag. She quashed those thoughts because that was an issue for later. Now, they needed to be warm and as dry as possible.

It took a lot of maneuvering, a few vicious curses and whimpers, but Jane got both herself and Colm into her down-filled mummy bag. She and Colm lay on their sides, bodies pressed together, with him facing away from her. They couldn't move much—actually, not at all—but they'd be warmer and drier together. Wadding the bag's hood under Colm's head, she covered his skull with her hat. Then she flipped up her jacket's hood, positioning it to face the right way so that the elements would once again be expelled by the waterproof material.

She heaved a long breath as the snow continued to pile around them. Soon, it would cover them.

Jane must have fallen asleep because she startled awake as a clump of cold plopped onto her nose. Her eyes sprang open, and she stared up at a mass of white, which meant that they were coated in the stuff. Her dad had told her that in the case of an avalanche, she needed to claw her way upward, toward air—that even a small hole of fresh air might be a lifeline. People died in avalanches from asphyxiation, the snow becoming their tomb.

"Colm. Wake up. I need you to help me." Urgency punctuated Jane's words.

"Wha..."

"Help me make space around us. For oxygen."

"Are we covered in snow?" He sounded less groggy.

"Yeah. It's been coming down for hours. Push your feet out and up. Make as big a space around you as possible." He snapped his jaw shut, but not before he whimpered, no doubt from the tug on his wound. Jane lifted her legs, too, sucking in a hard breath as her knee protested, and they pushed upward hard. They did it again. After the third repetition, Colm was sweating profusely.

"Great," Jane said. "Now, poke your fingers up, into the snow above you repeatedly."

"Why?" He panted. This was too much for both of them, but they didn't have a choice.

"Breaking through the snow lets more oxygen into our space. We're going to need that if the accumulation is too great for us to dig out."

"Like an avalanche?" Colm asked.

"Yeah. Like that."

She felt his breathing grow labored, and his grunts turned deeper, pained. Still, he kept at it, trying to give them a shot at survival.

"How'd you learn that?" he asked.

"My dad." Pretty much every skill she'd learned had come from her father. Well, and Cynthia. Jane paused, trying to think of a life skill her mother had taught her. None came to mind because a weekly manicure wasn't a necessity. Shaking her head, Jane returned to poking holes, doing her best with her shorter arms and fingers. The snow refilled the holes quicker than she could make them, but she rejoiced with each prickle of cold air. That meant more oxygen—another breath.

"T-tell me more about him," Colm said.

Jane heard the fatigue in his voice, but he gamely went on. His back must be on fire. Jane worried about his wound, but that was secondary to breathing. *Everything* else was secondary.

"He was into wilderness survival, and I wanted to be like him once I realized my mother was shallow." More like a full-blown narcissist, but her mother's shortcomings had no bearing on the current state of affairs.

Jane pressed her lips together and punched harder into the wall of white. A pile of snow fell onto the sleeping bag covering her hip, and for a moment, the cold air whipped over her gloved fingers, and the thick blackness of the night permeated her vision. Thank God. It wasn't too deep. Yet.

Jane and Colm would freeze to death in those temperatures. Their best bet was to remain here, buried in the snow.

*Buried.* She shivered at the image, barely choking down a vicious wave of hysteria.

"So, he was a good guy, huh?" Colm asked.

Jane latched on to the question, thankful for the momentary

reprieve from the fear, like snow, that pressed down on her. "Yeah." A thick breath in and out. "He's—he was—the *best*."

"He taught you useful skills." Colm's arms wavered. He had to be exhausted. Jane was. Still, they kept hitting and digging. "Chase was a good mechanic. He could change a timing belt or transmission oil, but he wasn't great at the wilderness survival stuff. We...ah...weren't as prepared for this as we should have been."

Jane knew those words cost him, but she also knew that after what he'd survived, there wasn't a place for ego. Wilderness stripped away most of the constructs of modern living.

Jane both loved and loathed that. Through this experience, though, she'd come to understand her father better.

"You learned," Jane said.

"Had to." Colm cleared his throat. "The first couple of days after Chase and Lorna...died, I wished I'd gone into the military—had some kind of survival training. If I get out of here, I'm taking classes."

"When, not if," Jane said. "We made it this far. The park's border isn't that far..."

It was, but she didn't want to admit she might not be able to do more than hobble. Eventually, someone would come across them. She and Colm just had to make it to that point.

"Where Chase, Lorna, and I were camping—what, hundred miles from the nearest town? You've put in maybe fifteen miles per day, which is amazing over this terrain. But we still have a long way to go," Colm said. "I'm not giving up. Just trying to be realistic."

"They'll be searching for my dad and me," Jane said. "We checked in with the park service, and Cynthia—she's basically my aunt—will sound the alarm. She probably already has."

At Colm's stoic silence, Jane's heart broke.

"You don't have anyone?" Jane asked, her voice tentative. But talking was good. Talking kept her mind off how tired her arms were.

"Not anymore." Colm's movements slowed. So had Jane's.

"What happened?" she asked.

"My parents died in a car accident about a year ago. This trip was, in part, for them. They always wanted to see the redwoods. I was going to do it for them."

Warmth blossomed under Jane's breastbone. What a thoughtful gesture.

Colm's hands thudded to his sides. "I can't anymore."

Jane wasn't sure if he spoke about digging them out or talking about his life. When Colm turned his hand over, opening and closing his fingers, she realized they were bare.

"Jeez! Your hands are freezing. Tuck them back under the sleeping bag. I'll finish this."

"Okay. That's probably good for now." She pulled the packet of jerky from her pack, along with the small supply of trail mix. "Let's feast."

Colm chuckled. "I could eat."

"Said like every guy I've met."

They chewed in silence. Jane scooped up some snow and tossed it in her mouth, then pressed closer to Colm as she shivered.

Colm lay on his uninjured side. He started to lift his arm, but let it fall back in front of him, "I was going to hug you, but it hurts."

"You did more than enough," Jane said. "I'm the big spoon in this relationship."

That drew a chuckle from Colm, then he groaned. "I'm twenty-five and single. Just so you know."

"We're trading ages now? I'm twenty-two. Also single and so thankful for that."

"There's a story there."

Jane gave Colm the abbreviated version of her few months with Scott. "I've found that most of the guys my age aren't interested in doing more than having a good time."

"Hmm. I was that guy a few years ago. Losing my parents made me reevaluate a lot of things in my life," Colm said. "I want what they had—my parents. What Chase and Lorna had."

"Wow. A man who admits to looking for commitment. I'm impressed."

Colm chuckled. "It's been an evolution."

"Have you graduated or are you still in school?" Colm asked.

"I'm a senior." She detailed her years at Dartmouth, then her return to Bozeman for the second ACL surgery. "I took biology classes because...well, I didn't know what else to do." She shrugged. "My dad has a fairly cool job. I mean, had." A pall settled over her.

"Hanging out in the wilderness sounded a lot more fun before I actually tried it," Colm offered. He must have heard the grief in her voice.

"Right? Well, anyway, I didn't have a better idea, so I went into biology. It's okay, except I don't really love animals. Not like my dad did."

"I ran into a cougar. Between that and the bison, I totally get it."

Jane smiled. Something else they shared. "Exactly. But last year, I read a paper on trees and how the organisms work together, sometimes across a whole forest. They'll share nutrients and communicate about drought...I'm boring you."

"No. That's fascinating. I had no idea."

Jane's cheeks flushed with pride. "That's what I want to study. I was going to tell my dad this weekend. I...I think he would have liked my choice."

"He would have because he would have known it made you

happy. I can hear the passion in your voice, Jane. Based on what you told me about your father, he'd want that for you."

Silence fell again. But it was cozy. Jane could almost pretend they were snuggled together in a tent. She pushed those thoughts away. They were warm enough not to get frostbite, and they were safe from predators for now.

"I went into computer programming because it was easy," Colm said. "Everything's always been pretty easy. I mean, my parents always had enough to take care of me and help with college. Even when they died, I got their life insurance settlement, money from their house. I hadn't realized how lucky I was that they took care of me even in death until now, though."

"And now that you realized that?" Jane asked. Her eyes were heavy, but she didn't want to sleep. Talking to Colm was easy after so many days alone. His presence made her feel connected, wanted. As silly as it was, she felt *safe*. Or maybe it wasn't silly. After the last few days, Jane was desperate for security, and she was the one cuddling the rifle.

"Now...I don't know. If we get out of here—"

"When. Repeat after me: when we get out of here."

"When we get out of here, I want to do something worthwhile. That will make a difference, so no one else has to suffer like we have."

"I like that," Jane said. "I like that a lot. You're a good man, Colm."

"High praise, since you said the same about your father."

A smile caught at the edge of her lips, tipping them upward. She'd been wrong about Colm, and she was woman enough to admit her mistrust was misplaced. He'd proven to be a much better person than most. She didn't know anyone else who'd rush into a bison stampede for her.

Her dad would have. Cynthia might have.

Silence settled over them again. Jane wondered if he'd fallen asleep when he said, "I saw you with him. You, your dad, and the other woman."

"You did?" Jane's aching fingers twitched, and her pulse pounded.

"Yeah. I wanted to warn you, but I couldn't get to you in time. You'd walked off, and I knew the other woman had a phone. I was about to approach her when the killer showed up."

"The killer?" Jane asked. "Other woman with a phone?"

But Colm didn't answer. He'd slid into a deep, much-needed sleep, leaving Jane confused...and more concerned than ever about Lavinia.

* * *

HUMANS WERE CREATURES OF LIGHT. Whether or not they realized it, they timed their lives by the sun's rising and setting. But with only white walls that had turned dark as the snow and night possibly fell, Jane lost the concept of time. Because of the darkness, she couldn't read her watch, not that knowing the actual time would help much.

And that scared her more than anything else she'd faced thus far. Without an idea of time, she didn't know how long the oxygen in their potential tomb would last. She couldn't tell if the snow had stopped, but she knew it was too deep to kick out—she'd tried. Eventually, when her breathing turned ragged and her head throbbed from lightheadedness, she gave up.

She couldn't sleep. She needed to know what Colm had planned to tell her about the killer. If Colm had seen the shooter... he made it sound like it wasn't Lavinia. But it had to be. Her father said no one else was in the park.

Her father had been wrong, though, because Colm and his friends were nearby.

She stared at the "ceiling" of her tomb, though she had no clue how long...but long enough to need to pee. The more she thought about it, the worse she had to go and the more the snowy walls pressed in.

"Colm?"

Nothing.

She shifted as much as she could, trying to take in his features, which was difficult because their air pocket had collapsed around their legs a while ago. She'd done her best to shift it, but any movement now strained her.

"Colm?"

She touched his neck, unsurprised to find his skin too hot. Just as she'd feared, he'd contracted a fever from infection. Could be from the water he'd drunk, too. But all his issues were exacerbated by the diminishing oxygen.

She lay back down, the rifle digging into her hip, her throat tight. She would die in the snowy grave that she and Colm built.

No.

*No.*

Jane gritted her teeth and repeated her mantra to herself: when she got out, she'd pee and find her father's murderer.

She blinked as wooziness spun through her mind.

She was going to get out. She had to, but she felt bad. Dizzy. Wrong.

"Help." Jane blinked, then blinked again, and breathed the word, which settled on her lips.

She tried to lift her legs, but they were leaden, much too heavy to raise above her head.

At least she didn't have to pee any longer. She glanced over at the man next to her.

"I'm sorry it's ending like this," she said. "I really like you. I wish...I wish we'd met at a different time, different place."

Jane closed her eyes and let herself think about her father. She missed him. She'd hated leaving him.

Of course, he'd deserved more...better from her mom, but also from Jane.

"I wish I could have told you how much I loved you. How much I respected you," Jane whispered. "Because I did."

Tears spilled from her eyes but clung to her lashes and skin. Cold, *too* cold.

She was tired...too tired to stay awake.

"At least this way won't hurt," she mumbled. And as she drifted off into that semi-darkness, the rifle still pressed into her side, smelling of gunpowder, she remembered Colm had mentioned a walnut stock.

Walnut was lighter than other hardwoods, so it was often used, but she'd seen the rifle pointed at her father. Just a flash of it. And the smell of gunpowder bubbled the memory forward: the firearm had a large loop—good for people who wear gloves. *That* distinctive detail was how her father knew it was a Henry.

Lavinia had carried a Henry. Jane had stared at it, worried the woman would raise it and shoot them.

But Colm said the killer, not the woman, as if they were two separate people. If that were true, there were two other people Jane knew with Henrys: Scott and her mom, who called it her best-luck shot.

# TWENTY-FOUR

WHEN DETECTIVE TARA FREMONT showed up at the frat house where Scott lived, the other guys in the living room eased back, though they'd all remained close enough to hear Tara ask Scott if he'd heard about Jane's disappearance.

The young man nodded. "Yeah, I heard. Amber told me. That's my girlfriend. She heard Dr. Sorenson was dead, and Jane was missing. That sucks. Though I have to say Dr. Sorenson was way nicer than Jane."

His smooth, Ken-like face with the smattering of light freckles on his nose made him appear less threatening than his six-two frame suggested. His hazel eyes held hurt and anger from Jane's treatment.

Well, well, that was promising. Tara smiled at Scott as she put away her badge.

"Anywhere we can talk privately?" She raised her eyebrows and shot pointed looks toward the five guys lingering at the periphery of the untidy room with its sagging leather sofas, large television, and multitude of game consoles with wires strewn haphazardly across the unvacuumed rug.

"Um, sure..." Scott stood there, clearly at a loss. "My bedroom, I guess."

"Lead the way," Tara said.

Scott's room was small, with an unmade twin bed covered in random piles of clothes so that the muddle was like a strange art installation rather than a place to relax. Equal parts sweaty socks and cologne caused Tara's nasal passages to burn. Scott grabbed the backpack and three thick books off his desk chair.

"You can sit there..."

Tara flashed him another smile. "Thanks."

"Course." Scott dumped the new items on the bed, creating a silo atop a rumpled hoodie. He settled against the mattress, atop two pairs of jeans and countless T-shirts, unperturbed by the unevenness of his seat.

"So...Jane. Have you found her?" Scott asked.

While he seemed without artifice and imagination, Tara withheld further opinion. She'd interviewed too many people whose façade eventually cracked.

Tara shook her head. "That's why I'm here. I hoped you could talk to me a bit about her. And her mother."

Scott shrugged. "I don't know Jane as well now that we've broken up. She's got some friends she met last year when she transferred in."

"Can you give me any names?"

"Erm, Lucy Cahill and Sierra Garcia."

"Do you see Jane often?"

"Nah. I mean, that would be awkward, what with me being with Amber, and because I dumped her."

Not the story Tara had been fed, but then, Mindy wasn't reliable. Cynthia appeared more so, and she'd noted that Jane spoke of Scott with disappointment and hurt—as if he'd let her down.

"You did? Why?"

"She wasn't fun. I mean, I knew she'd just had surgery, but she never wanted to go to parties, come to my competitions..."

The kid came up for air, a faint blush on his cheeks. Tara held his gaze for a moment. "Hmm."

"I'm part of the fraternity leadership, so I was expected to be at the parties," he said. "But Jane just wanted to chill on the couch. And, like she meant just chill..."

Tara was beginning to see why Mindy held a grudge and why Jane broke up with Scott. "Tell me about your competitions."

"Oh! The rifle club. That's what I'm about."

"You're *about*?" Tara stressed the second word just slightly, making it more of a question. A faint buzz lit over her skin.

"I've been competing with the 4-H club since I was seven. Top shooter for nine consecutive years. Ten now, after I won the competition for the state." His chest puffed out. "Jane wouldn't come to the event. Said her knee hurt. That was the end for me. I mean, I need a girl who understands—"

"So, you're a good shot," Tara interrupted. She was not interested in more of Scott's self-aggrandizement.

"The best." Scott's white teeth flashed. "That's why I'm here on scholarship. Why this frat wanted me so bad."

Tara digested that information. "Care to give me a list of your firearms?"

He rattled off six different rifles and two pistols. Tara would check those he'd named against the database, but she didn't think Scott had lied to her.

"Where were you Saturday night?"

"Here. At a party we hosted. You know, Rush Week. Amber gets the importance of showing the kids a good time."

Tara chose not to think about what that could mean, but at least his party attendance would be easy enough to corroborate, which Tara did before leaving the frat house. Scott helped set up for the party, starting at noon on Saturday. But by seven or eight, none of the guys in the living room seemed to remember much beyond the party being epic.

Tara pursed her lips, realizing she wasn't going to get a firm alibi from anyone. The next time anyone saw Scott was after one in the afternoon on Sunday, when he settled in at the frat house kitchen table for breakfast—cold pizza, of course—with the rest of the guys.

Unfortunately, that left plenty of time for Scott to have driven to Yellowstone and back out. She'd have to wait for the medical examiner to give her Matt's time of death, which should come in the next day or so.

"Can you tell me anything about Jane's mom?" Tara asked as she headed toward the front door.

Scott shrugged. "She wasn't home a lot. I heard her tell Jane I was around too much, too much of a distraction. That's when Jane moved in with her dad. Her mom was just...annoying, you know?"

"Anything else?" Tara asked.

"I heard Mrs. Sorenson tell Jane that she should be smarter because love wasn't all that great, but money had never steered her wrong." Scott dropped his gaze then, the tips of his ears pink.

"What about Jane's dad? Did you go over there ever?"

Scott shrugged. "Oh, sure. He was always nice to me—you know? I'm *really* sorry to hear about him."

"But not Jane or Mindy?" Tara was worried about the young woman. Blizzards were terrifying when you were close to home. She couldn't imagine Jane's fear and agony if she'd been caught unaware. That poor young woman had already watched her father's murder.

Scott dropped his gaze again, but Tara read the rest of the statement loud and clear: Scott wouldn't have grieved a moment for Mindy.

"Course I don't want Jane dead. She's okay."

"What about that other thing?" One of the frat guys moved closer, looking nervous but excited.

"What other thing?" Tara asked. She'd been ready to go.

"Um...you tell, Brian. You're the one who saw," Scott said.

"Surprised me." Brian puffed up his chest, pleased to have something he considered important to share.

Tara raised an eyebrow.

"I mean, I hung out with Jane and Scott sometimes, so I knew Mrs. Sorenson, right? I'd never seen her on campus before. But then, last week, she was behind the science building with another guy. *Not* Jane's dad."

On a hunch, Tara pulled up a picture of Charlie. She showed it to Brian. "This is the guy?"

"Yeah! That's him. He was loading up an ATV last weekend. Sweet machine. We used to ride one at Jane's." He grinned.

Tara shook both young men's hands. "Thank you so much for your time. You've been a big help."

TARA DROVE TO HELENA, about an hour from Bozeman, right after her conversation with Scott. The sun was low against the horizon, and she had to sit up straight for her visor to block out the worst of the glare.

On the way, she got a call from a park ranger on a satellite phone from Horton. She answered using her Bluetooth tech.

"Fremont speaking."

"I found the ATV," Horton practically crowed.

Tara's stomach soured. "No sign of Jane?"

"None," Horton mumbled.

"Tell me about the ATV," Tara said, trying to salvage Horton's good mood.

"It's Mindy's."

"You're sure?"

"Yep. Matched the VIN since it's a different color and without a plate."

"Where?"

"Off 191, tucked behind a clump of pines."

"Is it a sweet-looking machine?" Tara asked. She had to explain what Brian had told her.

Horton snorted. "Looks like an ATV. Kids today can barely use the language."

Tara chuckled, glad for a brief moment of levity—especially when Horton joined in. This job would wear them down even quicker without these tiny moments of...well, humanity.

"Needed that," Horton said. "Thanks."

"Welcome," Tara said. "Back to business: that road wends its way through the park, so the ATV's driver could have driven out from either side of the park, meaning into Wyoming or Montana."

"Right. That's not much help. It's with forensics now, and they'll go over every inch of it, hoping for some DNA."

They could get lucky and find out who Matt's killer was.

"Anything else?" she asked.

"A park ranger named Ben remembers the large black SUV that had supposedly carried Lavinia out of the Montana side. Description matches Mindy's Escalade."

"Better and better," Tara said.

"Thought so." Horton's tone was smug with delight.

"Though I wish we knew where Jane was. The storm's getting worse."

"I know. And me, too." Horton's tone turned somber.

Tara sighed, thinking of her daughter. "So, I'll go talk to Lavinia, probably tomorrow. I hope she can shed more light on the office politics between the three professors. It's got to be one of them or Mindy, maybe two of them working together."

"Or all three," Horton said. "They disappeared, by the way."

"Who?"

"The two professors. In one of the snowmobiles. Betty—the park ranger—said the woman—"

"Cynthia."

"Yeah. Her. Was desperate to get to Jane."

Tara pursed her lips. "I don't like them being in the park. It's too easy for Jane to have an accident or disappear if they were to find her."

"Agreed. But there's not much we can do with this snow. It's coming down in buckets. I'm not sure if I'll be able to get back to Bozeman."

"That sucks." Tara gripped the wheel, glad it was Horton and not her out there. "While I got you, let me tell you what else I learned from Scott..."

Tara parked a few minutes later because she'd pulled up to Jordan Rathon's expensive office building. She studied the art prints for something worth noting while waiting for the dark-haired, middle-aged receptionist to let Jordan know she needed to speak with him.

The woman tried and failed to contain her excitement as she spoke in staccato tones that carried across the marble-tiled space.

"Mr. Rathon, there's a *detective* here to speak with you."

A pause. "Yes, yes, of course I'll show her to the conference room."

That palatial space was up two floors. It took up half the building, a wall of windows letting in the sickly light that seeped past the darkening clouds and thickening snow.

The gleaming table was expensive, with thick legs and ornate carvings that could easily seat sixteen. A large monitor hung on the longest of the three non-window walls, the volume down on the news station that offered an updated financial ticker.

Jordan Rathon was a trim, handsome, if bland, man in his mid-forties. He looked the type who golfed instead of hunted. He was pale-skinned, pale-haired, pale-eyed...probably all directly associated with his pallid personality. Jordan's suit was well-made, probably pricey, and a dull black. His tie, the standard sharp red, was also boring. He didn't wear a watch or cufflinks. His cheeks were slightly flushed, but Tara couldn't tell if that was from excitement, embarrassment, or makeup.

She held out her right hand and flashed her badge in her left.

"Thank you for seeing me, Mr. Rathon. I'm here regarding your relationship with Mindy Warner."

Jordan pulled out a seat for her and motioned for Tara to take it. Since it put her back to the windows, she did.

"Mindy Warner?" Jordan settled at the head of the table—a power play—and unbuttoned his suit coat. "Yes, I know her. We've been seeing each other for a few weeks."

"Her ex-husband was shot in Yellowstone, and her daughter's missing..." Tara let the rest of the sentence dangle.

"And you're checking in on her associates to see about alibis. Well, I can't give Mindy one this weekend, but I attended an accounting convention in Denver. What do you need to prove that?"

Tara smiled. "I'd like the name of the hotel and some of your colleagues. It's routine. I'm sure you understand."

Tara could tell he didn't like the request, but he wouldn't fight it. He would, however, make a point of ignoring any future calls from Mindy Warner.

"So...it's murder? I mean, I can't imagine you coming here if it were a hunting accident."

Tara leaned forward and widened her eyes. "*Definitely* murder. And we're worried about Jane. It'll be all over the news tomorrow—we don't want anyone to head into the park and get hurt during the incoming blizzard."

"Right, of course. Erm...what makes you suspect Mindy?"

"Well... I can't say what we've found." She lifted her eyebrows and knew her eyes gleamed as she mentally ticked off what they had on Mindy: mud all over her brand-new Escalade, a contentious relationship and divorce from her ex-husband, and her ATV was found in Yellowstone.

Jordan cleared his throat. "You can't tell me."

"It's an ongoing investigation," Tara demurred.

He nodded. "I guess you'd like to know how Mindy and I met."

"If you'd like to tell me. And think it's pertinent."

His expression sped from distaste to worry. "Oh, I'd say it's pertinent." He picked up his phone and dialed an extension. "Stewart, please come down here. I need legal counsel."

Tara's good mood fizzled as she waited for another suit to enter the room. But instead of stepping in, he pulled Jordan out and huddled in the hallway, whispering about strategy, no doubt.

Tara's eyebrows rose when Stewart stepped into the conference room. "Follow me. Jordan thinks you'll find this very interesting."

# TWENTY-FIVE

## TUESDAY

SNUFFLING STARTLED Jane from the gray of groggy, achy semi-consciousness. Everything came back, speeding through her mind, and she tried to relax so she could listen.

Scratch… scratch… snuffle. Digging.

"Help!" She slammed her fists against the roof, and snow fell onto her face. Jane sputtered even as she squinted against the harsh winter sunlight at the faint, gleaming blue of the sky high above the tips of the pines. Fresh air hit her nose, and her lungs expanded in a galvanizing gulp.

Her head swam and pounded, feeling pinched and too big all at once, but she continued to gasp greedily.

"Oh, my god. Ohmigod, ohmigod, ohmigod…"

Thick, brown claws broke through the snow mere inches from her face, causing her to press back. More digging. More snow on her face, in her hair, even her ears. But, most importantly, *air*.

She dragged in another deep lungful with gusto even as she raised her feet, tugging Colm's up with her. She began kicking at the rest of their ceiling even as she wiggled her arms free of the snow-covered sleeping bag and clawed at the hole, expanding it as she gasped and cried.

She was alive. *They* were alive.

She hoped, at least. Colm had to have made it if she had. But he hadn't made a sound—not even in distress—when she'd started kicking at the dome above them.

Before she could check, a masked face, led by a black nose, twitching whiskers, and pointed teeth, poked into the hole. She screamed, flopping back, away from the critter as far as possible.

Not a bear—thank God, thank God! She'd had enough of bears to last her many lifetimes. This creature was too small, even for the black variety. Plus, the nose was too long.

"Wha..." Colm coughed, his voice groggy. He coughed again.

"You're alive," Jane cried out, relief flooding her chest. Before she could reach for him, the beast resumed digging. Her next glimpse of its features caused her eyes to widen.

"The badger..." She knew it was the same one because of the dirty bandage around its paw. Her father had told her that badgers typically had relatively small territories with an average of two square miles, but some in Illinois patrolled up to seventeen miles. Clearly, this particular mammal had a larger-than-average territory.

Her father also told her that badgers used their muscular front legs, topped with long claws, to dig out ground squirrels and other rodents as a quarry, but she'd never heard of an animal digging up a human—a bit like a Saint Bernard used during avalanches.

The badger shoved its face deeper into the hole and hissed as it closed the space between them, nose moving, seeking. Colm wiggled, trying to extricate himself from the sleeping bag, but Jane and the snow the animal dislodged pinned him.

"What do you want?" Jane asked.

The badger disappeared from the hole, but Jane heard its claws sinking into the ice-laced snow above Colm.

"What's it doing?" Colm asked. His voice was scratchy.

"It's okay...he's my friend," she said.

Her mind was sluggish. From the cold, no doubt. She must be close to hypothermia. *That* was why she hadn't recognized the badger she'd saved earlier.

Yesterday? The day before? She had no concept of how long she'd been buried...long enough for hunger to tense her stomach and her bladder to express its displeasure.

A hole emerged over Colm's face and rapidly enlarged, resembling Jane's, baring his torso to the pale, stark light of the plain. He winced as he shifted, so Jane placed her hand on his shoulder. "Hang on. Let me dig the rest of the way out, and then I can help you out, okay?"

His terse nod confirmed how poorly he felt, and Jane's stomach twisted as worry cloaked her shoulders.

The badger disappeared from the hole, and Jane shifted further forward. Her knee still ached, but it didn't flare in agony like it had when she'd destroyed the tendons last year, that second time. Maybe the long hours in the snow helped reduce the swelling. It had also caused her other muscles to ache, and her neck flared in protest at her sudden movement.

Jane had maneuvered enough to get her feet under her hips, and she pushed her shoulders through the hole the badger had made that she'd enlarged. It took a few minutes for her to wiggle out of the bag, then shove more chunks of icy snow away. She used her arms to pull herself out of the hole and took in snow, snow, and *more* snow piled in drifts at the forest's edge.

No bison. No bears or mountain lions. Thanks to all the forces in the universe.

She was not in fit enough shape to take on another large predator.

As she brought her knees toward her chest, the snow caught around her torso, making further movement challenging. The badger approached, its little nose snuffling at her. This time, Jane clamped her jaw and forced herself to remain still. Its whiskers quivered, and its nose eased closer. The bright, black eyes—like the shiniest jet—fixed on her. Its brown fur over its eyebrows shifted, seeming to rise, almost as if it asked, "Well? Are you coming?"

"H-h-hi." She licked her lips. "Hey, fella. Good to see you again. Want to help me out of here? Then I can get Colm out."

She reached toward her only genuine hope, then pulled back when the badger made a low, guttural noise and flinched backward. Her teeth chattered.

"It's...it'll be okay." She said this to herself, not the beast. Well, maybe for the mammal, too. "Yeah, we're okay, buddy. Right? I mean, you found me, and that's *so good*. I probably wouldn't have gotten out of that hole by myself. It's deep—look at Colm. It's got to be two feet. That's a lot of snow. Thank you, little guy." Jane's hips were stuck. She wiggled them, but the snow held her down. She turned to the badger. "Will you help me out? Please?"

She held her jacketed sleeve up to the predator and held her breath, aware of each of her chilled fingers in her gloves and the pulse slamming against the delicate skin of her wrist. It could either help her out or bite her, scratch her...again.

The striped, fuzzy mammal snorted, its mouth jittering before relaxing in a strange, jagged line that somehow articulated its confused frustration with her. With a hissing whistle of a growl, the badger lunged forward, mouth agape, teeth gleaming.

# TWENTY-SIX

MINDY SAT at the police station again. Tara could tell that Mindy hated the precinct, which actually made Tara's day.

The place was a bit brooding, full of low-end, institutional finishes and the tar-like smell of burned coffee. Phones rang, and people bustled around...while others settled into hard seats as if the weight of the world sat upon their shoulders.

Earlier that morning, Tara had stopped by Lavinia's place, but the woman hadn't answered her door. After a moment's hesitation, Tara had rapped on the neighbor's door. A young, bookish woman had answered as her gaze had swept Tara in a quick glance.

"You looking for Lavinia?"

"Yes," Tara had said. "Have you seen her?"

The other woman had shaken her head. "Not in a few days."

"I'm getting worried about her. I'll drive back by later. I'd like to talk to her." Tara had asked for her information after flashing her badge and wrote down the woman's details. But right now, Tara focused on Mindy.

"Thanks for coming in," she said. She wasn't *actually* thanking Mindy. It was a formality. "We wanted to update you on my conversations with Jordan Rathon and Scott Pembleton. They were...enlightening."

Mindy leaned forward, eyes wide, seeming to hang on their every word. Tara was pretty sure Mindy was reorganizing her shoe collection in her mind.

"We found Dr. Sorenson's body about a hundred yards from where we believe he was initially struck," Tara said. Mindy nodded. "We believe Dr. Sorenson went after the assailant. Three of the seven gunshot wounds indicate close-range entrance and exit wounds, lending further credence to our theory."

"So, Matt's dead, and you haven't found my daughter," Mindy said, slumping into the chair. "Same old, same old, detective. Why are you wasting my time by telling me this?"

"What Detective Fremont is saying is that Dr. Sorenson did his damnedest with the last of his strength to give your daughter a chance to run," Detective Horton said. He'd made it out of the park—barely. And he was in a sour mood, thanks to Charlie ruining his crime scene.

Mindy rose, a growl ripping from her throat. "Fabulous. Just great that Matt *died* for Jane. Because now my daughter's out there, in that godforsaken wilderness."

Horton shot Mindy the squint-eyed look that Tara disliked so much because it worked, even on her. As expected, Mindy returned to her chair.

"I'm sorry. I'm just so worried about Janie...out there, alone, with no one to look after her. Matt promised." Tears streamed down her cheeks, smearing her makeup, but Mindy never wiped her eyes. "My *baby*. She's alone. In a storm. With a crazy killer."

"Why didn't you tell us about the mud on your SUV?" Tara asked, hoping to throw Mindy off from her rant—and because she had a different direction she wanted to take this conversation.

Mindy stared at her, the silence stretching out so that Tara could take in Mindy's red-rimmed eyes and the mascara streaks on her cheeks. "Why would that be relevant?"

"Because, according to the CCTV cameras that caught you leaving Bozeman and those that timestamped your return, you had plenty of time to go into the park, shoot Matt, and return to your house."

Mindy's mouth slackened.

*Didn't see that one coming, honey? Oh, there's more...a lot more.*

Horton shifted in his seat, but neither Mindy nor Tara looked at him. The two women grappled in a battle of wills, and Mindy seemed to finally realize that Tara was a formidable opponent. This was Tara's job, and she was an excellent detective.

"I...I showed a property in Gallatin County. It's next to the Climbing Arrow...only about ten thousand acres, but expansive... what does this have to do with finding Jane?"

"We know that, just as we know you could have had time to slip over the border into the park, four-wheel to Matt and Jane's location, and shoot him before you headed back to the ranch where you were supposed to meet your client. We found the ATV, by the way. In the park. There's blood on the back. In... say a day, two tops, we'll get a report back on that and DNA." Tara leaned forward. "*We'll know.*"

Horton slid down in his chair, eyes half-closed, arms crossed over his barrel chest, letting both women know this was Tara's rodeo. Smart man.

Tara pulled a file folder from her satchel. She spun it around and placed it on the table before Mindy.

"While we're waiting for those results and word on your daughter, I'd like you to explain your purchase of an additional life insurance policy you took out on Matt right before your divorce. The one in Jane's name that you had Jordan Rathon create nearly a year ago. He was very keen to give me all the details."

"Why does it matter?" Mindy sniffled. She looked around for a tissue. There were none. Not today. Tara had removed the box before Mindy showed up.

Mindy drew her purse into her lap and pulled a tissue free. She dabbed her eyes and nose. All the while, she watched Tara and Horton, no doubt trying to read their faces.

"Well, for one, I'd like to know if Jane was in on the scheme." Horton's gaze homed in on Mindy, and Tara noted that he hadn't been taken in by Mindy's emotional outburst or her tears. Good. That was progress.

"She must be, seeing as the first time she got her father alone, he's dead. As you two planned it." Detective Horton's words reverberated around the space, making Mindy flinch.

"Jane? You think *Jane* would kill her father?"

"Yeah. *Jane*. Who's in the woods with a 'crazy killer' that no one has seen or heard from. Pretty convenient for a marksman to show up in Yellowstone after the season—when it's just her word we'd have to take for what happened out there," Tara said. "Especially now that we know you set Jane up so she will inherit a large amount of money out of the scenario."

"She's the second beneficiary," Mindy snapped.

Gotcha on that one. But Tara didn't smile because she wasn't convinced Jane was as innocent as Cynthia Bianchi said she was—not after Jordan Rathon handed over the large life insurance policy Mindy and Jane had taken out weeks before her divorce. The timing was suspect. Tara's heart ached for Matt, who had cared for both these women and died because of it.

"When did you tell your daughter about the life insurance?" Tara asked. "Her signature on the forms tells us she must know about it, though Jordan Rathon said she never came into the office to sign—her part was digital."

Tara didn't add that Jordan worried Mindy had signed those documents for Jane. If she could build a case against the daughter to get justice for Matt Sorenson, she would.

"Did you have her move in with Matt so that he'd let down his guard?" Horton asked. "What percentage did you promise her if she killed him?

Mindy looked between the two of them, her chest rising and falling in a quick burst. She shoved back from the table, toppling her chair, which hit the ground with a sharp crack. "We're done here. I want my lawyer."

# TWENTY-SEVEN

THE ANIMAL'S teeth sank into the sleeve of Jane's jacket, at her biceps, and it tugged, thrashing its head back and forth as it used its sturdy rump to hoist her out of the snow.

Colm bellowed as he struggled to help Jane.

"No, no. It's okay, Colm." Gently, Jane pushed him back with her free hand, letting the badger yank her over the two feet of snow that had fallen over them. Jane collapsed face-first, breathing hard, thanks to the blooming pain that radiated outward from her knee. She laughed.

She was free and alive. How *amazing* was that?

The badger released Jane's jacket and skittered back. It was sitting on its haunches but on the verge of running.

"Thanks for the help, little guy," Jane said.

It sat there, panting...staring. Waiting.

"Oh," she said. "Yeah, just a sec..."

She pulled out the jerky bag that had been tucked into their sleeping bag. She swallowed down her concerns over the tiny stash of meat and trail mix left and tossed the badger the most significant piece of jerky.

"Thank you," she said.

The badger darted forward, sniffed the prize, and snatched it in its mouth. It shot her a look before trotting off into the forest.

"That was...something." Colm grimaced as he scooched upright. He squinted as he glanced around the pristine, empty meadow.

"My dad had that connection with wolves. They just *knew* they could trust him not to hurt them."

"I don't think it works like that." Colm panted as he worked to pull himself from their burrow. His color was both too pale and too red. Heat radiated off his body in a thick wave.

Damn.

Well, Jane shouldn't be surprised. Bison horns must have years of organisms floating over their surfaces—many of which the human body couldn't tolerate, especially a young, formerly healthy man who'd been through massive trauma and nearly a week of malnourishment. There was only so much a body could handle.

"Well, no offense, but you haven't been around the best examples of humanity out here—your friends excepted." Jane stared at the space where the badger had disappeared. "I guess he thought digging us out was easier than hunting for his next meal. And I guess he'd followed us this far since he knew I had food. Good thing. We were pretty close to suffocation."

Jane shuddered, trying to shake the last of the lethargy from her muscles. Those moments had been...relaxing, peaceful, and all the more horrifying for it.

Colm collapsed next to her in the snow. He rolled onto his back with a wince and stared up at the sky. "I don't think the badger saved you only for the jerky. If that was the case, he could have taken the backpack." He swallowed. "That moment, when you were tending the badger, was the one nice thing I've experienced this week. I bet it was for him, too."

Jane stared at the vast blue sky, too, unsure what else to do or say. Eventually, her body's needs kicked in.

She shook out two more pain pills from her limited supply. "Take these. Then, we should cover some distance. I need to pee."

"Me, too."

"Well, let's head for those trees." They were about a quarter mile, maybe more, from where they sat in the meadow.

Jane might have been better off physically than Colm, but her swollen, disjointed knee made walking through the snow drifts impossible. She gathered their belongings, tucking them into her backpack. Her knee didn't welcome the additional weight.

"Not going to make it far," he gasped. "My back is on fire."

"Right. Okay. Um...Behind this drift?" Jane gestured to the mound of snow ten or twelve feet in front of them, thankful that was as much terrain as she needed to traverse.

"Yeah. Sure."

They shuffled toward the mound of snow.

"I remembered something," Jane said. "Right before I fell asleep." She told Colm about the gun she'd seen and how her father told Jane it was a Henry before he died.

Colm's teeth chattered, and his cheeks were fiery red. "You said the rifle had the same stock as the gun I saw him pick up after he shot the woman. I didn't see the gun he used on Chase and Lorna, but we can expect it was either the one he used on your dad or the one he used on the woman."

"The woman has to be Lavinia." Jane squinted, willing her body to move faster and with fewer aches. "You're saying she's dead."

"Yeah. I checked on her. No pulse. Shot in the chest. Close range." Colm panted, and he seemed even hotter now. His body was unhappy with this exertion.

"Like my dad."

"And my friends." Colm's eyes had rolled back in his head,

and he flopped down hard. Jane fell to her own knees, her vision dimming as the pain from her injury lanced through her body. She crawled toward Colm and growled as she struggled to flip him over.

"You're freaking heavy," Jane said. He rolled, and his mouth sputtered open in a raspy gasp.

"Same MO," Colm said, clearly not wanting to discuss his fall.

"This snow sucks." Jane sympathized as she wrangled the sleeping bag back out of her pack and draped it over Colm. She gritted her teeth and tried to pull herself upright, but her knee hurt too much.

"Give me a minute."

He chuckled. "Not going anywhere. Need a nap."

"Sleep away," Jane said, relieved that Colm wouldn't watch her next few embarrassing moments. After doing her best to clean up, she got her clothes rearranged with minimal snow inside them to melt down against her flesh.

The hygiene trip took a profound toll on her energy, and Jane's teeth chattered so hard as she made the painfully slow crawl back to Colm that she worried she'd break a tooth or three.

She flopped beside him, thankful at that moment for his searing heat.

"You're cold," he mumbled. "C'mere."

She snuggled closer.

"Colm?"

"Yeah?"

"I'm scared," Jane whispered. She bit her lip and squeezed her eyes shut. "I can't walk well, let alone run."

"And I'm not at peak performance," Colm said. "But you know something, Jane? You have a lot of great skills."

"So do you," Jane said. "You've been out here longer than me."

"I got lucky. I found you."

Her chest warmed, and she tipped her face so her nose was

buried in the crook of his neck. He made her feel gooey and warm in the best way. There wasn't artifice with Colm. They'd both been stripped down to their most primal selves—and they fit. Jane hadn't understood what that meant. She'd been searching for some meaning for her life since the pandemic. She hadn't realized she'd find it in a deep connection to a man during the lowest point of her life.

"We can stabilize your knee, find you a branch to use as a crutch," Colm said. "As long as we're careful, we can do this."

He was right about her leg, but Jane didn't mention they were almost out of food. Worse, they had no shelter. At least the sun shone down on them, so more snow wasn't a concern, but it was cold. Too cold for them to survive a night outside.

For a moment, Jane almost wished that the badger hadn't dug them out. That method of dying—through cold and asphyxiation might have been preferable...at least less painful...to whatever came next.

"I'll carry you out of here, Jane." Determination graveled through Colm's voice. "We've come too far to lie down and take death."

Jane kept her cheek on his chest while Colm rubbed a soothing hand up and down her back.

They rested together, trading childhood stories and favorite foods.

"I can't believe you prefer curry to a burger," Colm said. "That's so..."

"Un-American? Weird? Unnatural?"

He chuckled. Some of his color had come back, thanks to another round of pain pills that reduced his fever.

"Nah. It's just so you," Colm said. "For the record, you do eat burgers, right?"

"Of course. This is beef country, and my grandparents own a ranch. It's just not my favorite."

"All right. Well, when we get out of here, we'll hit an Indian restaurant, and you can eat bowls of curry."

"What will you eat?" Jane asked.

"Meat. Naan. That yogurt dip. Don't care as long as I fill up."

Jane handed Colm another piece of jerky, and he raised it in thanks. "It's amazing how much I like this right now."

Jane looked down at the final piece in the bag. She glanced up at Colm, who was chewing, his eyes closed, his expression blissful. When he finished the piece, she handed him the last one.

They must have dozed off again. Colm's temperature had risen significantly, telling her the medication had worn off. She lifted her head and groggily noted it was still light. The sun was in the west and lowering, so it must be mid-to-late afternoon.

A snuffling sounded from behind Jane, and she rolled over, clenching her teeth as her knee jostled. A huge, horned beast with a wedge-shaped head and a wet snout nuzzled into the grass nearby. Lifting its head, it munched lazily.

Jane tensed as the bison ambled closer. It froze and slowly lifted its head, nostrils flaring wide as it scented Jane and Colm.

Not again. Oh, no. No, no, no...

Jane shrank back against Colm, trying to be as small as possible, even as the scream burst past her lips. The animal slammed its hoof into the ground as it lowered its massive head.

# TWENTY-EIGHT

"JANE!" Cynthia sprang up, the cry for the girl on her lips even as the scream echoed through the air, covering tens, maybe hundreds of miles of empty wilderness. Those vibrations of sound were a blessing but also an added layer of fear atop the thick, soft blanket that had settled over her as they waited in the cabin.

That morning, the snow had been too deep to push out the door, so they'd whiled away the hours in the small space. Cynthia spent a lot of it pacing while Charlie seemed content to sit and stare out the window.

Cynthia couldn't understand how he could be so calm in the aftermath of Matt's murder. She felt like a live wire, sizzling with tension as another moment passed with tortuous slowness.

It was during their lunch of reconstituted noodles and weird chunks of meat that Cynthia drummed up the courage to continue their conversation from the night before.

She smiled. "Glad we talked last night. Mindy's role in Art's death has always bothered me."

"I can see that," Charlie said.

His gaze had flitted to her, checking her, throughout the morning. She cleared her throat. "What did you do? When you found him?"

"Oh. Well, I dropped my rifle and ran to him, checking for a pulse. I performed chest compressions. That's about when you ran in."

Cynthia froze, her breath halting for a painfully long moment before she dipped her spoon back into her bowl. She clutched the utensil more tightly to stop the shaking from being so noticeable. She had run in *with* Mindy and Matt, which was why Cynthia knew Charlie had lied to her. *He'd* been the one to shoot Art, not Mindy.

She'd missed that before. Her story had been muddled, she knew, as had Mindy's, Charlie's, and Matt's. They'd given different accounts to the lead detective back then. Matt had probably been protecting Mindy, but Cynthia had been terrified that Charlie was involved physically, romantically with Mindy...and Art's murder.

Fear wrapped its long fingers around her throat as she realized that because of her decision to protect her pride and her then-husband, Jane might well be in terrible danger now.

Cynthia wouldn't let anything happen to Jane. No matter what, she'd get Jane out of the park safely.

Rising from her chair, she went to the door and opened it, once again staring down at feet of snow. She peered up at the sky. The clouds had broken apart, and more blue shone through.

"We need to go. Get Jane—"

"Slow your roll, Cyn," Charlie said. "We'll find her."

Cynthia offered a tremulous smile, not saying what they both were thinking: there were over two million acres to traverse, which equated to an area bigger than Delaware and Rhode Island *combined.* Jane was the proverbial needle in a haystack. But they'd heard her.

They'd find her, no matter what.

At that second scream, their gazes met and tangled, urgency spurring them on as they completed their tasks in record time.

"She's *alive*," Cynthia murmured, unable to push the words out any louder against the pressure in her chest. Tears sprang to her eyes, and she dug faster. "She's alive."

"And with someone," Charlie said. "Or attacked by him. That other voice sounded male, don't you think? That didn't sound like Lavinia. There can't possibly be another person out here in this mess, can there?"

"I don't know. I don't..." She had to take a deep breath. "Right now, I'm going to focus on how good it was to hear Jane's voice."

"Right. Yeah. Makes sense. I'll call it in."

Charlie picked up their radio, which he'd silenced yesterday against the indignant squawk of the NPS ranger in charge of the search and rescue. No way Charlie and Cynthia would turn back without Jane, so they'd decided to save the battery.

Cynthia focused on clearing the snowmobile, not paying attention to Charlie's conversation, though she heard the shrill voice on the line.

"Okay, so you heard that." Charlie bumped her out of the way to continue with the dig out.

"Wasn't paying attention...we don't know if the snowmobile works or where she is or—"

This time, Charlie comforted her with an embrace. "We'll figure it out, Cyn. *All* of it. You, me, the past, which doesn't matter. Our future together. All right?"

Cynthia lowered her head, bit her lip, and nodded, hoping she'd played that role correctly. And Charlie hadn't noticed anything different in her behavior. Being with him, trapped out here, had been a near-impossible feat of play-acting.

Cynthia had never been good at that.

"Any idea how far a scream can travel?" she asked, tamping down on the overwhelming desire to run out the door and into the snow, screaming Jane's name. Cynthia wouldn't get to Jane faster that way, and she wouldn't keep her safer by splitting up from Charlie.

Jane was priority one. Charlie's lies, his past deeds, came second.

But she didn't—wouldn't—trust him. Not with Jane.

Charlie fiddled with the motor, probably trying to warm the gasoline inside it.

"Ah, yeah. It's something between half a mile and a mile."

Cynthia's hands stilled, then she balled them into fists. Jane had been trying to get to one of these cabins, most likely. She'd been doing what her father told her, and she had to be close, maybe within a mile of where she and Charlie slept last night. So damn close.

"Whatever happens out there..." Cynthia began. "Whatever happens out there...I don't want to be alone anymore. I...I want you... I'll move in," she rushed to finish. She smiled up at him, her stomach a mass of nerves.

"With me?" Charlie rose to his full height, his gaze never wavering. "You'd move in with me? And you wouldn't leave? You're *sure*?" Charlie demanded again. His gaze was sharp, like a bird pinning a moth with its beak.

As she'd expected, he liked her saying that because he thought he'd fooled her *again*. Cynthia needed him to get Jane out of here, and her pride could withstand one more hit.

Cynthia licked her lips and met his gaze. "Yes. I'm sure. I love you, Charlie. I always have."

But for the first time ever, Cynthia lied to Charlie. She had loved him. She didn't now—couldn't—after what he'd done to Art. Drawing a breath, Cynthia realized she was *finally* free of him. She wouldn't ever trust him again.

Cynthia finished gathering their sparse belongings and tossed them into one of the side bins before sliding onto the frigid, hard plastic seat. At least that would warm up, thanks to her body heat. But this was going to be a brutal, cold ride.

"We should travel in concentric circles up to a mile and a half," she said as Charlie settled before her. "Which way?"

Another scream rent the air as the snowmobile blasted to life.

"Go left," Cynthia said. Charlie did, and she clung to him, needing him...for now. But the moment she could, she'd take Jane and run straight to Detective Fremont.

# TWENTY-NINE

AFTER THE INITIAL CHARGE, the bison determined Jane and Colm weren't enough of a threat to trample, but Jane didn't trust them. She wanted to move, but she was too afraid, and Colm was too sick to try.

As they lay in the snow, Colm's fever worsened. She needed to get water *in* their bodies. *One step at a time, Janie.*

Just as her father taught her. Their top priority was slaking thirst, so she repeated her process from before to fill her Camelback while keeping an eye on the bison who'd moved to the other side of the valley. Once the snow was melting, Jane dug out from the sleeping bag and settled her knee into the snow, burying her leg and hoping the cold would quell any additional swelling. Unlikely after the many hours, but the cold was Jane's only treatment option. She popped one of the Advil in her first-aid kit to assist with reducing inflammation, wishing she could take two, but knowing she needed to save the others for Colm to bring down his fever.

"Colm, I need to check your wound," Jane said.

"Sure." He rolled onto his side, tucking his good arm under his ear. She lifted his layers and gasped at the redness and swelling around the wound.

"Um...it doesn't look great," Jane said.

"It's been throbbing for a while."

"Why didn't you say something?" Jane asked.

"There's little we can do for it," he replied.

"I still wish you'd said something. I'll clean it with snow again, then add more of the cream."

He was quiet while she worked, but she could tell by the rigidity of his back and shoulders that her ministrations hurt him. She applied the antibiotic cream liberally, smearing it into and around the gash.

"I don't have enough bandages, so I'm going to wrap my T-shirt around you. It's clean...ish."

"Sounds great. Probably cleaner than anything I'm wearing."

Jane finished the task and re-smoothed his clothing, then pulled the sleeping bag over his shivering form.

"I'm sorry. I know that hurt." She cleaned her hands in the snow, locking her jaw against the cold.

"If it helps stave off infection, it's worth it," Colm said.

"Why don't you drink some more water?" Jane suggested.

Colm obediently drank from the proffered straw, wincing as the cold fluid hit his overheated mouth and throat.

"Thanks." He smiled, but his eyes were too bright. Illness had definitely taken hold.

They needed to get out of this valley...and away from the bison herd she could make out at the entrance. She couldn't tell yet if they were heading closer to her and Colm or not, but she couldn't wait too long to move.

Because the bison would be back—and they wouldn't take kindly to Jane and Colm's presence.

After nibbling on the dwindling supply of trail mix, she took a few cautious sips of the water, opening her mouth as soon as she swallowed to ease the ache in her teeth.

Good thing Colm burned with fever. The chill might help reduce his internal temperature to a healthier level. Maybe.

She glanced up again. The bison were farther away. Not even Colm's funny name for the beasts could ease the anxiety she felt near the fur tanks.

With a grimace, she shoved the snow from her knee. It was still sore, but she bent it a little. When she palpated the top, she felt no shards of bone crinkling under the skin.

"Not shattered." That had been her fear: her femur in pieces. Not that her leg was in good shape, but at least bone shards weren't floating through her body, causing inflammation like Colm's.

"Colm? Can you drink?"

He remained asleep, something his body clearly needed. Still, Jane wanted him to have the fluids he needed to fight off the infection.

"Colm, please wake up."

She rested on her side as she brought the straw to Colm's mouth. He lay there, water dribbling along his cheeks until he choked on it. She lifted his head a bit and tried again. He sputtered, but he swallowed. She tried again, but Colm turned his head away. He thrashed, caught in a fever dream.

"No," he cried out. "No!"

One of his fists slammed into Jane's bad leg, and she dropped forward, protecting her injury even as a scream ripped from her lips.

Noise rushed through her ears, and the nuts she'd eaten pushed up her throat. She swallowed, not because she worried about vomiting, but because she couldn't stop whimpering and crying.

The pain...

It was all-consuming.

Colm rose from the makeshift pallet, wild-eyed. The sleeping bag slid off his body, pooling at his feet. He staggered toward her, tangling in the material, and fell hard into the snow. He flailed, pushing from the soft mass Jane had created when she'd filled her water pouch earlier.

The pain in her leg ebbed from a sharp stabbing to a duller pulse. She could sniffle back fresh tears.

"I'm all right," she croaked.

Colm had flopped onto his back. He stared up at the sky, spread-eagled. He shivered, his eyes too bright and cheeks crimson.

"I don't think I am." Colm turned his head to look at Jane. He studied her face, his countenance softening. "It's okay. I got to spend some time with you."

The urgency created strength, and Jane slithered closer. "Don't say that. Please. It sounds like you're giving up."

He squeezed her fingers. "I'm okay with that, as long as you get out. Live your life. Saving you is worth it."

"No, Colm. You're *not* going to die. I'll...I'll think of something." She gripped his chapped, feverish hand in hers.

She pulled out the last pain pill and set it on his lips. "Take this. It helped before."

Colm swallowed the pill and more water, all while Jane silently melted down. She couldn't lose this man, too. Not after watching her father fall, crimson blooming over his chest.

"Ah, Jane. I wish I could have spent more time with you." His smile was endearingly lopsided.

"You will if you hold on for me, okay?" Jane snuffled. She brought his hand to her cheek. "Just *hold on*. We'll get that curry. You'll love it."

"Do my best," he mumbled. "Tired."

"Drink a little more."

Once he had, Jane glanced around, awed by the majesty, thrilled to the roots of her hair by the beauty, the silence...the sheer magnitude of its *wildness*. If she let the negative thoughts in, they would destroy the pleasure she'd found in the park and the connection she'd been building with her father.

Gripping Colm's hands harder, she searched for an answer...

Then she heard the low thrum of a motor.

Jane dropped Colm's hand to grab his rifle, swinging it up to her shoulder with practiced ease. She sighted toward the sound, but her scan brought up nothing. Keeping a grip on the firearms, she turned to meet his gaze.

His eyes brimmed with fear and that extraordinary inner fortitude that had kept him going all this time.

"Could be help, but it could be the killer," Colm said. His fear surrounded them, almost as if it had its own smell.

One of those two groups had a greater incentive to find them.

# THIRTY

CYNTHIA'S FINGERS clutched harder into Charlie's side, but before she could shout anything, he'd turned the snowmobile toward Jane's most recent cry. The going was slow—too slow—thanks to the densely packed vegetation, but eventually, they burst into a large meadow. Cynthia caught her breath.

"*Jane.*"

The silly knitted hat with a pompom atop sat on her head. The one Jane and she had painstakingly knitted during Jane's failed attempt at fiber arts. That hat was ugly, misshapen, and perfect. *So perfect.*

Wait. Not Jane's head. Because Jane sat up and waved an arm, her other hand pressed against the person in her hat.

The walkie-talkie clipped to Charlie's waistband crackled. "... check in..."

Cynthia snagged it. "We found Jane! *We found her*!" Cynthia rattled off their coordinates from her GPS.

"Who is that with her?" Charlie vibrated with energy, clearly unable to contain his animosity toward the person lying on the ground. He better not try anything stupid...

Cynthia hopped off the snowmobile and slogged through the

drift before Charlie cut off the engine. She fell to her knees beside Jane and caught the younger woman in her arms, muffling Jane's cry against her thick winter jacket.

"You're here. I can't believe you're here." Jane clasped Cynthia tighter.

She cupped her dear girl's cheeks. Her face was thinner, and there were thick, purple shadows under Jane's eyes. Exhaustion settled over Jane, making her movements slower than usual.

But she was alive. And whole.

"Of course, I came for you, sweet girl. I'm sorry it took so long." She smoothed Jane's hair back from her forehead, cataloging each scratch. Jane had suffered. Cynthia pressed her lips together, tearing up. "I thought...Jane, you scared me. Us. We've been so worried..."

Jane pressed her wet cheek to Cynthia's, but neither woman moved to wipe their tears away.

"Watch her knee," a rusty, thin male voice said. "She's hurt."

Cynthia glanced at the other person in the snow. She gasped as she realized a man lay shivering under a sleeping bag. Battered by sun and needing a wash and a good meal...or fifty. His eyes were glassy but sharp with intelligence, and his teeth chattered. His clothes weren't thick enough to withstand the elements.

He couldn't be much older than Quincy...maybe a bit younger than her graduate student. But even injured, this man had a stability to his presence. Her grad student was a chihuahua, whereas this man was an injured wolf.

"Who are you?" Charlie asked, towering over them all. His hands were on his hips, and his scowl grew darker with each passing breath. Cynthia's good mood plummeted.

"Charlie," Jane squealed. She moved as if to get up, then grabbed her knee as she cried out. Charlie dropped to his haunches, concern for Jane wafting off him as he laid his big, gloved hand on her shoulder.

"Hey, now. Easy, Janie. Easy."

"You know these people, Jane?" the man asked. He edged closer to the rifle Jane had dropped in the snow while his eyes darted around and his mouth pulled tight with worry. His hand wrapped around the stock.

"I do. They're family." Jane clasped Charlie's hand. "I'm so glad you found me." Tears built in her eyes and spilled over her cheeks as she turned to her father's best friend. "Charlie. Charlie, Dad's dead."

"We know." Charlie's words were sharp. "We've been looking for you since I helped the rangers carry him out of the woods."

Jane pulled back, confusion and anguish flitting across her features. Charlie didn't notice Jane's change.

"Where'd he come from?" Charlie glared at the prone figure. The young man stared back boldly, unwilling to bend to Charlie's aggression. While she understood Charlie's emotions, she didn't like how he scared the kids.

"He was in the woods," Jane said. "We met up a couple of days ago. His friends were murdered a few days before Dad. Colm saw the killer and chased him." Jane said as she shifted, putting her slight form between Charlie's growing ferocity and Colm. While Charlie continued to glare, Jane gave them a brief overview of Colm's last, harrowing week in the park.

"I...I thought it was Lavinia. She was in the back of Dad's Jeep, and...and...then, Dad...he was shot..."

"Breathe, honey." Cynthia rubbed Jane's back in long strokes.

Charlie's chest expanded as he inhaled hard, processing the information. "I can't believe...she's Matt's grad student...why..."

Charlie swallowed hard and turned away, pressing his fists to the sides of his head.

"Just give him a moment," Cynthia said. Her worried gaze tracked Charlie before she focused on Jane. "Oh, honey. What you've been through."

"Why is he *that* upset about Lavinia?" Jane asked.

"What if Lavinia's *still* in the park?" Colm asked. Jane shot him a look. Colm's expression had shuttered, but his eyes held horror of death. There was fear there, too. Well, Colm didn't know her, didn't know Charlie, so mistrust after what he'd been through made sense.

"Lavinia's still in the park?" Cynthia asked slowly. "That doesn't make sense. I mean, I can tell you she never returned to her student housing. The police are looking into her as a missing person and a person of interest in your father's murder."

"Police?" Jane asked.

Cynthia nodded. "Obviously, there's a lot to catch you up on."

"You said Lavinia had reason to hate your dad," Colm said. Again, there was something off about his voice. He craned his neck to follow Charlie's movements.

"She does," Cynthia said. "Every grad student's worst nightmare is getting thrown off a project before a paper's published, before they get their degree in hand. It means starting over on a different team, taking additional years to graduate, and more money."

"*What* was Matt thinking?" Charlie waded closer, the snow nearly to his knees. He scrubbed his palms down his cheeks. "*You know* grad students have killed for less than that. Hell, we've joked about it at lunch..."

Charlie stomped off again, needing the moment to cool off.

"That guy's got a lot of anger..." Colm's gaze trailed Charlie's form.

They remained quiet. Jane frowned, glanced at Colm, then asked, "Back at the location where...where...Dad died." She swallowed a thick, wet sound. "There would have to be shell casings for the bullets, right?"

"Probably," Cynthia said with a shrug.

"Have the police gotten in there?" Jane asked, her mind racing. "Did they find any casings?"

"Yes," Cynthia said. "They were there, but I don't know about the casings. Detective Horton didn't mention those to me."

"Can we find out?" Jane asked, getting more animated.

"Why?"

"Because..." Jane glanced at Colm, gauging his reaction to her bringing Cynthia in on his secret.

"Because we could compare them to the ones I've kept from my friend's murder. And if they matched..." Colm said.

"That's really smart." Cynthia thought for a moment, then nodded. "We'd have a better trail to connect to the killer.

Jane, Colm, and Cynthia glanced around, and Jane shivered, biting off a whimper.

Charlie stomped back and gestured toward Colm. "I get the Lavinia angle, I really do, but how do you *know* it wasn't this kid who shot Matt? He just shows up..." His voice broke, and his finger shook as he pointed at Colm, who tightened his grip on his rifle. It was empty—no more bullets in the chamber—but Jane assumed Colm wanted it nearby, preferably in his arms...like a security blanket.

"Stop, Charlie. I know you're upset about Dad." Jane's lower lip wobbled. "I know. But it wasn't Colm. He's a victim, too. Plus, he-he saved me."

Cynthia rolled her lips back into her mouth, unsure she believed that statement. But then, finding Jane out here had been a leap of faith, and here they were.

"And that's not the killer's rifle." Jane sniffled.

"What?" Charlie demanded.

But Jane pressed closer to Colm, her nose in the center of his chest. "The bison." Her voice cracked.

Cynthia frowned. "They're moving this way. We don't want to create a stampede."

Colm groaned while Jane's eyes widened. "Not again. I just can't face the bison again."

The bison edged closer, the herd's leader scenting the air. Jane and Colm clutched each other as they began to shiver harder.

It was clear they'd had a run-in with the animals—and it hadn't ended well.

"Let's load up the kids." Cynthia studied Jane's interactions with Colm. Jane had brought Scott around more than once, and Jane had never been this comfortable with her ex-boyfriend before.

Colm closed his arms around Jane, even though it seemed to pain him. "It's okay. I've got you."

"No! We're not going through that again." Jane's breathing escalated as she lifted her head, wild eyes seeking Cynthia's. "We need to leave."

"Whoa! We're okay for a second. Breathe, honey. Tell us what happened—" Charlie began.

"*Now.*" Jane shook with such force that her knee bounced, and that caused her to collapse over it, holding it. "I can't...not if there could be another stampede. One of *them* gored him."

"After another one trampled you," Colm shot back. "We barely made it out of harm's way. It was..."

"Horrible," Jane rasped.

"All right. Let's get you loaded up for the ride out." Worry entered Charlie's expression. "Janie, it's going to be bumpy. How bad is your knee?"

Jane took a deep breath and released it, determination settling on her face. "Bad. But I can handle it."

"I'm sure you can." Cynthia squeezed Jane's hand. She rose from her crouched position with a grimace and noted Colm's red cheeks, too-bright eyes, and blue-tinged fingertips. She pulled off her gloves with her teeth and tried to work them over his hands, but he was much larger than she was.

"I got this, Cyn." Charlie pulled off his outer gloves and then yanked off a pair of thin, supple inner ones. "These aren't as warm, but they'll help." He worked them over Colm's red knuckles, and Cynthia had to close her mouth as she noted the emotions swirling in Charlie's eyes.

Charlie went back to the snowmobile, grabbed one of the blankets they'd brought, and wrapped it around Colm's shoulders. Then Charlie set about reorganizing the small trailer they'd towed behind them. Cynthia couldn't help but remember the morbid reason it was there: to haul Matt's corpse from the park. Instead, they had two twenty-somethings who needed medical help.

"He's in poor shape," Charlie muttered to Cynthia. "Might have the onset of sepsis. See if you can get some water in him."

She grabbed their spare canteen. "How are we going to fit them both?"

"With difficulty, but we'll make it work." Charlie narrowed his eyes in concentration, his jaw set with determination. "Somehow."

Cynthia offered Colm the water and set about wrapping Jane's knee. Jane's pants were tight there because of the swelling, and the flesh was hot even through the material. Like Charlie, Cynthia's concern escalated as she realized how careful they would need to be—even as time was of the essence.

Colm drank the water but seemed to fade out of consciousness. He must have used up all his energy trying to protect Jane. Warmth built in Cynthia, pushing out the concern. Colm clearly cared about Jane. And Jane appeared just as protective of him.

"His back's a mess," Jane said. "And I don't think he's eaten enough. For days at least, if not longer."

"Well, this is about as good as I can make the space. Hopefully, you two will fit," Charlie said.

"We crammed together in the sleeping bag," Jane said. "This is spacious by comparison."

Cynthia hummed, refusing to blurt out any of her thoughts.

Charlie squatted and picked up Jane while Cynthia grabbed her sleeping bag and pack. Once Jane settled into the sled, Charlie trotted toward Colm. He stared down at the younger man, a scowl forming the longer he looked.

"We won't leave you here."

"Glad to hear it," Colm said. Cynthia picked up on the faint tremor in his voice.

"But just because Jane trusts you doesn't mean I do. Or that I'll let you near our girl without making sure you're not a threat to her or to Cynthia."

"I'm not—"

"You mentioned casings."

Colm's eyes flared. With a quick motion, Charlie twisted, gripping Colm's shirt in his fist.

"No..."

Colm gripped tighter at the cloth barrier, but Charlie had already fished out a bullet casing from Colm's pocket. Colm gasped, possibly from the pain Charlie's action caused, but as much from the metal in Charlie's palm. He displayed it to Cynthia and Jane, his eyes flashing with triumph.

"Just as expected. You know a lot more about Matt's murder than you told Jane, don't you, Colm?"

# THIRTY-ONE

CHARLIE'S EXPRESSION was that of a triumphant prosecutor who'd just slam-dunked the perpetrator to life in prison.

"No, I don't, and those aren't from *my* gun," Colm said.

"From whose, then?" Charlie crowed.

Colm clammed up tight, but he shot Jane a beseeching look. One that also accused. She'd told Colm these people were family.

People she trusted. Jane's head went weightless for a moment as the world shifted, reorienting into a terrible possibility she never could have imagined even moments before.

But Colm had saved her life.

Sure, Charlie and Cynthia were here with her. These three people should all have her best interest at heart, but something wasn't right. Something *really* wasn't right. She inched closer to Colm. Fumbling, she managed to entwine their fingers, trying to show him without words that she believed him...and that he may have been right about who had just roared into their world.

They'd found her. They were the ones looking. Colm had told her that would be the killer, something she'd believed wholeheartedly until Cynthia and Charlie appeared.

Bile rose hard and fast up her throat.

"I'll keep a close eye on you," Cynthia said. She glanced between Jane and Colm before meeting Jane's gaze, hers firm. She glanced between Jane and Colm before meeting Jane's gaze. Hers didn't hold worry. Cynthia's held confirmation.

"Promise."

The word didn't reassure Jane at all. No, it slammed into Jane's chest as a threat of something already decided.

Jane and Colm shared a long look. They didn't have a better choice now but to go along with Charlie and Cynthia.

After a brief fight that he clearly lost, Cynthia took Colm's empty rifle from his stiff fingers. He swallowed hard when his eyes slid to the holster at Cynthia's waist. Charlie had one, too. Most experienced hikers had a pistol or rifle in these woods. His eyes flicked back to Jane, then down to the holstered weapon.

Colm rose, staggered, and fell into the trailer next to Jane. She tucked blankets around him and fussed to get them right. Colm remained quiet while Charlie clambered onto the machine and started the motor. Cynthia settled behind Charlie and glanced over her shoulder, her gaze assessing.

"I can overpower Cynthia for her pistol," Colm murmured once Cynthia turned away, leaning her cheek against Charlie's back as they glided and bumped over the snowy terrain back toward civilization. "Her *loaded* pistol, which will give us much better odds. We just needed to separate Cynthia and Charlie."

Jane nodded her understanding, even as she marveled at the surreal situation. "I understand. You're right. We need a firearm." For a brief, beautiful moment, Jane had been so sure they were now safe.

# THIRTY-TWO

VOICES PULLED Jane from her reverie. She wouldn't say she'd been unconscious...just not that interested in focusing on the spike of pain that shot from her knee all the way to her jaw with each bounce or turn on the snowmobile.

Colm clutched his shirt as his face contorted with anguish. "I didn't think to hide them better. Now that Charlie's touched one of them, that'll distort the evidence."

*One of them.* The casing Charlie took from Colm's pocket.

*Singular.*

But Colm had said *casings*. As in, he had more than one.

"How did he know it was in my pocket, Jane?" Colm asked.

Her gaze snapped to his as that thrum ratcheted up to a howl. "Maybe your shirt bulged or...I...don't know."

"Me, either." Colm chewed his battered lip. A drop of blood appeared there. "Lavinia—you know she's dead. I told you that."

Jane gave a jerky nod. "Yes, you did. But we don't know whether they know that, which is why you let them believe she's still alive and in the park, right?"

He nodded. "That and I didn't want them to know I'd been

following them if they're the killer. Right now, they think they have the upper hand."

They did because Charlie and Cynthia were healthy and had firearms.

"At least we're out of the bison meadow," Jane said.

"We need to go to the spot where she died," Colm said.

"Lavinia?"

"Yeah. There's something there." Colm wiggled, cursing and gasping, and finally pulled out a small piece of plaid. He cupped it so that neither Cynthia nor Charlie would be able to see it.

"The killer wore a ranger's uniform. I couldn't shoot an innocent, so I waited...and Lavinia died."

Jane's eyes slid shut. When she opened them, Colm had fisted the fabric. "The killer's shirt caught on a tree branch, ripping it. This was underneath."

"You took that from the crime scene?" Jane breathed.

"I left part of it. But yeah. Like the casings."

"Do you have one from Lavinia's death, too?"

Colm shook his head slowly. "I thought this was more important, and I wanted to find you—warn you."

JANE MUST HAVE DRIFTED off again, lulled by the vibrations of the snowmobile. She hadn't planned to sleep, hadn't thought she'd be able to, not after Colm's revelation.

She dreamed of her father—of them talking just outside the little Army Corps of Engineers cabin where they'd spent their first night in the park.

Dad tossed the clump of algae-crusted dirt, where it hit the bark of the Douglas fir and exploded into tinier particles of rich, black, life-giving soil. He laid his hand against the tree, skimming the rough bark.

A pang hit her because this was a dream. He wasn't real. "I'm going to miss you," she mumbled. She inhaled his familiar scent again. But it was off...a hint of something that shouldn't be there...

Something *sinister*. Deadly.

"Ah, Janie. I'll be with you. Whenever you need me," he said.

But even as the words left his mouth, he staggered.

"Dad?" Jane cried.

He dropped to his knees, causing Jane to let him go. But she fell next to him and grasped his shoulders.

"What is it?"

"You *know* who killed me," he rasped.

He pressed his hands to his belly, and they came away covered in his blood.

"No! Dad, no! I'm not losing you again—"

"You know, Janie," he muttered.

Jane's eyes popped open, and she gasped for air. They were still in the trailer attached to the snowmobile, gliding over a meadow. It differed from the bison's field—smaller and with steeper ridges that rippled upward toward the cloud-laden sky. As the snow melted, purple flowers atop narrow silvery-green leaves emerged, drooping back into the pristine snow.

"You okay?" Cynthia asked.

Jane nodded, trying to regulate her breathing. Charlie drove over the plant as he cut through the meadow.

Jane stared into Colm's feverish eyes. She had to make a choice: she must trust him as she had at the bison's meadow, or she must allow Charlie's skepticism to change her opinion of the man she'd slept with—the man who'd saved her life. Colm stayed silent, patient. Jane closed her hand around his.

"We need to make a stop," Jane called up to Cynthia. "To the place where you last talked to Lavinia on Dad's sat phone."

Cynthia frowned. "Why?"

"Because...there's something there we need to find."

"Jane..." Cynthia said. "Let's just get you out of here, okay?"

"We *have* to go," Jane insisted. "That's where my walking stick is. The one Dad made for me. Please, Cynthia. I can't lose that, too."

She hadn't left it there. She'd dropped it when her father told her to run. But Colm said they had to go back to the spot where she and her father left Lavinia—where Lavinia had died—and that was the best lie she could create right now. If Cynthia called her on it, if she knew that Jane had dropped her stick in the clearing where her father died, that would implicate Cynthia in his murder *and* Lavinia's.

The fear had grown after her dream, screaming at her now that she and Colm weren't safe.

That Cynthia and Charlie hadn't braved the storm to save her.

What to believe? Who to believe?

Jane had to trust her gut. And her gut told her Colm was telling the truth.

"What does she want?" Charlie asked, glancing over his shoulder.

He and Cynthia spoke, but Jane couldn't hear all the words. Eventually, they came to an understanding, and Cynthia turned back toward Jane. "No. I don't think we should go there simply because we can make it on the way back. I don't like deviating from the path we told the rangers we're taking."

That gut feeling had merged with the anxiety that she'd begun to feel ever since Charlie pulled the casing from Colm's shirt.

She and Colm were with two of the people who would most benefit from her father's death. The stupid Wolf Project would pass to Cynthia and Charlie. But if this were about revenge or money, then her mom would benefit more.

Any way Jane looked at it, Jane trusted Colm more than anyone else. So, if she needed to lie to Cynthia and Charlie to steal away, she would. And she'd make sure she and Colm made it out of the park.

# THIRTY-THREE

THE GOING COULD HAVE BEEN FASTER, but the warming temperature and melting snow slowed them down. The snowmobile lurched and sputtered before jolting to a stop. Jane bit her lip to keep from crying out while Colm hissed in pain.

His cheeks had reddened during the ride, which could have been from the sun and the reflection it cast off the snow. Jane's own skin felt tight and burned. But Colm's eyes seemed less focused... glassier.

Jane glanced up at Charlie, who slammed his fist into the snowmobile's steering wheel.

"Sorry, kids. Because of the hydrothermal activity in the area, the snow melted more quickly here, and there's not enough snow for us to skim," Cynthia said.

"How far to the spot where I dropped my walking stick?" Jane asked.

Charlie pulled out a GPS device. He gestured forward. "Should be just through those trees."

Jane climbed from the trailer with Cynthia's help, testing her swollen knee. To her surprise, she found it tender but not as painful as it had been right after the bison stepped on her or when she had torn the tendons. Maybe they'd held. Maybe it was just bruised and strained.

Colm struggled to sit up. Cynthia bent in to help him. She offered him more water, then said, "Walking will be difficult, I know, but the other option is leaving you out here."

Colm glanced toward Jane. His eyes had sunk into his skull, and worry nibbled at her. She walked over to Colm and took his hand. It was burning up. The last round of medication shouldn't have worn off that quickly.

She'd heard Charlie's comment about sepsis, and she knew Colm wouldn't have a lot of time if he had a blood infection. She wasn't sure she could do anything else for Colm right now besides keeping him hydrated. He needed to see a doctor and get antibiotics. Soon.

"You okay?" she murmured.

Colm's lips quirked. "Been better. Not sure I've been worse."

That wasn't the answer she'd hoped for. "Thanks for stopping," she said to Charlie and Cynthia.

"Wasn't like there was a choice," Cynthia said on a sigh.

Maybe not, but it allowed Jane to reconfirm Colm's story—and see Charlie and Cynthia's reaction to Lavinia's corpse.

With a steadying breath, Jane walked forward. The clearing was silent. She didn't see Lavinia's body.

Maybe Colm had lied.

As she dropped her head forward, she glimpsed white. It stuck out among the dead leaves and mud. Brown, white, and green plaid. Camouflage colors that were perfect to blend in with the surroundings.

She bent down, wincing, and grabbed it, squeezing the fabric in her hand. It was the same one Colm had. Relief loosened her limbs. He'd been telling the truth. He'd wanted her to see that—to know, without a shadow of a doubt—that she could trust him. She had, but this had helped.

A lot.

Because now Jane had to fight her instincts about Charlie and Cynthia, people who'd cared for her as long as she could remember.

She glanced up at him as he shuffled closer. "I don't like this," he muttered. "Any of it. We need to get a gun, Jane. And we need to get out of here. Got any ideas for a distraction?"

"No, and we can't take the snowmobile, which would have been our best and fastest bet." But it was useless without snow.

Part of her wondered if that had been why Charlie drove here—he'd have known about the hydrothermal activity. He'd know that the ground stayed warm much longer in these areas.

"Jane? Honey? Are you all right?" Cynthia asked. She started walking back toward Jane and Colm. Jane's heart clobbered her sternum. Cynthia was acting overprotective. Or she was keeping tabs on Jane.

"Did you find my walking stick? I really want it back." Jane clutched her elbows even tighter to her sides as she tucked the scrap of fabric into the inner pocket of her jacket. She breathed out, relief hitting her hard when she got away with that sleight of hand.

"No. Did you?" Charlie asked Cynthia.

A longing rose in Jane. She wanted one of the sharpened walking sticks that she and her father had carried in. It would help her balance her weight...and offer her a weapon of sorts.

"Lavinia's not here," Jane mumbled to Colm.

"She was."

Jane looked around, trying to spot anything related to death. She stilled as she noted a blood trail and broken foliage. She tipped her head toward it while Cynthia tried to get reception on the walkie-talkie, but the device only emitted static. Colm's eyes widened, and he dipped his head, acknowledging the scene.

"We must be in a depression," Cynthia said. As she shoved the radio into her pocket, a piece of paper fluttered out.

"Or we're out of range," Charlie said.

"It's getting dark. Let's head to the cabin. It's not too far. Maybe a couple of miles that way. We can ease back out of here on the snowmobile." Cynthia's finger shook. The older woman cut a glance toward Jane before she turned back to smile at Charlie. "You'll get us there easily, just like you found Jane. We'll rest until morning. I don't think Colm's in great enough shape to handle hours of bouncing yet. Plus, you always say night driving is dangerous."

Cynthia was lying to them...or to Charlie.

"Normally, yes, but does that make sense in this situation, Cyn?" Charlie asked. "Maybe it's better to head straight out of the park."

"We can't," Cynthia sounded desperate. "If it gets dark, we won't be able to see well. We could run into a...a...boulder."

Cynthia seemed really fixated on getting to the cabin. Jane frowned, trying to think of why.

There were beds...and food...and batteries and walkie-talkies. Did Cynthia want her own way to communicate with the outside world? Maybe she didn't trust Charlie either.

Too much was happening, too many variables. Jane struggled to decide which, if either of her father's friends, she could trust.

Neither. Jane trusted neither, and that realization unsettled her. Her breathing sped up.

Colm had returned to the snowmobile. He bent down and retrieved a paper. His step stuttered, and he gasped low. He shifted his body so that his back was to Cynthia and Charlie. He held out the paper, which Jane scanned. Her lips thinned as she read the words.

*Cut funding.*

*Six months to complete data.*

She glanced up at Colm and gave him a faint nod. Yes, this was important. It was the motive Jane hadn't been able to figure out. The reason Cynthia and Charlie would kill her father.

The reason she shouldn't—couldn't—trust either of them.

Jane snatched the paper from Colm's hand just as Cynthia turned back toward her. Jane somehow managed to shove the memorandum into the interior pocket of her coat, where she'd housed the scrap of flannel fabric. Then she clasped Colm's hand, wanting him to know she wouldn't leave him. He'd saved her life, and now she'd save his. Even if it was from her father's closest friends.

But there was nowhere to go. Not at this moment. Colm had had his rifle before, but now the firearm was useless...and back at the unusable snowmobile that they couldn't start and back out of here quickly enough if Cynthia and Charlie decided to use their pistols. Plus, Charlie and Cynthia had food and fresh water. Jane had the frozen snow she'd forced into her Camelbak.

It would be much better if they could collect some supplies and sneak away at night. She hoped Colm understood that.

Cynthia continued to study Jane. She frowned. "Are you feeling okay, honey?"

"Just wishing that walking stick had been there." Jane offered a smile, but it felt more like a grimace.

"I can support some of your weight," Cynthia said, moving closer.

"No, no, that's okay. Colm and I...er... we're used to supporting each other."

Colm bit his lip at this blatant lie, but Jane didn't want Cynthia touching her. Not now.

"Want me to carry your backpack, at least?" Cynthia asked. "Here, give it to me. There's no reason for you to have the extra weight."

"Don't touch it," Jane cried. Her breathing escalated as

Cynthia grabbed the strap. She twisted away, desperate to keep what little she had—the water pouch, the Jeep keys. "Don't. Please. D-dad gave it to me."

Cynthia dropped her arm, the shock in her expression morphing to understanding and then pity. "All right. I won't take it."

"Leave us alone," Colm mumbled.

"What's that?" Cynthia asked, still frowning.

"Could I have some water? I'm thirsty," Colm said.

"Oh, yes!" Cynthia pulled out a stainless-steel bottle and handed it to Colm.

Colm drank from the water bottle even as he kept his gaze on Cynthia and Charlie.

Cynthia sighed, her gaze dropped to the forest floor. She gasped. "Oh my...Charlie, look! There's blood here."

Cynthia had noted the same bloody trail Jane had pointed out a few moments before. "We have to follow this—see what it is. You kids stay close to me."

Colm groaned softly. He leaned in for her gun, but Cynthia drew it before he could reach it. Jane's heart sank. That had been their best opportunity to get protection.

Cynthia could shoot well enough to run off a predator like most Montanans. She'd taken Jane to the shooting range a few times back when Jane was in middle school and high school to ensure Jane had the skills to live at the edge of the woods.

Cynthia had always found her mark on the paper targets. Now, Cynthia's firearm made Jane feel even more vulnerable. Cynthia, the woman Jane had looked up to and wanted to emulate, had found her when the park rangers couldn't...and hadn't even let Jane make a call on the walkie-talkie for backup.

"You got an extra pistol?" Jane asked. She studied Cynthia's reaction.

"No, honey, and we both know I'm the better shot," Cynthia said. "Plus, I don't want to add additional trauma to your ordeal."

Charlie nodded. "Exactly. I don't want you to have that weight on your shoulders along with everything else. Don't worry, Cynthia and I will take care of you."

He shot her that grin that Jane loved. It was a little self-deprecating and charming. This time, it caused Jane to shift closer to Colm as if Charlie meant taking care of Jane...as he had her father?

"I'm paranoid," Jane whispered.

"No, you're not," Colm murmured back.

"Oh, my god! That's...that's Lavinia!" Cynthia cried. She raised her pistol and took aim at the animal tearing into the woman's body that lay, so still, motionless on the ground. One, two, three shots at the alpha wolf Jane and her father had viewed just days before. The animal growled, snapped, and finally, slunk away.

"Why did you do that?" Jane whimpered. "Why did you shoot him?"

"Jane!" Colm cried.

"It's Lavinia! She must have stayed in the park and killed Matt," Charlie said. "My god. We were just talking about that—how a grad student would kill to keep their spot."

"I didn't aim at the wolf, Jane," Cynthia said. "He's fine. I was just scaring him away from Lavinia's body. Oh, the poor girl."

Cynthia tugged on Charlie's backpack, yanking him to the ground next to her and the prone corpse.

"She's dead," Jane mumbled. Charlie said it louder.

"There's nothing we can do for her, Cyn. Plus, she...she killed Matt." He dropped his chin to his chest, his shoulders heaving.

"She wasn't a threat..." Jane mumbled. That thought galvanized Jane because she and Colm were similar to Lavinia. They'd seen or heard something they shouldn't have, and they were next.

Jane wouldn't let Colm die simply because he'd been in the wrong place. No, and Jane wouldn't die either. No time to head back to the snowmobile—not that there was anything on it of use since Charlie had the pack with food and additional supplies on his back.

The only choice left: she and Colm needed to disappear. Now.

# THIRTY-FOUR

JANE AND COLM HOBBLED ALONG, moving much too slowly for Jane's comfort, until the shadows congealed, forming a blanket of pure black. Jane never let go of Colm's hand. She felt his body temperature rise and his limbs start to shake.

The infection was spreading, made worse by this forced exertion.

He needed to rest, which meant she needed to find someplace safe.

With each break in the trees, Jane clocked the sun and did her best with her internal compass to keep them en route back to her father's Jeep which was on the road that led to Wapiti and Cody and to *civilization*. How she missed the concept.

Both Charlie and Cynthia would be able to track them, thanks to the snow and mud. But the darkness would give Jane and Colm some cover. Jane couldn't worry too much about the tracks because she had to care for Colm...and keep moving.

"What's the plan?" Colm asked, panting. "Need you to talk—keep me awake."

Jane's stomach clenched at this new revelation. "We're heading toward my dad's car. If it's not there, we'll still be closer to the park's exit—closer to a park ranger. I think I know about where those barracks are, so I should be able to get us there. But it'd be better—easier—to get to my dad's car."

Faster. More likely for Colm to survive.

With each step, more of Colm's weight sagged into Jane. She gritted her teeth, trying to bear the additional stress on her knee without complaint.

"Who was supposed to collect my dad's Jeep?" Jane mumbled to herself.

"What?" Colm's voice had become raspy and thready.

Jane's knee throbbed with her next step. *They* needed to sleep, she amended.

"My dad's car. I have his spare set of keys. He left the other in the Jeep. If we can find it, we can get out of here."

Colm sank to the ground, his body wracked with shivers. "If it's still there."

"It *has* to be there." Jane needed something to go right for her and Colm. She had to believe in her dad's Jeep. "Okay...I'm going to talk this through aloud. Help me out."

Colm nodded, his hot breath puffing against her temple.

"What do I know about this? Cynthia, Charlie, Lavinia, and Quincy are all working on the project."

"So, if one of those people drove your dad's car out of Yellowstone, they wouldn't rouse suspicion for being here." Colm leaned his head against a tree and his eyes drifted closed.

This man continued to astound her. He was helping her unravel the terrible mystery of why and how Jane and he had become victims.

"Seems like," Jane said.

Colm coughed. It was dry and rough. Jane dropped to her knees and offered him the straw from her Camelback. Colm shook his head.

"Germs," he muttered. "I should have thought of that before. Get you sick, too."

"Drink the water. It'll help fight the infection." She hoped. At least the fluid would give his body a better chance to flush itself. "Here, I'll pour the water into the canteen Cynthia gave you."

"You swiped that?" Colm asked.

"No, you did. I just picked it up when you dropped it. I planned to pick up more supplies from them, but leaving while we had the chance was the smartest choice. I'm sorry I don't have more. Like food."

Task completed, Jane handed Colm the water, then steadied his hands around the bottle and to his mouth.

He went back to leaning against the tree. "On the plus side, not even a burger sounds good right now." He opened his eyes and said, "Do you agree now that the killer could be Charlie or Cynthia?"

"It would make sense," Jane said. "They both come in and out of the park often. The rangers know them."

"Who did your dad trust more?" Colm asked.

*That* was the question. Charlie, his friend since elementary school or Cynthia, who'd seemed so steadfast up until Jane found the memo in her pocket.

"What did Lavinia say to me?" Jane pursed her lips. She struggled to remember *Dr. Bianchi said...*

"She could have been talking to either of them. They're both Dr. Bianchi." Jane made a sour face. "Not much help."

"But it is," Colm argued. "One of them told her...something. If it was Charlie, then he shot her to shut her up."

"That makes sense," Jane said. "But I can't rule out Cynthia. She wore the same plaid we found on the tree branch."

"Which was under the ranger uniform shirt," Colm said. "We never found any bit of a brown shirt, and that's bothering me."

"On TV, the bad guys burn those clothes."

"But Cynthia was wearing the shirt. So, right now, both Cynthia and Charlie are suspects. I wish..." Colm's voice cracked, and he shook his head sadly. "I wish I could help you more, tell you more. But I only saw the person for a minute."

Jane looked up, her attention riveted on Colm's face. "Tell me *exactly* what you saw."

"I..." Colm closed his eyes. His brows tugged tight over his nose as he struggled to parse the memories.

Jane understood. The first gunshot aimed at her father had taken her by surprise. Then, her entire focus was on her dad—getting to and *saving* him. She hadn't even considered the potential threat to her safety.

If her dad hadn't yelled at her to run, Jane would be dead.

"Blue hiking boots," Colm said.

Jane's heart sank, and her nose stung with Colm's revelation. "You're *sure*?"

He nodded, his eyes never leaving her face.

Jane's pulse thudded in her ears. Blue.

*Charlie's boots.*

"I tried to look at their boots when they were loading us into the trailer," Colm said. "I'm pretty sure Cynthia had on brown ones."

"She did." Jane choked up, tears pressing at her eyes, but she refused to let them fall—not for Charlie, not until she mourned her father at the very least.

"I'm sorry, Jane."

"Sorry that my father's best friend murdered him?"

He met her gaze. "You're sure?"

Jane nodded. Colm gathered her close to his side and kissed the top of her head. "Yellowstone hasn't been the trip I expected," Colm said.

"You can say that again."

Colm's arm tightened. "At least we know who shot Chase, Lorna, Lavinia, and your father."

"It's cold comfort," Jane said.

"I don't think sleeping out in the open in smart," Colm mumbled. "And I have to sleep. So. Freaking. Tired."

"There's a system of caves nearby. One of my dad's wolf packs dug out a ground-level one for a den not too far from here." Because the female wolf's injured leg wouldn't allow her to climb. At least, that's what her father and Jane hypothesized after seeing her drag the limb behind her.

"When we passed it, I saw an opening that was a few feet off the ground. Not much climbs up there, and it was big enough for both of us. Plus, the wolves' scents will keep away other predators. We'll hole up there until morning."

"Yeah. Sure." Colm rubbed his cheeks, no doubt trying to rouse himself enough to walk.

"I'm not losing you, too. You've grown on me—like algae."

That brought out a weak chuckle that turned into a hacking cough. Jane bit her lip, tears pressing at her eyes and stinging her nose.

"You saved my life, and now your life is my responsibility."

"Just as you were your dad's," Colm murmured. "I get it. But I don't want to be a burden."

"You're not. Don't ever think that again." Jane understood now why her father made her run. He must have seen something—known who the shooter was. He'd known the type of rifle, at the very least.

That selflessness wasn't something she'd ever take for granted, and it was something she could pass forward to Colm. He deserved a future as much as she did. Now, she just had to implement the plan so that he had the chance.

THE CAVE WAS ten feet deep with a convenient rock screen that blocked some of the wind and was only a couple of feet off the ground, which Jane managed to maneuver into well. Climbing took the last of Colm's strength and opened his wound, but maybe that wasn't such a bad thing. After she tended to him, Jane sucked the last of her water from the bladder. She stared out at the sky for a long moment while her limbs shook with the need to move—to get out. Instead, she lay down beside him.

Colm had sunk into a fitful, feverish sleep the moment he stretched out.

She forced water into him all night, keeping vigil as she thought through options.

Sneak past Charlie and Cynthia. Jeep. Or the barracks.

Jeep.

Best way out of the park.

It was far...possibly too far for Colm to travel, and it would put her knee to the test.

But it didn't matter. That was their plan—an achievable goal. Maybe.

It had to be.

Jane rose with the first blush of dawn. Colm roused when Jane brushed back his dirty waves from his hot, dry forehead. The fever had increased even more. Colm's eyes sank into his skull, and he appeared to have lost twenty pounds overnight. His sunken cheeks and cracked lips gave him a macabre, skeletal appearance.

He was out of water after her failed nighttime efforts to keep him hydrated. So, fresh water was the first order of business, and then Jane could create some sort of travois to drag him through the forest.

It was risky, but she couldn't expect Colm to walk. He could barely lift his head.

"We're not that far from a beaver dam that Dad and I saw coming in. It looked abandoned, and I'm sure the water's not as fresh as we'd like, but there's a stream feeding it. I'm going there to refill our canteens."

"Not smart. Let me come with you," Colm said.

Jane squeezed his shoulder. "I would, but you need the rest. It's just for a few minutes—less than an hour."

"Jane—"

"I promise on my father's soul that I will come back, Colm. I'll come back for you."

Colm didn't look convinced, but he didn't argue. His eyes slid shut. Jane bit her lip as her worry that he'd never open them again grew.

They must exit the park today. Colm was out of time.

# DEEP IN THE FOREST

## WEDNESDAY

A reddish haze filmed everything. Colm had fallen into the sun. It was that hot. His muscles ached, and his head throbbed with each pulse of his heart.

But the wound on his back burned and seemed to bubble over with heat.

Like a stew. Boiling.

Jane.

She'd left.

To get water.

He was hot. Thirsty, so thirsty. And tired. Limp with exhaustion.

Good thing she'd left. She needed to get out.

He couldn't even sit up. He groaned, agony shooting to his fingertips and toes, into his mind.

Everything hurt. So hot. Stupid to hold out for a date.

Last thought. Sinking...drifting...

Sometimes, you really didn't get what you most desired.

He jolted. Groaned. Mind alert. Danger.

"There you are." Cynthia slid deeper into the cave.

"What were you two thinking, running from us like that?" she chided.

Cynthia was here...real or a hallucination.

"Where's Jane?" she asked.

Colm bit his tongue.

"Too parched to answer? Okay, drink this."

She dropped to her knees and brought a stainless-steel water bottle to Colm's cracked lips. The cool metal was welcome against his fevered skin. Cynthia was real. Here.

He wasn't alone. He guzzled the water with involuntary greed before he realized she might poison him with it.

Death lingered nearby. Might as well slake the terrible thirst.

"You're not the killer," Colm said.

Cynthia frowned. She peered into his eyes. Colm's breathing grew more rapid.

"No. I didn't hurt anyone."

"Charlie did," Colm mumbled.

"Yes." Cynthia's voice was ragged and her eyes filled with the same painful understanding. "I have some acetaminophen and broad-spectrum antibiotics. I think you have sepsis."

"Feel like I'm dying."

"You might. Take the meds." She pressed the pills to his lips.

He stared into her eyes, searching as his sluggish mind struggled with the risk-reward ratio. She might kill him faster, or she might give him a fighting chance. Jane. That date. Selfish to want it. Couldn't help it. Wanted more than this.

Eventually, he opened his mouth.

# THIRTY-FIVE

JANE PASSED the wolf's den when she heard the unmistakable sound of a twig snapping behind her. Whirling as she dropped into a crouch, Jane grit her teeth as her knee protested, prepared for the alpha wolf's angry reprisal of her nearness to the pack.

Charlie's grin caught her off guard.

"I'm so glad I caught up with you," he said.

"Wh-why?" Jane asked. Dread bubbled up faster and faster, a toxic stew that left her guts a muddled, angry mess.

He tilted his head. "Oh, Jane. I think you know."

She did. The moment Colm mentioned the boots, everything clicked into place. "Where's your Henry?"

Charlie's smile turned softer, full of pride. "I don't own a Henry. Officially, I never did."

Understanding hit Jane, and nausea roiled through her. Oh, this man was so savage in the pursuit of his goal. "It was Lavinia's rifle. You killed her so that you could use her gun to shoot my dad. And, as long as it took a few weeks to find either of them, the time of death would be too close and too hard to differentiate."

Charlie's smile widened. "You really are a smart young woman. The best part is, I set it up so that people expected

Lavinia to go crazy when your father rejected her. She couldn't understand, wouldn't leave him alone, kept telling people about the promises he'd made her."

"That *you* had made for Dad. That my mom will corroborate." Bile ravaged her throat.

Charlie's smile widened. "Got the idea from your mother last time she and I were...er...together."

Jane's throat convulsed. Her mother had an affair with a murderer. "Where's Cynthia?"

Charlie wrinkled his nose. "That woman has *always* been a nuisance. That's why I had to be sure she didn't get the deanship. No way that bleeding heart do-gooder was going to be my *boss*. Ridiculous."

"What lie did you tell about her?"

He smiled again, wider than before—like he relished what came next. He lifted the pistol and leveled it at Jane. "None. I just let Matt know my wife wanted kids. That would make her work secondary. Not great for the deanship."

"Cynthia is looking for us," Jane said, her voice sure.

"She claimed we'd do better if we split up." He chuckled. "A first time for everything—even Cynthia growing confidence."

If Cynthia had found Colm, she could save him.

"Colm saw you in the woods when you killed his friends."

"I wondered." Charlie shook his head. "Shame about those two kids. I'd thought they were you and your father." He chuckled, and it made the hairs on Jane's skin stand up straight. "It was late—almost full dark. I took out the man quickly."

Jane swayed, her vision tunneling at the casual way he talked about murdering people.

"You can imagine my surprise and disappointment in finding out it was some random couple."

Jane's hands fisted. This wasn't the congenial man she'd

thought she'd known. Now, without the amenable mask, Charlie was cold. Viciously so.

"It was a bad coincidence. Bad intel, as they say. Lavinia told me you and Matt were leaving earlier than you did. Maybe because Matt told Lavinia that. Doesn't really matter. I still killed Matt and Lavinia. It took longer than I expected, but now I get to finally get rid of Cynthia. That's a bonus I hadn't planned on."

"Why?" she asked.

Charlie's expression filled with regret. "Your father was an enormous asshole, Jane. He didn't leave me any choice."

"How can you say that?" Jane demanded. A faint rustling drifted on the wind...toward the wolf's den. Charlie might not know it was there, not if Cynthia had been playing him.

Her desire to get to the cabin made more sense. She'd planned to incapacitate Charlie on the way there, then use the snowmobile to pull Jane and Colm out. But Jane hadn't been sure who to trust, so she'd abandoned them both.

Stupid of her.

A gold-tinted brown shape slunk from the den behind Charlie. The female alpha. If he could shoot people without compunction, he'd shoot the wolf. Jane's heart ached because her choices were limited, and if she made the one to save herself, she might cost the female and her pups their lives.

Her father would be so disappointed.

"He planned to take me off the project," Charlie said. "He told me when I received the memo. He said I deserved it for sleeping with his wife."

*The memo.* Jane had skimmed it, but...but...part of her reeled from the realization that her father's death, her risky flight through the park, and Colm's injuries and losses stemmed from a *funding feud.*

How disgustingly basic.

So much pain and trauma over one person's greed. No, not just greed. Ego. This was all about Charlie.

"Write your own grant. You're charismatic..." Jane gagged, unable to continue.

Charlie laughed. "Why would I want to do that? It was easy being the second author on this project—glory without the work."

"You always were in his shadow," Jane said. "Followed him to Montana State. Second author. Gah, you must have hated him."

"I did."

Before Jane could form a response, a growl thrummed through the air.

Charlie stepped closer, and Jane pivoted so that she had to back up closer to the den. He'd either seen the wolf by now or heard her.

The beaver dam was to her left now, along the thin animal track. The wolf was maybe ten feet behind her.

"You know where we are, don't you?" Charlie eyed Jane, excitement lighting up his eyes.

Jane nodded, mute.

"It seemed fitting. Poetical even. You dying by wolf."

"No, *that* death made sense for my father."

Charlie tilted his head. "Maybe. But I enjoyed shooting him. Very satisfying to watch him bleed out, even if it was from fifty feet away."

"How did you know about the wolves?" Jane asked. "Cynthia didn't tell you." But the piece was already there, staring Jane down. "Lavinia. She told you everything that happened in the lab."

Charlie winked. "Got to stay a step ahead."

Her heart raced as she glanced up at the sun. It wasn't yet midday, so the alpha male might still be out hunting as he'd been the last time Jane and her father came through the area. If so, Jane had a chance...as long as Charlie didn't know the female was lame.

"Understand, Jane. I *am* sorry about this, really. I'll hate seeing you suffer, but I'm not cut out for prison."

Jane's stomach heaved at the callousness. This man...Jane had never known *this* man. He was so willing to believe his beautiful lies that there was no way Jane could convince him otherwise.

Jane inched to the right just a little, even as she stepped back, trying to get out of range of the female wolf whose snout was now visible in the cave's opening. The growls grew in volume as the mother wolf told Jane to back off.

"Cynthia's not part of your scheme?" Jane asked. She *had* to be sure.

Charlie scoffed. "As if she'd agree to something so mercenary. She's an even bigger believer in right and wrong than Matt was. Really, if the two of them had gotten together, everything would have worked out. But Mindy got pregnant, and I got stuck with Cynthia. Your father messed up *everything* when he went all moral high ground and refused your granddad's money. The only option left is your trust fund."

Jane remembered Charlie throwing her up in the air, Jane spreading out her arms and legs, laughing. Thrilled by his attention. He'd been her fun uncle. The one with the joke.

"You and my mom had a long-term affair, then. And I'm just... an obstacle."

Jane glanced back, knowing Charlie wouldn't pull the trigger on his pistol unless he had to. The mother wolf's lips peeled back to reveal her teeth. Her fangs dripped saliva, and the whites of her eyes narrowed, showing off a pinprick of gold.

*That's when they pounce.*

Her father's words came to Jane right before she threw herself to the side, landing hard, with a grunting howl, on a rock.

The wolf's lame haunch slowed her enough for Jane to roll away...but, as expected, the wolf lunged again, at the closest target, latching onto Charlie's leg just above the knee.

Oh, how Jane appreciated that bite—the pain Charlie must feel as the teeth ripped into his flesh and tendon.

Charlie cried out as blood dripped through his pant leg. He'd dropped the gun as he used both hands to wrestle the wolf.

Taking a huge breath, Jane rolled toward the pair and snatched up the gun. No way would she let Charlie shoot the animal. But even knowing what she did, Jane struggled with the idea of killing Charlie. That path led to more blood and pain. More death.

The cycle had to stop.

She raised the pistol upward and pulled the trigger, then again. The shots reverberated through the forest as she ran, and birds squawked and fluttered from the trees. Jane popped off a third shot. His injury would slow him down, but it wouldn't stop him from following her, trying to kill her. A life sentence in prison or the death penalty awaited him. He had too much on the line to quit now that he'd admitted to the murders.

She darted down the narrow animal track...away from Colm and Cynthia. Colm needed water. He wouldn't last long without it.

Yellowstone would have taken Colm's life, and while it would raise eyebrows, Charlie could present the case that the park's wilderness overpowered Jane and Cynthia, too. As Jane's father had said to her the morning they started their hike *out here, we're just another part of the food chain.*

Charlie had fooled them all.

*Please,* Jane prayed. *Please, please, please.*

Jane ran, ignoring the growing pain in her knee. She gritted her teeth, refusing to stop. She needed to put distance between herself and Charlie. Between Charlie and Colm.

*She needed more time.*

The meadow appeared seemingly out of nowhere. The trees thinned, and Jane darted forward as quickly as she could...which wasn't that fast. Her leg ached, felt heavy, and seemed to drag behind her with each step.

A bullet slammed into the ground by her ankle, causing Jane to yelp and shift direction. She immediately re-corrected back toward where the last bullet had been—just as another bullet slammed into the ground three feet from her other foot. She pushed harder, her knee screaming up and down her nerve endings.

Charlie had *another* gun. Of course, he did.

Less than fifty feet to the beaver dam. Jane gritted her teeth as she committed to a genuinely terrible scheme.

# THIRTY-SIX

THE POND'S water hit like a vicious slap, sucking all the air from her lungs. Jane opened her mouth on a scream that withered into a whimper as the cold fluid closed around her. Icy tingles threaded through her clothes, around her fingers and toes, against her scalp. A shot rang out from above, the bullet slamming so close to Jane's face that she felt the heat.

Instead of pushing upward for air as her instincts demanded, she forced her body to sink lower, using her arms and good leg to move through the pond. Her lungs ached, and her eyes throbbed—possibly from tears, definitely from the murk floating past her face and catching in her hair.

*There.*

The branches and trees that formed the abandoned beaver lodge coalesced in the gloom. Jane swam down, then up into the domed building. As her face burst through the water, she gulped great lungfuls of the stale air, hissing out her exhalations as quietly as possible. Small cracks of light peeked through the thatched roof, indicating that the spot hadn't been abandoned for long.

Jane shivered, experiencing the same fear as a trapped beaver that gets chased back into its home because, of course, Charlie knew where she was. And he'd drive her out of this temporary shelter. She needed a new plan.

Jane clambered up onto the dry area at the back of the den, violent shivers wracking her body. She tried to be quiet, but she must have failed because a bullet slammed into the tree trunks that made up the roof above her, sending bark and debris spinning through the air. Jane flinched back, stifling her yelp.

"It's over, Jane," Charlie called. "The pond will freeze over eventually, trapping you. Maybe I should let that scenario play out —it would save me from trying to explain a bullet wound if they find you before a bear or scavenger does. All the predators are out looking for a good meal to help tide them through the coming lean months of winter."

Jane pressed her cheek to her sodden knee. Her backpack was soaked—and still on her back. That meant her cell phone's internal circuitry was probably fried...even if she could find a location with reception.

She was well and truly alone. Despair welled, creating lethargy.

Just give up. Give in to the inevitable...

*No.* She would *not* give up. Colm needed her. He'd pushed himself hard yesterday, fighting his body's need for rest just so they stood a chance today. Jane had promised to get back to him.

That promise mattered, and as long as she continued to breathe and could so much as crawl, she would not quit fighting for that future.

Charlie shot again, causing another shower of bark, but the structure held. Jane blessed the beavers for their engineering skills. A moment later, a loud thud caused the edifice to shudder. There was another mighty thud, and daylight peeked through the hole. Jane saw Charlie rear back and slam his forearm into the beaver's den.

Another thwack sounded as additional logs rolled loose,

thumping and bumping down the side of the hut. A few shifted inside, the ends dropping into the water, which pushed the beaver-chewed ends skyward. Jane scuttled back and crouched in the shallows where the hut remained intact.

He stopped slamming his body into the lodge. A long moment of silence ensued. Her knee gave out along with her earlier defiance. She was exhausted. Frigid. *So done.*

"Come on out, precious," Charlie crooned—just like he used to sing her silly songs when she was little. "I'll make it quick. Nothing to fear."

Tears slid from her eyes down her cheeks. When she didn't answer, he body-slammed the beaver's house again, and a dozen of the five- or six-inch lodgepole pine trunks shifted, some of them tumbling into the pond and onto the ground. Jane caught a glimpse of his face.

*That* was real—the viciousness in his eyes, the coldness of his features. He slammed against the lodge again, shifting the saplings. The sharp-edged points were a weapon. *If I could get one, I could use it...*

Some of those poles were over twenty feet long, much too unwieldy to use as a pike or lance.

Jane flinched back as another gunshot blasted the stillness. Charlie grunted, his body thrown forward against the deteriorating roof, eyes wide and mouth open in shock.

"God *damn* you, Charlie Bianchi," Cynthia screamed.

She must have followed Charlie. Whether out of love or suspicion that he shot Lavinia, Jane didn't know. Didn't care. All she knew was that she was no longer alone.

Cynthia fell on Charlie, hitting and kicking him as Jane peeked through the hole created by the broken lodgepole pines. Charlie turned to face Cynthia, and the two of them, backlit by the sun, grappled.

"Shoot him," Jane hissed. But Cynthia didn't. She seemed

incapable of realizing that she had the advantage with her firearm. Charlie must have dropped his when Cynthia shot him before. The wound inflicted by the wolf and Cynthia's bullet had slowed Charlie, giving Cynthia a chance.

But they needed more than a chance. Charlie must be stopped. The fastest way out of the den was the way she'd come in.

Jane bit her lip as she forced herself back into the icy water... through the muck...and up to the pond's edge. She popped up, gasping, in time to see Charlie leveling his pistol toward Cynthia, a look of triumph on his face. He hadn't dropped his firearm as Jane had thought. He'd simply needed to get both hands on it again so he could fire it.

Jane reached forward and caught the edge of his jeans with her stiff, prickly fingers. Gripping the damp, rough denim of his pants leg with all her strength, Jane yanked downward into the water as hard as she could, just as Cynthia brought her gun up and whacked the barrel across Charlie's cheek. Charlie reeled. Jane's arms trembled as she let go of his pants and clawed her way from the frigid water.

Cynthia lurched forward, her mouth twisted in a terrible grimace, her eyes streaming with tears.

"Everything—everything you ever said, *ever did*—was a lie!" Cynthia raised her arms and sighted the weapon at his chest. Jane saw the determination in her features and the pain in her eyes. Killing Charlie would destroy Cynthia. Jane didn't want her to live with that blot on her conscience.

Charlie shuffled backward, arms up to cover his face and shield himself from another of Cynthia's blows. Blood streamed from his nose and from his leg wound. He deserved worse, but Cynthia didn't. He lowered his arms, triumph forming when Cynthia didn't take the shot.

Charlie wouldn't win—he wouldn't take someone else from

her. Jane lunged at Charlie, slamming her fist into the wolf's bite. He screamed as he stumbled backward. The dirt at the pond's edge gave way, and his heel sank into the water. Charlie flailed his arms and shouted as he fell backward onto the hut with its jumbled, shot-up logs.

Cynthia and Jane gasped, then gagged at the sight.

From the outside, the beavers' den was in worse shape. Many of the lodgepole pines had popped out of position, thanks to Charlie's shots, their gnawed ends poking outward like a World War I trench fortification. Charlie had landed on one of those beaver-chewed ends, and a good four inches protruded from his right side, just above his belt. He gasped and sputtered, staring up at the sky. His breathing turned shallow, and blood pooled at his midsection as he clawed at the area with his bloodied hands. Blood dripped down his side into a puddle at the pond's edge.

"I hope it's as painful as my father taking bullets to the gut," Jane ground out.

"Help," he rasped. "You...gotta...help..."

"No one's going to help you, *murderer*," Jane said.

Cynthia's gaze turned to Jane, and she stumbled forward.

"*Jane.*" Picking up steam, Cynthia rushed to Jane's side, tugging her sodden, shivering body from the pond's edge. "Quick now, that's it. Up, up! Move. You need to circulate that blood so you don't lose any extremities."

Cynthia wrapped one of Jane's arms around her neck, rubbing at Jane's numb hands and fingers. Cynthia shivered as the frigid water slid down the back of her neck and chest.

"You can't...leave...me...here..." Charlie tried to sit forward, but the two-inch-thick tree held him fast.

Cynthia wrapped her other arm around Jane's waist. The adrenaline that had fueled her back into the pond and her subsequent tussle ebbed from her, and she shivered with such an intensity she worried that she'd bite her tongue or that her legs wouldn't support her next step. Cynthia and Jane glanced back. His pistol lay at his feet.

"*If* he reaches it, maybe he'll put himself out of his misery," Cynthia murmured. All the while, she hauled Jane as the younger woman stumbled across the meadow. "But he's not the priority. You are. Let's get to Colm. Get you both out of here."

They entered the forest, where the air turned colder, and Jane shivered harder. "Not much farther, Jane. You got this."

"T-t-two miles," Jane shuddered as she nearly tripped again. "C-c-can't f-feel my f-f-feet."

"No, honey. Not two miles. My pack's with Colm. Just around that bend. See it? It's what...let's say...a half mile."

They had to cover a full mile, and they both knew it, but Jane appreciated the lie. She needed it to continue to track forward.

Jane's knee throbbed—a good thing because she knew she had circulation there. But her fingertips and the entirety of her feet were...missing. As if they no longer existed. The thought of frostbite and amputation caused Jane to whimper, but she kept moving.

"You're walking." Cynthia understood the panic suffocating Jane, so she kept the younger woman moving. "Let me pull off your gloves." Cynthia shifted and worked the wet material from Jane's hands. She chafed at Jane's skin before shoving one hand against her soft tummy. Cynthia sucked in a breath, then hissed it out. After a grunt, she hooked Jane's other arm around her neck again and pushed Jane's hand against her skin by her jaw.

Jane couldn't imagine Cynthia's discomfort, but the older woman continued to walk and talk.

"Already better, right? You were so brave. Come on, come on. Jane, you got this. *You got this...*"

"Colm?" Jane mumbled. She pushed another foot forward, then another, just as he had the day before. She had to get back to him.

"He's in the cave. I gave him antibiotics and acetaminophen. He'll be feeling much better by the time we get there. You'll see. Another step. That's it."

Jane's eyelids were heavy, and no matter how much Jane wanted to pry them open, they wouldn't listen. A faint rush hit her ears. She gritted her teeth and tottered forward.

The next while seemed to happen in snapshots. Walking, stumbling, dappled light...Colm's exclamations...hands stripping her sodden clothes, blessed warmth, the soft inside of her sleeping bag that smelled ever-so-faintly of her father's cologne.

Jane wasn't sure she remained conscious, but she'd flinched at a sound...a gunshot. She was sure that was the sound. Jane lifted her head from where it lay atop Colm's chest. She blinked and then squinted against the sunlight. She shifted.

"Jane's awake," Colm said. "She's got some color. Finally. And her fingers aren't icy anymore."

Cynthia's face appeared pale, salt tracked from dried tears down her cheeks, and her eyes were red and puffy.

"Oh, thank God. *Jane.*"

Cynthia embraced the younger woman, who was caught between the overheated bodies of Colm and Cynthia.

"We have to get out of here. The rangers are searching for us. They must have found Lavinia by now."

"How?"

"Unlike Charlie, *I* gave the rangers actual updates." Cynthia frowned. "I didn't understand why he was so angry that I insisted on the walkie-talkie when he wanted to separate and search for you. I didn't contact them until a little before I found Colm—I worried about you..."

She'd come after Jane. She'd fought off Charlie and saved Jane.

Jane touched his cheek. It remained too warm, but not dangerously so. "You look better," Jane said.

"I feel better." He shifted and grimaced, and Jane knew his wound bothered him. Whatever Cynthia had given him was a stopgap measure. His wound, at a minimum, needed proper treatment, not emergency field medicine.

"If you're ready," Cynthia said. "Let's find those rangers."

She pushed upward and touched her lips to his. He kissed her back, his larger hand cupping her skull. Jane luxuriated in the feel of his embrace, of his show of affection—of the deepening of the connection between them.

She pulled back and stared into his brown eyes. They were filled with wonder as he slid his hand from her head to touch her mouth. "Best kiss of my life."

Jane smiled as she pressed another to his palm. "For luck."

# THIRTY-SEVEN

"DAD'S JEEP IS CLOSEST," Jane said. "Whereas the cabin is an additional mile and a half deeper into the park. We can drive to the ranger station from there." The altercation with Charlie had caused her knee to swell once more. "And you don't have another dose of meds for Colm, so it's our best option."

"You're right." Cynthia sighed. "Let me look at your fingers and toes."

After an excruciating examination in which Jane was speechless, thankful that circulation had returned to her extremities, she dressed in Cynthia's long johns, sweater, and two pairs of thick wool socks. Her boots were still sopping, but she needed the protection for her feet, so she reluctantly put them back on.

"If we're lucky, police will have left the Jeep there," Cynthia said. "But, if we're not...it's still a long way, Janie."

"I know," Jane said. "But it's on the road, and that's the way home."

The three of them trekked from their spot. Colm remained in better shape than he'd been in since the goring, but both he and Jane needed to rest often. Predictably, Colm's fever rose as the medicine wore off long before he could have another dose, his skin taking on a terrifying cherry-red hue.

After the first mile, their walking speed slipped lower than a drunken amble, but they kept moving. Cynthia brought up the rear, sniffling, though she tried to keep her tears private.

"He admitted to killing my friends and your dad?" Colm asked.

Jane swallowed. "Yes."

Colm put on a brave face as they trudged along another track that slid southwest, away from the wolf's den and the beaver dam. Jane clutched her elbows as nausea swirled through her body.

"Did he...did he say why?" Colm croaked. He pressed his lips together. His eyes were glassy, but Jane thought it was from emotion, not just the fever.

"He thought they were Dad and me," Jane said, her breath catching on the pain in her chest.

Cynthia filled them in on the manhunt for the preschoolers who'd wandered away from their parents' campsite.

"Do you think they found them?" Jane asked.

"With the manpower they pushed at it, yes. But that's why Charlie and I were the only ones looking for you."

"Do you think he lured the kids away?" Jane asked. "I mean, if he could kill innocent people..."

"He'd do something like that." Colm's voice snapped with bitter anger. "He was unfeeling enough, devious enough, to lure kids away if it would help him achieve his goal."

"I guess you're right," Cynthia said.

"Enough now," Jane whispered. She took Colm's hand, easing her chastisement. But Colm bowed his head, acknowledging that his anger wasn't helpful. "You need to conserve your strength."

"I'll manage," Colm said.

With no other choice, they trudged onward, and Colm struggled to keep up. Jane's worry turned to his collapse.

Twilight slid into the complete darkness of night, and still, they kept moving as if realizing that they might not get back up if they stopped.

Eventually, Colm's legs gave out, and he tumbled forward, faceplanting into the turf. Cynthia cried out and rushed forward, slowing his descent to the ground. Jane wasn't sure how much farther she could go. The moment she stopped moving, exhaustion slammed into her, and Jane swayed.

"I'll make a travois," Jane said.

"Good idea. The antibiotics wore off. He's sliding into sepsis shock."

# THIRTY-EIGHT
## THURSDAY

WHILE JANE COULD FEEL ALL her fingers and toes, and it was a blessing, they still burned and ached, making walking miserable. Still, Jane plodded onward, doing her best to pull her half of the sled she'd fashioned. Dawn broke first with the birds, which twittered as they flitted overhead from branch to branch. Shadows shrank as larger patches of light shifted through the trees and the sky slid from velvety purple to mauve, and finally, blue.

"What day is it?" Jane asked.

Cynthia frowned. They'd been quiet for hours. "Thursday."

Six days. Jane had been in Yellowstone for *six days*. Her father's death, the running, Colm's appearance, Charlie's admission, the desperation to save the man who'd saved her...all in six days. Most people didn't experience that much in six *lifetimes*.

Jane trudged forward while her eyes leaked tears, but she'd long since pressed her lips together and tugged Colm's toboggan forward.

"Let's rest." Cynthia wavered on her feet as she slowed her pace, and Jane noted the deep bruises under her bloodshot eyes. Cynthia plopped down on the ground, too tired to take her standard care of ticks. The older woman had slept little since discovering Jane was in trouble, and they were all feeling the effects of their time in the park.

Neither of them was sure of how much distance they'd covered. Jane's mind floated, and her body ached. She fished out the Jeep keys from the front pocket of her backpack. She studied them, hoping their internal connection had dried during their trek.

*Just...just...please. Let us be close.*

Holding her breath, Jane prayed as she pressed the lock button. Up ahead, lights flashed through the shrinking gloom, and the horn beeped.

"Oh, *thank God,*" Cynthia breathed.

She bent down and grasped the sled's wooden handle...and that's when Jane saw the large, bloody patch on Cynthia's side.

# THIRTY-NINE

"HE *SHOT* YOU?" Jane asked, startled.

Cynthia shrugged. "No. I don't think so, anyway. It happened so quickly."

"How bad is it?" Jane asked. At Cynthia's blank look, Jane lifted her chin and used it to point to Cynthia's side.

"Can't be too bad since I've been able to keep going this long." Cynthia licked her lips. "When Charlie and I were grappling, one beaver's tree trunks stabbed me, I think. Probably not a bullet. The bleeding's slowed."

"But not stopped?" Worry, already looming in Jane's mind, exploded. She struggled through a couple of breaths as she pushed it down, pulling at the edges of her fraying composure.

"No." She offered Jane a wry smile. "But it's at my hip, which has increased at least a pant size this year. It's only a flesh wound."

Jane appreciated the attempt at levity but refused to let the older woman deflect. "I'm worried about you, Cyn. Let's get in the car. Get you both medical help."

Jane's arms quivered from exertion after she and Cynthia muscled Colm into the Jeep's backseat. She covered him with one of her father's extra blankets while Cynthia leaned against the Jeep's front panel, clasping her side.

"I looked." She swallowed. "It's...bad. Worse than I expected. I don't think I'm in good enough shape to drive," she said as she lifted her head. "Too lightheaded."

"I already planned to drive us out, Cynthia. Get in and rest."

Cynthia offered Jane a watery smile as she wrapped her in another one of the blankets Jane's father kept there. She helped Cynthia to the passenger seat before rounding the hood, her own gait uneven. Didn't matter. She'd be off her leg momentarily. One last task. Just one.

Settling into the driver's seat, Jane pressed the ignition. The vehicle started, and she shot off another heartfelt thank-you that no rodents had eaten through the various lines leading to the engine.

Cynthia had her eyes closed, and her breath was shallow. Colm's cheeks were a shocking raspberry, and his breath was too fluttery.

No time to waste. Jane backed away from where she and her father had left the car a few days before. Her breath caught once again as she turned forward and faced the beauty of the view. Yellowstone was *awesome*.

For all its beauty, Yellowstone had taken so much from her. Jane turned the wheel, pressed the gas, and pointed the Jeep toward civilization, ignoring the flat tire on the back passenger side that thumped against the pavement and the wheel well.

She'd fallen asleep on the road, but her foot slipped off the gas pedal, and the Jeep coasted to an easy stop, idling until Jane awakened and drove again.

Nothing else was in the woods. At least, nothing Jane saw.

She wondered about Charlie...how much he'd suffered while impaled on that pole. If it had been challenging to pull the trigger on himself.

If she'd ever get the image of her father's desperation out of her head.

She worried over Lavinia and whether any law enforcement had recovered her body.

But mostly, Jane worried about Colm and Cynthia. Much as she wanted to roll down the window to air out the smell, she'd been afraid to do so, especially now that Colm's thrashing and teeth chattering had stopped.

She hadn't looked back—hadn't dared to check on him.

Two hours after they climbed into the Jeep, Jane slid the car into a spot next to the ranger post that led to Cody, the heater blasting and Jane's eyes drooping to dangerous levels.

Betty came out, eyes wide.

"We need help," Jane said.

JANE'S HEAD swam from the voices and ambulance sirens. She wrapped the thin, crinkly blankets tighter around her, hating her separation from Colm and Cynthia.

She asked after them, but no one gave her an update. The ride to Cody's regional medical facility took ages, but Jane was warm and dry. She'd shed tears when she'd removed her still-damp boots.

"What time is it?" she asked the paramedic who'd been reading her vitals.

"About one in the afternoon."

"Oh."

"Why?"

"I was trying to determine how long I've been awake."

The paramedic took Jane's hand. "You're safe now. You can rest."

Jane shook her head. "Not until I know about Colm."

"The guy with you?"

"Yes."

"Are you related?"

Jane didn't hesitate. "Yes."

While they weren't family by blood, they were bonded by experience and that mind-boggling connection that came from finding a missing piece of herself. Colm was part of her, just as she was part of him.

"I'll see if I can get you an update."

JANE AWAKENED WITH A GASP, shooting upward in her bed.

"Easy! Take it easy." Cynthia reached over to press her palm to Jane's shoulder. She sat in a chair next to Jane's bed. She wore a pair of scrubs, and her hair was still damp.

"Are you okay? How's Colm? Did he make it?"

Cynthia pulled herself forward. "I'm okay. Needed twenty-six stitches in my fat ass. I'm on antibiotics. So are you. You still have your fingers and toes, thank goodness. And they said your knee is okay. Strained, badly bruised, but the tendons didn't tear." Cynthia gestured toward one of the bags of clear fluids dripping into the tubing that led to the needle in the back of her hand.

After what she'd been through, the idea of passing out while people touched her gave Jane the heebie-jeebies, but she was alive. And she had more pressing worries. Cynthia hadn't mentioned Colm.

"Colm? Cynthia, what about Colm? *Please*...he's alive?"

"Yes, he is." Cynthia smiled. "And he seems to be recovering well now that he has his antibiotic cocktail and stitches—he only needed twenty-one. They have you both on fluids to counteract the dehydration."

Jane sighed. "Probably why my head's pounding less."

"Probably," Cynthia agreed.

Silence grew. Jane kept her eyes closed, unwilling to face the ugly truth between them.

"Charlie took the batteries from the walkie-talkie. That's why I couldn't get through to anyone on our way out."

"Oh."

Cynthia cleared her throat. "I thought I was patching through, but I was so busy talking...I'm sorry, Jane. I made a bad assumption, and we paid for it. I let the detectives know. Horton—he's the older guy—said a forensics team will retrieve Lavinia's body," Cynthia said.

"You said something about kids?" Jane asked.

"Right! The ones who got lost. They're back with their parents."

"And Charlie?" Jane asked since they were both thinking about him. "The rangers or police found his body, too?"

Cynthia's face was stark, the lines around her mouth and eyes deeper than Jane had ever seen them.

"He wasn't there."

Jane absorbed the answer. "Did he fall into the pond?"

"I got little more out of Detective Fremont and the park service than I just told you. Detective Fremont wants to talk to you, by the way."

"Yeah. I figured someone would." Jane wet her lower lip. "I'm sorry, Cynthia."

Cynthia reached over and clasped Jane's hand. "You never apologize to me. *Ever*. It's me who owes you an apology. I...I brought him into the park, let him get near you—"

"And saved my life."

Cynthia shook her head, then swiped at her wet cheeks. "You

were doing a mighty fine job of that all by yourself, Janie." Cynthia had to pause and swallow as the emotions overwhelmed her. "I'm proud of you. Your dad is—would be—so proud, too."

Jane scooted closer and hugged Cynthia, not wanting to linger on her dad. Not yet. "You had to make some hard choices—"

"No," Cynthia pulled back and cupped Jane's cheeks. "I made the *only* choice. The right choice. For you. For Colm. And for me." Her gaze pierced through Jane's soul with a fierce intensity that could not be ignored.

"I want to see him," Jane said.

"I'm sure you do. He's asked about you, too." Cynthia smoothed Jane's gritty hair back. Jane desperately wanted a shower. "I just came from his room next door. He's asleep, which he needs to heal."

Jane leaned back against her pillows and stared up at the ceiling. They'd survived Charlie and Yellowstone. Together and because of each other.

Was this how military comrades felt? Some of those units were so close, closer than any family, because—Jane surmised—they'd traversed through the valley of death together.

Colm had a life back in Philadelphia. Jane wouldn't blame him if he wanted to get back to it. To leave the blood and gore and pain of his trip West behind.

She fisted her hands on the pristine, thin sheet, sending a waft of the bleach and illness that clung deep in the fabric.

"Whatever comes next, it'll be his choice," Jane said.

"You've both been through a lot, honey. Maybe you both need time to process..."

"I'm sure we do. In fact, I know so." Jane bit her lip as her mind flashed through the past week. She looked up at Cynthia. "I survived, Cyn. I did that. My dad would be proud of me. I'm proud of myself. But I-I need to grieve. Not just my dad, but me.

I'm not the woman who stepped into those woods. I'll never be her again."

# FORTY
## FRIDAY

"OOH, Janie, what you had to go through," Mindy sniffled as she settled into the chair next to Jane's hospital bed. At least Jane was showered and in clean clothes. She'd never take either for granted again.

"Thanks."

Mindy had chattered, explaining how the stupid police had considered her a suspect. How they should spend Jane's trust fund money. Did Jane want to go to Italy, like she'd always planned?

Jane stared at the ceiling, quiet, throughout Mindy's gabfest, busy processing her mom's affair with Charlie.

Mindy shifted as she stopped talking. "You know you don't have to stay here—"

"But I do," Jane interrupted.

"You can return to Dartmouth now that your dad's not making you stay. Even without the scholarship, we can pay the tuition—" Mindy began.

"No."

Mindy pursed her lips but then nodded and smiled. "That's why I'm proud of you. Your certainty is awe-inspiring."

"Dad had it." Jane leveled a look that she wished would pierce

Mindy's soul. "With you. He loved you *that* much. And you cheated on him with his best friend."

Mindy's hands trembled. "That's ridiculous. How did you... are you suggesting..."

She pulled her purse up into her lap and glared at her daughter as she straightened her spine and looked down her nose.

"Just who do you think you are?" Mindy demanded.

"Matt Sorenson's daughter," Jane answered. Her eyes flicked behind Mindy, and she frowned at the two people who stood just inside the room's door. But Jane had expected the audience, so she pushed herself into a seat as she leaned forward, closer to her mother. "I'm Matt Sorenson's daughter. He made me the woman I am today."

Mindy fell back against the chair's back support. "It's the drugs. It has to be the medication. Janie, you've had an ordeal. I don't hold it against you that you said those horrible things to me."

"Charlie chased me to the beaver dam, and while he did, he told me some interesting things." Jane locked eyes with Mindy, focused on what she needed to do.

Anger settled in Jane's belly, a welcome friend that fueled her through this necessary confrontation.

"The most interesting thing was that you two started having an affair after you got pregnant with me. That I was simply a way to try to force Grandpa Sorenson to give you and Dad money for me."

Mindy sputtered. "That's ridiculous. I'd never—"

Jane raised her eyebrows. "But the most disgusting thing—the reason I no longer want anything to do with you—is the fact that Charlie told me *you* drove him into Yellowstone."

"So what if I did? That's not a crime. I had no idea what the man had planned. And anyway, Charlie's dead, so it doesn't matter."

Mindy squealed when a hand clamped around her wrist that she'd slid into her handbag.

Detective Fremont squeezed a little harder. "Don't even think about touching that pistol."

Detective Fremont held her service sidearm in her other hand while Detective Horton moved around the chair, his own Sig Sauer pointed at Mindy's chest.

Mindy lifted her sweaty hand from her handbag. "I-I-I *just* wanted a tissue," she stuttered.

"And I *just* want to hear about this drive into Yellowstone," Fremont said as she holstered her Sig. She kept hold of Mindy's hand as she moved the purse out of Mindy's lap, handing it to Horton.

"You record that like we planned, right?" Jane asked.

"Every word." Detective Fremont shot Jane a genuine, warm smile that made her look fifteen years younger. "Thanks for following up on that for us."

Detective Fremont slid a handcuff around Mindy's wrist. Jane's mom yelped and fought.

"Don't," Horton snapped. "Don't make us restrain you in front of your daughter. She's been through enough."

Mindy didn't listen. She fought and cursed and screamed. Within a breath, her cheek dug into the linoleum floor, and both her hands were cuffed tightly at the small of her back.

"I have one more question." Detective Fremont hoisted Mindy off the ground with little effort.

"I'm not answering anything," Mindy spat. "I want my lawyer."

"Sure, sure," Detective Horton said.

"You want to ask her, Jane?" Detective Fremont asked.

Mindy raised furious eyes at her daughter, but Jane was focused on her dad's confession at the start of the trip, on how fierce his protectiveness had been when he'd told her to run.

"Did you suggest killing Dad to Charlie?" Jane asked.

Mindy sniffed. "I'm not saying another word without counsel."

"Tell me, Mo...*Mindy*," Jane corrected.

Mindy's smile turned sharp, as cruel as the words she hurled next. "Who said he's your actual father?"

# FORTY-ONE

COLM HELD Jane's hand as she recounted everything that had happened since he passed out. Even now, with the drugs and fluids, Colm felt shaky, on the verge of collapse. His medical team said to give it time.

It wasn't like he had a choice, but he hated the weakness invading his limbs, especially because it gave him too much time to think.

"I can't imagine how you feel." Colm shook his head.

His *clean* head. The shower earlier that day had been a religious experience. As soap sloughed away days of dirt, body odor, desperation, and guilt, a new emotion took root: hope.

Even traveling across the country with his friends, Colm hadn't been hopeful—hadn't considered a future because he'd felt like it didn't really matter.

He'd been glad to get out of Philly, awed by the mountains and wide open skies. But now, he'd found a sense of rightness, of connectedness, through Jane and Cynthia. They'd both fought for him to the end.

He couldn't ever repay them, but he could find purpose so that he showed them how much their belief in him mattered.

Jane had showered, too, and her light brown hair framed her face, showcasing the dark blue of her eyes. Like him, she was thinner, her cheekbones more pronounced, and they both bore scratches and bruises. Jane's knee was swollen, and his back would scar when it finally healed.

After a rough inhalation, she said, "I get it if you want to leave my mess—this place—

behind. I won't hold it against you."

Pain radiated from the laceration when Colm shoved upward. "You wanna get rid of me?"

Jane's eyes filled with tears, and she shook her head. Fingers shaking, Colm touched her chin, then cupped her cheek as he looked into her eyes. "You'd be good if I stuck around?"

"Yes."

"Would you like me to stay?"

Jane licked her lips. "Yes."

"So I can take you on that date. Curry. Naan. The yogurt dip."

"Yes." Jane's chin wobbled, but she firmed it and met his gaze with her clear one. She clasped his hand where it now cupped her cheek. "I want you in my life—if you'll have me."

"Damn straight I will."

"But...I need to tell you, Colm, I'm not exactly sure who I am now."

"I get that. I feel the same. Maybe we can take time to figure it out together."

She swallowed even as she nodded. "I'd like that."

This time, he kissed her, and it was even more glorious because they could take their time, get to know each other's quirks.

"I've been making a list of things to do. Top priority is a place to stay," he said as he pulled back. He scooted over and patted the narrow slice of bed. Jane slid onto the hard mattress, and a worry Colm hadn't realized he carried eased. He'd gotten used to having Jane close, and he hadn't rested well with her farther away.

"I called Chase's parents. That was rough," Colm said. Jane hugged him tighter. Sometimes, they'd learned, there weren't words to ease the pain. "The detective here had an officer in Philadelphia give them the news. So, I didn't have to tell Mrs. Spinetti on the phone that Chase was dead. She said she didn't blame me. That helped."

"I get that."

They lay together while Colm ran his palm up and down Jane's spine, shocked by how easy it was to talk to her, be with her.

"Cynthia's going to need me," Jane said.

"She has us," Colm replied. "We'll survive what's next. Heal. Build a life."

"I like that idea."

"Me, too."

"Something else to look forward to, after our date," Jane said.

CHASE'S and Lorna's bodies were recovered during Colm and Jane's stay in the hospital, but Charlie was still missing. The park service and law enforcement officers from Wyoming, Montana, and even Idaho made regular treks into the park to search. So far, they hadn't been successful.

Colm hoped Charlie Bianchi got ripped apart by a mountain lion, but he kept those thoughts to himself, especially around Cynthia. She was a nice lady. He was glad that she and Jane got along so well. They'd needed each other that past week, especially since Jane's mother had implicated herself as part of Charlie's plan.

He also appreciated Cynthia's dry wit and sharp observations.

She'd invited him to move in with her while he was still in the hospital, and after he'd talked to Jane about it, he'd agreed. For one, he wasn't quite ready to be alone again, and that made him feel...unsettled. He'd never minded living alone before, but after those first days in Yellowstone, before finding Jane, when his sanity started to crack, Colm discovered he liked people a lot more than he'd thought. Well, good people.

Cynthia's bungalow reminded him of his parents' place. Cozy, not too big, lived in. Colm had been surprised by how easily he'd settled.

The hospital set him up with a counselor, and those daily talks were helping.

But, as Jane noted, he wasn't sure who he was now. The time in the park, alone, surviving, changed him, too.

Colm told Cynthia he planned to make a full recovery. He refused to accept less. So far, so good.

The night of their date arrived a week after their return to civilization. Jane had driven her own car—a Subaru—to pick him up. She'd given him the keys to her father's Jeep, not ready to drive it again. Jane had returned to her father's house a few days before, and she'd admitted to nightmares. The dark circles that remained under her eyes confirmed her struggles.

Jane had chosen a small neighborhood restaurant in Bozeman, away from the media circus that descended once the press got wind of the story. Settled in a booth in the back of the small, warmly decorated space that smelled of exotic spices, Colm stared at Jane. She wore a dress—he liked that. He liked the knee-high heeled boots more.

"I've been thinking," Jane said.

"Let's have it," Colm replied.

"I don't think I can handle staying alone at my dad's house. I..." Jane bit her lip. "It's still fresh for me there. I plan to deal with his death. I *will* deal with it."

"But the memories slam into you when you're not prepared."

"Yeah."

Colm took her hand and squeezed. "I had the same reaction when I saw the van. I'm giving it to Chase's family."

"That's sweet."

"They deserve all of him they can get."

"You're right. So...Cynthia invited me to stay with her, too, for a few weeks," Jane said. "Then, hopefully, I'll be ready to move back home."

"I like the idea of living with you." Colm smiled a little. "A lot, actually."

"Me, too," Jane said. "I got used to it, and I miss being the big spoon."

Colm laughed. "Never thought I'd hear that one."

The curry arrived. Jane dug in, and Colm gamely tried a bit of his. It was good. The spices were the same that scented the air. The sauce was flavorful, warming. The naan was fluffy and smelled of garlic.

"Food's good. Just like you promised," Colm said.

Jane smiled. "I'm glad. So...I had something else to tell you. I'm going back to classes next week."

"You ready for that?"

Jane shrugged as she spooned up another bite. "I need to go. I want to finish my degree." She hesitated. "I'm seeing a counselor there, so I'm already on campus once a week. Plus, I want to be close by, at least some of the time, for Cynthia."

"Are people bothering her? I'll be her bodyguard."

Jane shook her head. "Cyn's tough. Capable. I think I'm her biggest weakness. Well, both of us. She's definitely madly in love with you."

Colm smiled, but it was shy. "She means a lot to me, too, and not just because she saved my life. I like helping her. She deserves love."

"She does."

After they completed their meal, Jane captured both of Colm's hands. "How are you?" she asked.

"I'm...getting there."

Jane nodded. "I get that. Totally. I'm struggling with the details that have come out about my mom and Charlie."

"I can't imagine that's been easy."

"It's not." Jane dropped her gaze to the tablecloth. "But I'd rather know than not. And...well, I have to keep pushing forward for my dad."

"Would he want you to do that?" Colm asked.

"Doesn't matter. I need to. Continuing to live my life is something I have to do—for him and for me." She bit her lip, raising her gaze. "I'm hoping you'll be part of that. But I'm not ready to jump into a romantic relationship with both feet."

Colm nodded. "That seems like it'd be a Band-Aid that's covering up the broken bits."

Jane sat back in her chair, tension leaving her shoulders. She kept hold of Colm's hand. "Exactly."

"I don't want to push you, Jane. I don't want to push either of us. But I did have some news. Good news, I think. I'm going to be on campus with you next semester."

"Oh?" Jane sounded guarded.

"I'm going to get a master's in criminal justice." Colm sucked in a breath, wishing it would slow his thudding heart. "Like you, Yellowstone changed me. I'm not sure how much—or even how yet—but I know that I can't tolerate anyone else going through what we did."

"Ah. That explains your talks with Tara."

Colm smiled. "Some. But I don't want to work for the police."

Jane tipped her head to the side. "What's your plan, then?"

"The Bureau of Alcohol, Tobacco, and Firearms."

Jane's eyes widened. "Why's that?"

"Because I can make changes on a larger scale, help more people who could be Lorna, Chase, or your dad.

Jane studied him. "You've given this a lot of thought."

"Yep."

She smiled back. "I'm excited for you."

# FORTY-TWO

AS THE WEEKS PASSED, the twenty-four-seven coverage of the manhunt for Dr. Charles Bianchi slowed. At Colm's urging, Jane obtained a DNA test and ascertained she was Matt's biological child. Not that her genetics would have changed how Jane felt, but the confirmation soothed her—even if it did add to Jane's anger toward her mother.

The horror Mindy's words evoked at the mere whiff of an idea that Jane was related to Charlie made her draw inward.

"Don't shut me—us—out because your mom's a hateful person," Colm said one night as they sat on the couch in Cynthia's living room.

Jane glanced over at Cynthia, who'd halted in the kitchen's archway, now hovering, unsure if she should enter the living room.

Jane licked her lips, her gaze bouncing between the two of them. "I'm sorry. I didn't realize I'd pulled back so much or that it was hurting you."

"We're all handling the fallout the best we can, and I think doing it together is better than only turning inward," Colm said.

Cynthia slipped into the armchair next to the couch and reached for Jane's hand. "What's bothering you?"

Only weeks ago, Jane wouldn't have been able to say any of it aloud. Now she admitted, haltingly, how small her mother had made her feel, how angry she still was, and how little she believed she deserved Colm's and Cynthia's friendship. They listened with quiet patience, and Jane found unexpected comfort in simply being heard.

Better yet, over the next few days, Cynthia offered insights into her parents that soothed some of Jane's worst moments. And over time, the three of them had formed an impenetrable unit that Mindy couldn't pierce—though she tried.

At her father's funeral, a couple of weeks after Jane's and Colm's first date, Jane came face-to-face with her mother when Mindy threw herself in Jane's arms, tears dripping down her cheeks.

"I didn't mean it, Janie. Please, please don't be mad."

Revulsion ripped through Jane until she peeled her mother off. "Why are you here?" Jane demanded.

From the corner of her eye, Jane noted Colm heading toward her, and the rapid thud of her heart slowed.

"Because my husband—"

"Ex-husband."

Mindy quivered. "—Died, and it's my responsibility..."

"No. My father isn't your responsibility. Nor am I your responsibility." Jane narrowed her eyes as she leaned back into Colm, who slipped an arm around her, comforting her even as he stood quietly, allowing Jane to handle her mother. "And, until you decide to be honest with the police about what happened with your lover and my father's killer, I don't want to be around you."

Cynthia arrived, flanking Jane's other side, hand on the younger woman's shoulder. The three of them stared, unmoved, as Mindy sobbed and dabbed at her eyes. "You're being unreasonable..."

"Want me to get someone to escort Mindy out?" Cynthia asked.

Jane nodded.

"Janie! I can't believe you'd throw me out of my husband's funeral."

"*Ex*-husband," Jane repeated through clenched teeth. "Now, leave me to bury my father in peace." Jane turned her head into Colm's chest. He brought his other arm up, embracing her, never saying a word.

Cynthia returned with security guards, and Mindy left. Jane's fingertips and lips tingled as tears clogged her throat. Colm rubbed her back, and Jane melted farther into his warmth.

"That was brave," Cynthia murmured.

Jane met her gaze. "But was it right?"

Cynthia gave a helpless shrug. "I don't know what 'right' means anymore."

Jane compressed her lips into a tight line. Once she mastered her emotions, she slipped from Colm's embrace after offering him a thank-you and a smile. She made her way up the funeral home's aisle. She stared down at her father's serene face. No one would know he had five bullet wounds to the abdomen. No one could tell that his last expression was filled with pain and fear—for her.

He lay there, as peaceful as could be. Jane inhaled, released it, and then repeated the action. "I'll get you justice, Dad. That's all I can offer you now. But I promise you that."

MINDY STRODE out of Matt Sorenson's funeral under Detective Tara Fremont's watchful eye.

Detective Horton sidled up next to her. "Had a sighting," he said.

"Of Bianchi?" Tara asked. That was the one loose end, and Tara remained frustrated.

"Picture's blurry, too far away for a positive ID."

Tara stopped and turned toward him. "If you don't have the positive identification, then why'd you tell me?"

"Because you were right about Mindy. About Bianchi. About Jane." He grimaced as if the following words pained him to speak. "I figure you got a good gut for this work."

Tara slapped his shoulder. "Don't hurt yourself with the compliments. I'm already aware my track record's better than yours. And I didn't say I was sure Bianchi's alive. I said I needed actual proof to close the case."

WEEKS PASSED after Jane's father's funeral, interspersed with extended interviews with the police and district attorney, nightmares, homework, and an attempt at normalcy.

A park ranger recovered a revolver from the beaver pond, and it was coated in Charlie's prints. Colm identified it as the firearm Charlie used to shoot Lavinia. The following week, less than a mile from Lavinia's murder site, the police forensic unit dug up the brown ranger shirt with Charlie's blood.

Detective Horton had shuttled back and forth from the park to help with the searches around Lavinia's and Matt's murders, as well as Jane's attempted murder. The older detective found Lavinia's Henry tossed in a creek near where the ATV was found. But the clincher for Charlie's guilt was the DNA evidence taken from the ATV itself and the ping from the cell phone tower that placed Charlie's phone in the park at the time of both Lavinia's and Matt's deaths.

"Charlie didn't plan as well as he'd clearly thought he had, and he wasn't anywhere near as intelligent as he assumed he was," Cynthia said one night over dinner.

"That's cold comfort, but it's a kind of win, nonetheless." Jane scooped up mashed potatoes and shoved the bite into her mouth.

Colm remained quiet, but he later told Jane he was glad Charlie's guilt was so well established. "I want justice for Chase and Lorna, just like you want it for your dad. I feel like we can move on, even if we don't know what happened to Charlie, because everyone knows he's responsible."

When Colm received his acceptance from MSU, he, Jane, and Cynthia celebrated at the Indian restaurant.

"The naan's grown on me," Colm admitted with a sheepish grin. "But I still prefer a burger."

"Me, too." Cynthia glanced back and forth between the two of them. "Thanks for letting me join in your celebration."

"It's our celebration," Colm said.

"And you're family," Jane added.

Soon, winter settled over Bozeman, and Charlie remained at large. Thanksgiving arrived, and Cynthia surprised Colm and Jane by inviting Quincy, Detective Fremont, and her eleven-year-old daughter.

Over their turkey dinner, Detective Fremont told them her department would continue to search for Charlie as weather and funding permitted. Jane didn't hold out much hope they'd find Charlie, but the thought counted.

The detective's gaze sought Jane's. "Do you want any details about your mother?"

Jane stiffened, and Cynthia patted her hand.

"I guess."

"As you know, Mindy never fessed up to planting the idea to murder Matt in Charlie's ear, but I'm certain that it happened. Proving it will be harder. The insurance company sued your mother for taking out a policy after her initial divorce proceedings.

From what I understand, the lawyer's confident the company will win."

"I'm glad there've been consequences," Jane said. "I wasn't sure what would happen when she admitted to her affair with Charlie. The public turned on her hard."

"I don't think losing her job at the elite real estate firm was punishment enough," Colm mumbled.

"It's more than she's ever faced before," Cynthia said.

Detective Fremont nodded in agreement.

"My mom texted me yesterday," Jane said.

All eyes turned to her. "She wanted to let me know she's back at her parents' ranch."

"Probably already scoping her next victim," Cynthia muttered. Her face drained of color. "Oh! I'm so sorry—that was thoughtless of me."

Jane shook her head. "Nah. She's looking for a rich man to marry."

The adults burst into laughter because that was so on brand.

Colm leaned over. "How are you feeling about the text?"

"I deleted it and blocked her," Jane said. "Mindy isn't part of my life anymore."

She refocused on the conversation, smiling at Quincy's story about botched research, then laughing at Colm's anecdote about a software upgrade gone awry.

She was thankful for friends and good memories.

# FORTY-THREE
## SPRING BREAK

THE NIGHT COLM, Cynthia, and Jane entered Yellowstone, she dreamed of her father. It was the first time she'd done so since he'd told her she knew his killer all those months before. Just like the last time, he showed up outside that tiny Army Corps of Engineers cabin deep inside Yellowstone's borders. This time, there was no blood...just a buzz of contentment that wrapped around Jane as they sat in the warm grass at the base of one of the big lodgepole pines and talked.

Her dad wrapped an arm around her, and she leaned her cheek against his shoulder, inhaling his aftershave.

"I'm thrilled you're interested in dendrology, Janie."

"Thanks, Dad. I wanted to tell you on our trip." She grimaced. He gave her shoulder a gentle squeeze.

"I don't understand how that ecosystem thrives below the earth's surface, but from what I've seen since we reintroduced the wolves, I know, without a doubt, that we're much more connected to each other, to the land and its biorhythms, than scientists imagined. So, my guess is that as you dig deeper..." His eyes twinkled as he let the pun sink in. "You'll find amazing correlations we haven't yet considered. How cool is that?"

He bumped her shoulder. "That'll require some outdoor skills."

"I'll use my trusty backpack you bought me. It worked great, Dad."

"Glad to hear that. Now, lay it on me. What do you want to research?"

Jane beamed up at her father as she told him about her plans for her master's degree. His acceptance and pride made everything better.

"I love that you found your passion, Janie. And Colm's been a great friend."

A pang of sadness slammed into Jane's heart. She could feel her mind pulling her from the dream.

*No. I don't want to wake up. I don't want to remember...*

Her dad hugged her close, and Jane embraced him even tighter. "Yellowstone will always be *our* special place."

"You died there," Jane pointed out.

"I did. But something wondrous happened." He smiled at her, love shining from his eyes. "You learned how to live without fear. You found Colm. You're living, not just going through the motions. *That's* what I wanted for you."

JANE SMILED as she pressed her tear-streaked face into her pillow. She inhaled the faint new smell that permeated the travel trailer. Because she and Colm were a little superstitious, Jane bought the camper by herself a month ago with some of the money her father left her...after she and Colm decided on the best option. It was big enough to sleep four, which was perfect for this trip she, Colm, and Cynthia had made into Yellowstone.

Jane rolled over and stared at the trailer's ceiling. That dream of her dad had been *normal*. Like he was still with her, even as he slipped away. She felt he'd given her his blessing...and told her goodbye. Her tears flowed faster but without bitterness and loss for the first time.

They were healing. Possibly renewing, Jane hoped.

"You all right, Jane?" Colm mumbled. He lifted his head from the pillow next to hers. His dark hair stuck up atop his head, and his eyelids drooped. He had a couple of days' worth of stubble on his face, and it looked good. He looked good. Healthy. So different from the man she'd hauled out of the park.

Jane snuggled closer. They still slept better together, and Jane was more than okay with that. They'd established trust in that snowstorm, and now they were building intimacy. She liked their slow progression.

Jane smiled. "Yeah. I am."

"This was a good idea," Colm said. "I wasn't sure at first, but we all needed to come back here—face Charlie. Plus, those wilderness classes I'm taking have boosted my confidence."

"Told you those would be useful. And you're better at starting a fire than I am."

He chuckled. "I'm better at tracking than you are, too."

"Well, that was a given. I'm so impressed you followed Charlie on that ATV."

"I had to. It led me to you."

They lay together for a long moment, luxuriating in their closeness, before Jane realized Cynthia wasn't in the trailer. "I'll go check on her," she said.

Jane rose and stretched. She marveled at how good her legs felt. As if she could hike between the ranger cabins...or run for miles. But she didn't have to do either. She, Colm, and Cynthia would take the ATVs to the next wolf stop to check in on the lame female, her alpha, and their pups—the reason the three of them were in the park.

Well, that and to scatter Matt's ashes that hadn't been buried, part of his request in his will. He'd wanted there to be a place Jane could visit, but he'd also wanted to be part of new life here, in the park.

Colm was excited to see the wolves, and Cynthia was hopeful the female alpha had regained use of her lame leg, giving the small pack a better chance at survival.

While Jane wanted to check on the wolves' health, there was one animal she hoped to see, and she didn't hold out much hope. Few people ever glimpse a wolverine or a lynx, after all. But if not this trip, then another.

They rose and dressed, and Jane settled next to Cynthia, who sat by the fire pit, percolating coffee in an old, well-used, soot-stained pot.

"What's the plan?" Jane asked as she picked up a coffee mug.

"I want to hike that way," Cynthia said, tipping her head.

Jane blinked, surprise coursing through her. "That's wolverine territory. Isn't it?"

Cynthia nodded, the tip of her nose red and her eyes slowly filling with tears.

Colm joined them. "Then why..."

"You think we'll find Charlie's remains there," Jane murmured.

Cynthia nodded again.

"He knew he was going to die," Cynthia said. "He knew the police were looking for him. His gun was useless once it ran out of bullets. All in all, an apex predator would be the quickest method, and wolverines don't tolerate intruders."

Jane bit her lip as she stared into the trees toward where Cynthia thought Charlie would have gone.

"I'd like coffee first."

"Not any breakfast, though." Colm scrubbed his hand down his face. "Can't believe I said that. Can't believe I want to skip a meal, either. But I don't think I can eat if we're going to find..." He shuddered.

Colm rarely called Charlie by name. Jane understood. To him, Charlie was his friends' murderer. Both Jane and Cynthia had more complicated feelings about Charlie. Not that they were happy to have been put in the position to have all those complex emotions swirling through their mind.

They weren't.

After finishing half of a mug, Jane rose from her spot and dumped out the rest. Colm followed suit, then headed back into the trailer. A moment later, the door banged open, and he returned with his trusty rifle and a new backpack he and Jane had filled together.

Jane went into the camper, gathered her own pack, running her hand down the side as she thought again of her father.

After locking the door, the three of them traipsed into the woods, silent due to their own thoughts but aware of their surroundings. They walked long enough for hunger to overcome their nerves. Cynthia offered them each a protein bar, which they ate while walking.

"This is familiar," Colm said.

Jane took his hand, unsurprised to find it shaking. While they could appreciate the park, the trauma Charlie inflicted wouldn't ever fully go away.

"We might not find him," Jane said, putting into words what they'd each been thinking.

"Let's give it another hour," Cynthia said. "If we don't find him, then we'll just have to assume Yellowstone meted out her justice."

Jane had just taken the final bite of her protein bar when she saw the blue boot. She stopped and gagged, finally managing to spit out the bite that had lodged in her throat. "There."

Cynthia and Colm hurried toward the spot where Jane

pointed. Cynthia dropped to her knees, but Colm stood, stoic, staring down at the footwear. Those blue hiking boots.

Jane joined him, sliding her arm around his waist. They watched Cynthia search the area. Colm nodded toward Charlie's jacket and cap. Cynthia stepped around a large boulder. Her eyes were red-rimmed and bloodshot, but she seemed more peaceful.

"Most of his skeleton is back there. It's pretty picked over—not too gruesome."

Jane nodded, and she and Colm traversed the boulders until they could see the bones. Jane expected to feel sorrow, maybe even anger, but instead, relief suffused her chest.

Colm's shoulders heaved. "God, I hate him."

"I totally get that," Jane said. "And I understand."

She scooted close enough to grip his free hand. Cynthia stood behind them, a hand on each of their shoulders.

"I'll take pictures," Cynthia said. "For Detective Fremont."

"Good idea," Jane said.

"It's over. Truly," Cynthia whispered.

"I hope he suffered," Colm muttered. He said it low, too quietly for Cynthia, who'd moved away to hear.

"I'm sure he did," Jane said. "And I'm sure it wasn't enough."

Colm blew out a long, slow breath. "And yet, it has to be."

"Yeah, it does."

She stood there for another long moment, working through her tangled emotions. Colm remained at her side, where he'd been since he saved her from the bison six months earlier.

Eventually, Jane lifted her face toward the towering trees, noting the light green growth of new pine needles. The branches swayed in the wind while the sun shone down from a bright, cloudless blue sky, caressing her cheeks.

"Bye, Dad."

Thank you for reading! Did you enjoy? Please add your review because nothing helps an author more and encourages readers to take a chance on a book than a review.

Want to see what's coming next from J.J. Cagney? Be sure to visit her website and sig-up for her newsletter at: jjcagney.com

Then, read THE HAUNTING OF BLACKWATER, by City Owl Author Marcia Armandi, available now. Turn the page for a sneak peek!

You can also sign up for the City Owl Press newsletter to receive notice of all book releases!

# SNEAK PEEK OF THE HAUNTING OF BLACKWATER

## BY MARCIA ARMANDI

***London, England, 1937***

Lina's dreams of a new life came to a halt the day her father was shot at Lydney Railway Station on his way to Blackwater manor, in Coleford. His death had been brutal, but here, lying in his coffin, Sir William Laroche looked at peace, his hands intertwined atop his black suit, his high-collared shirt neatly pressed. Lina unveiled her face and leaned forward. "I miss you." She gave him a final kiss, the coolness of his skin lingering on her lips—proof that his comforting words and warm embrace were now but a memory. She then heard the heart-wrenching words whispered by someone in attendance, "Orphan children."

Seven years ago, a heart attack claimed Sofia Laroche's life, leaving a bereaved family and Lina who, at thirteen years old, became a woman. Lina had promptly taken charge of caring for her baby brother, Mateo, as her mother had done. The task presented many challenges, but the boy, now eight, thrived academically and socially. Satisfied with Mateo's place in society and inspired by her post at the local library, Lina had applied for and been accepted to Oxford. She loved the idea of a career in mathematics. There was no room for mistakes in math. It was reliable, constant, so unlike the world in general. And, at times, she felt ill-prepared to confront that world—a world where death played an integral part.

Rumors of a world war circulated through the country, whispers and half-spoken thoughts gathering on the periphery like a far-off storm that had not yet overtaken the sunlight. Before her father's untimely death, she'd feared that when the lightning struck, not only would her father be taken but so would life as every Briton knew it. As a diplomat, William had been aware of the rising menace. Even more so of late, his meetings and telephone calls had multiplied. Lina's thoughts traveled back to the call that stood apart from the others.

Her father had been restless all morning. When the phone rang in his study, he dashed to answer it, neglecting to close the door. The stress in his voice made his words loud and clear. Lina could see him through the dim light of the hallway. He stood near his desk, his back to her, his shoulders slumped as if carrying an invisible weight.

"Nonsense. I refuse to believe that. The man is many things, but not that," William refuted into the receiver. And after a brief pause, he assured, "All right, all right. I will go there and settle this at once."

Lina hadn't thought much of the conversation. But now she wondered if that call was the first of death's plotting. Her gaze returned to her father's rigid body, and her fingers tightened on the edge of the silk-lined coffin. Was this the last time she would ever see him? Lina vaguely remembered the teachings of her youth about life beyond the grave—a topic she had never seriously considered. Moreover, she was convinced that paranormal accounts were fictitious, designed to instigate hope in an afterlife that didn't exist. But now, bereft of both her parents, she felt despondent and would have dearly loved a confirmation that death was not the end. The rawness of daily living, the regrets and disheartenments, and the tremendous responsibility of caring for her brother all seemed too much to bear. And with the assassin still at large, her despair threatened to consume her, trampling any hope that might have been born.

She took a stabilizing breath, repositioned the black veil over her face, and stepped away from the corpse to face the people awaiting the service. Dressed in respectful attire to pay homage to the solemnity of the event, they spoke in hushed voices while staring at the casket. Though many loved William, at least one person hated him enough to take him forever from his children. Lina scanned the chapel and found her brother huddled on a chair in the side aisle, twisting his hands. Her grief multiplied with each step she took toward him. How could she alleviate her own grief, let alone Mateo's?

"Lina, when are we going home?"

"Soon, darling, soon." She knelt in front of him, taking his hands into hers.

"I don't like it here. These people are scary."

"Oh, no, they are dressed in black to show their respect for Father, that's all."

Mateo shook his head. "No, not them."

"Who, then?"

"Him." Mateo pointed to the window at the end of the hallway.

Although the drapes swayed as if someone had brushed past them, Lina couldn't see anyone.

"I think he is very upset," Mateo remarked, shrinking in the chair.

"Well, don't you worry about him," she soothed, attributing his distress to their circumstances. As if losing their mother hadn't been enough, the boy was now fatherless at an age when he needed fatherly support and guidance most.

"I don't want him to look at me anymore."

"It's all right." Lina glanced at the hallway again, but still couldn't see anyone. "I'm right here with you." She slipped onto the seat beside the boy and pulled him close.

"I want to go home." Mateo buried his face in her arm.

"We will soon," Lina said, aware that what they called home

was about to change. Today they faced the funeral; tomorrow another trouble awaited.

At William's passing, his brother, Bartholomew Laroche, had become the children's legal guardian and the manager of their estate. Of course, William hadn't anticipated his own sudden death, or he would have taken measures to remove Bartholomew as executor of the family trust. Their relationship had deteriorated in recent years as Bartholomew's alcohol addiction had morphed him into a violent, unreasonable man. Stating health issues, Bartholomew hadn't bothered coming to the funeral. Instead, he'd busied himself with complicating the siblings' lives by demanding they leave their flat in London and move to Blackwater, the primary residence of the Laroche family for generations.

Preferring London, Lina's father had granted Bartholomew and his wife, Eleonor, charge over the manor. Lina considered a summer or two plenty of time to enjoy the countryside. And since she had spent several there already, she couldn't imagine it as a permanent home. It was too far removed from what she was accustomed to. Nonetheless, there would be no freedom until she turned twenty-one and the law permitted her to manage her inheritance and gain custody of her brother.

The more she thought of it, the angrier she became. Her uncle was robbing them of their home, friends, and even trusted house staff, having made it clear that the personnel would not be relocating with them. He'd also stolen her dream to attend Oxford, at least for now. Though Bartholomew hadn't brought up the subject, there was no way under heaven that Lina would let Mateo face Blackwater alone. They were all that was left of their little family, and she was determined to protect him.

William's agitated telephone call replayed in her mind. Had he been speaking of Bartholomew? If so, what had her uncle done? Did he have something to do with her father's death? After all, William had been en-route to visit the man when he met death as he'd stepped off the train. True, Bartholomew was a scoundrel who took to the bottle to solve his problems, but a murderer? It seemed farfetched, yet possible.

Now, more than ever, she felt vulnerable, powerless, and at the mercy of a man she hardly knew. He'd always been like a shadow lurking at the edge of her life, easy to ignore when her parents were alive. Now, the shadow would become the center of their lives.

Dark clouds hung low over King's Cross Railway Station, threatening to unleash a downpour. The siblings hurried into the building, scurrying past the other travelers. Covertly, Lina searched their faces. Perhaps with a miracle, her father would appear among them, but from his last destination, no one returned.

"Whoa!" Mateo exclaimed, staring at the train as they emerged from the train station onto the platform.

Grand and impressive, the Admiral Sutherland locomotive sat on the tracks. No doubt it had traveled far and wide, its passengers enjoying many adventures. Yet Lina wished she and her brother would never set foot on it. An incoming train rolled in just on the other side of the Admiral, clouds of smoke billowing into the sky. Lina's gaze was lost in the gray fumes, her thoughts returning to her father.

Why had he made this very trip? William had spoken of removing Bartholomew from Blackwater for his bad management, but Lina didn't think it would ever happen. In fact, she was almost certain it wasn't the reason her father had traveled there. *Why did you have to die? What's to become of us?*

Along with the unanswered questions, the feeling that they

should not go to Blackwater plagued her again. Ever since the family solicitor announced Bartholomew's decision, Lina had wrestled with a sense of foreboding about living under her uncle's purview. However, legally, she had no options. Running away was tempting, but she would not put Mateo in jeopardy. The small amount of money stashed in her pocket would run out within days, and they would be homeless. She could get a post somewhere, but she had no one to care for the boy. Besides, Bartholomew would soon find them, and their end might be worse than their beginning. At least, for now, she still had a chance to appeal to his sympathy.

Mateo pulled on her sleeve, and her attention returned to the present. "What are you thinking about, Lina?"

"The countryside," she answered, concealing her low spirits. "Getting out of London's gloom will be nice."

"Why do we have to go?"

"Because Uncle Bartholomew is our only family." She adjusted his hat on his black hair, and his brown eyes found her blue ones. His resemblance to their mother was a painful reminder of Sofia and how much Lina missed her. And now her own fair complexion would conjure memories of her father every time she looked in the mirror.

"I don't want to leave my friends," Mateo complained.

"I know. I know." Lina understood him well. She would miss her friends, Irene and Sherley, and their discussions at the library about their latest reads during coffee breaks.

"Will I ever see them again?"

"Of course, you will. We'll be back before you know it." Although she feared they would be forced to stay at Blackwater a whole year, she couldn't bring herself to tell him.

"But I don't like the manor. It's scary."

"Scary? Nonsense."

"Yes, it is. It's gigantic, and there are lots of strange noises."

Mateo had a remarkable memory. Even though it had been a while since their last visit, he still remembered. The manor's towering walls and obscure passages did make it quite menacing.

"Listen, there is nothing to fret." Lina's gaze found his. "I'll be with you every second of the day."

"That might be a bit too much," he said.

Lina laughed at the sincerity in his remark.

His attention jumped to a group of soldiers who'd stepped onto the platform, a common sight nowadays. Their loud voices and heavy boots drew notice. Mateo pointed "Look, Lina, look! Soldiers!"

"I see, I see." With a graceful move, she guided his hand back down to his side, wondering what kept the train attendant from inviting them aboard.

"Good morning, miss," a short, chubby soldier greeted her.

She nodded in acknowledgment. Mateo waved, enthusiasm present in the motion.

"Good morning, indeed!" another soldier emphasized, winking at her.

Lina produced a faint smile, not wanting to encourage them, for it was apparent they'd be traveling on the same train. Nonetheless, she felt a surge of pity. Some of them looked younger than her twenty years. And if the rumors of war became reality, the country's fate would rest on the shoulders of young lads like these. She looked down at her little brother. Thankfully he was years from military age, for she shuddered to think of him marching off to war.

The siblings were among the first to turn in their tickets when the train attendant finally summoned the passengers aboard. Lina purposely chose one of the first compartments. Since people tended to move farther down the aisle, she hoped no one would intrude on their space. The events of the past few days had left her starving for solitude and too weary for polite conversation.

"Give me your gloves," Lina instructed Mateo, taking off her own. "And your hat. We don't want to lose them." He did as he was told, and she placed the items inside their small suitcase. At least Bartholomew had sent for most of their belongings ahead of time. She secured the case on the overhead shelf and settled in beside her brother. "There, now we can relax."

Relaxing didn't seem to appeal to Mateo, who slid his body back and forth between his sister and the window. "What are we going to do at Blackwater? Will I go to school?"

"That, or a teacher will come to the house." Mateo's questions intensified her awareness of their precarious circumstances and what might await them at Blackwater.

The rhythmic chugging of the wheels grew louder as the train inched forward.

Lina's stomach churned with uncertainty, the distance between her and the world she had known increasing with each passing second.

"And what else?" Mateo wondered. His inquisitive mind seemingly sought answers to appease his anxiety.

"I think we shall ride horses, and if you are on your best behavior, you might get to have your own," Lina responded, knowing of his love for animals.

"My own horse?" Excitement filled him, but then a new thought occurred. "What if Uncle Bartholomew doesn't let me have a horse?"

Lina frowned. He must've heard more than he should have about their uncle from the house staff. Unhappy with Bartholomew's determination to relocate the siblings, they had openly expressed their opinions on the matter. "In that case, we'll find one in the stables we can call yours—it will be our secret."

Satisfied with her answer and probably musing about horses, Mateo leaned on her and finally sat still. Her blonde hair cascaded down her shoulder and brushed against his face. With a giggle, he tugged on a strand. Lina smiled and tucked him under her arm, feeling the tension in his body dissipate. It wasn't long until he was fast asleep, and when the train rolled into the next station, he snored softly. Some passengers disembarked, and new ones boarded, Mateo oblivious to it all. Lina leaned her head back against the seat as the locomotive pushed on, its steel wheels shrieking on the tracks.

"Come on, chap, come on! We haven't got all day!" The attendant's shouting startled Lina, and she peered through the window for an explanation.

With one hand, the attendant held onto the sidebar while motioning with the other for a late passenger to make haste. Lina's gaze drew to the color of the man's military uniform—blue instead of the usual brown—as he ran along the platform. *Hmm, a higher rank. Yet irresponsible not being on time.* It was a sentiment she'd gotten from her father, who was punctual to a fault, always on schedule. Her free-spirited mother was more relaxed about her relationship with the clock, which Lina had never picked up despite sharing many of her other traits.

As the train accelerated, Lina came to terms with the fact that sleep had escaped her. With a sigh, she dug into her handbag for the novel she had stashed before leaving their flat, and once she had it in hand, the title mocked her. *I Will Remember You Until the Day I Die.*

"Oh, how cheerful," she muttered. "I should have paid more attention." That morning had been nothing but stress-filled as she made sure Mateo had all he needed. Consequently, she found a new appreciation for her parents and regretted some of the things she had so easily censured them for.

"Excuse me, miss. Is this seat taken?" The soldier in the blue uniform pointed to the bench opposite her.

"No, it's not." *And I would like to keep it that way.* And to

Mateo, who had briefly awoken, she said, "Go back to sleep," patting his arm.

The boy leaned against the window, brought his legs up on the seat, and was soon comfortably back to dreaming. The soldier installed himself straight across from Lina, dropping his military bag beside him. She anticipated the conversation that surely would ensue. By sad experience, she had learned that some men were tediously dull when in the presence of women, as if their brains quit working. That morning's brief interaction with the soldiers had reaffirmed her feelings on the matter.

She detested flattering words and shallow conversations. Why could they not hold sincere, well-constructed discussions? At times, she dreamed of finding someone more interested in her as a human being than in her looks and of having a romance as special as her parents shared. But after some disappointment, she doubted she would. Besides, she could no longer afford to dream of it. For now, she had Mateo to look after.

Her first move was to avoid eye contact, hoping that time would be merciful, and they'd soon reach Lydney. From there, Bartholomew's chauffeur would take them to Coleford. She lowered her chin, pretending to be engrossed in the print in front of her. When the soldier drew a deep breath and stretched his long legs into her space, she responded by tucking hers closer to her seat.

The train continued its trajectory with a mind-numbing slowness. Now and then, from the corner of her eye, Lina caught glimpses of rolling hills and small villages. Momentarily, her thoughts wandered back to her plight, her mind working diligently to find a solution that didn't involve staying at Blackwater.

When her focus returned to the book, she found it difficult to concentrate. Though her fellow traveler hadn't said a word, she felt his presence. Perhaps speaking to him would have been easier to manage. With a few superficial exchanges, she could've started and promptly ended a conversation, thus mitigating the awkwardness in the compartment. Yes, she should've done just that, and when the soldier coughed, softly, as if calling for her attention, she seized the opportunity.

She lowered the book to her lap but was stunned to find his head tilted, his eyes closed, his features showing no signs of awareness—he slept. Whatever interest she had anticipated from him was nothing more than a product of her imagination. She was chagrined at first, but then smiled inwardly at her foolishness.

She let her gaze linger on him. Probably in his mid-twenties, he had fair skin with softly defined facial features and slightly wavy brown hair. The fit of his uniform indicated a well-shaped figure. Whether a sign of self-discipline or a strenuous life, Lina couldn't say. Yet, despite his pleasant appearance, what captivated her most was the serenity he emanated, a serenity that seemed to come from deep within. He slept as if nothing in the world mattered, as if he were an angel instead of a soldier, devoid of grief and concern. A wave of nostalgia swept over Lina for days that were planned and orderly—balanced. When parenthood didn't weigh upon her shoulders—when she had been the child who needed care.

The soldier made a slight movement, and Lina glanced away, feeling guilty for her perusal. She had condemned the very conduct she now displayed. Nevertheless, her gaze found its way back to him.

"What are you staring at?" Mateo's voice cut through the stillness of the compartment.

"Shh. Hush," Lina whispered, fearing that her uninvited assessment would be exposed. "We mustn't disturb him."

"But why were you staring at him?" Mateo sat up, rubbing his eyes.

Lina wasn't sure, but even though the soldier remained still, she thought she glimpsed an expression of amusement. "I wasn't," she lied, while the heat in her face confirmed that she was blushing.

"Is he a good or bad soldier?" On the topic of the atrocities committed by soldiers in other countries, the house staff also hadn't withheld their opinion. And Mateo hadn't missed a chance to listen, but at his age, it could be challenging to arrange things properly.

"Good. He is good." Her gaze returned to the man, and this time she saw his lips curl softly, as if suppressing a smile. She was now positive he was awake.

"Are you sure?" Mateo's eyebrows knitted together.

"Of course, I'm sure."

"Why isn't he wearing a brown uniform?"

"Sometimes they wear blue." She placed her finger on her lips, signaling for him to be silent.

"I'm bored." Mateo had had enough of quiet. "How much longer do we have to sit for? It's stuffy in here."

Lina didn't know whether to cry or laugh. Once Mateo got into a questioning mood, no power under heaven could make him stop. "We are almost there. I believe Lydney is the next stop."

"But I'm bored, Lina."

"Where is your car? The one you were looking for before we left the flat."

"Oh, I forgot about it." He fumbled in his pocket. "Got it." He waved the red metal car in the air as if it were an airplane.

"Oh, thank heaven," Lina muttered.

The toy entertained Mateo while his sister did her best not to look at the soldier again. He sat ever so still. Not long after, the final whistle shrieked like a banshee, and the locomotive slowed in preparation for its arrival. While Lina stowed the book in her handbag, she realized that even though she had wanted solitude, she was disappointed to have found herself ignored by the soldier.

The train came to a stop, and, letting out a tired yawn, the soldier adjusted himself on the seat. Lina grabbed her bag and sprang to her feet faster than intended, pulling Mateo up by his hand.

"Ouch, Lina!" Mateo wriggled his hand to loosen her grip. "You almost made me drop the car."

She seized the doorknob, the soldier stood, and the compartment suddenly became too crowded. He was more attractive than she had allowed herself to admit, which made her uncomfortable for a reason she didn't fully understand.

"Don't forget this." Reaching over Lina's head, the soldier brought her suitcase down from the rack.

"Thank you." Lina let go of Mateo to retrieve the suitcase while her other hand lingered on the doorknob.

Before she knew it, the soldier had wrapped his fingers around hers and finished sliding the door open. As she stepped into the aisle, he spoke again. "Have a wonderful rest of your day."

Lina turned, and his hazel eyes burned into hers, giving her the impression that they held an unsaid message. "The same to you, sir."

In response, he smiled and nodded.

*Ugh. I'm as daft as a brush. I should have said something more intelligent.*

Hand in hand, the siblings descended the train. And while they traversed the platform, the sorrow of the place overshadowed Lina with the unbidden image of her father collapsed on the station floor, his life slipping away. Her anguish was as tangible as the coward's bullet that had taken their father from them. Anxious for the day they would return to London, she turned to glance at the Admiral Southerland locomotive one last time.

"I don't think he got off here," observed Mateo, hurrying to keep up with her long strides.

"Who?"

"The soldier."

Lina said nothing. It didn't matter what the soldier's destination was. She would probably never see him again. And the long ride had given her time to solidify the purpose of her immediate future: to protect her brother and discover the truth about her father's death.

**Don't miss more from J.J. Cagney and discover all the details at jjcagney.com**

**Then, discover THE HAUNTING OF BLACKWATER, by City Owl Author, Marcia Armandi**

Lina doesn't believe in ghosts, but they won't leave her alone.

When her father is killed, Lina and her little brother Mateo are forced to move in with her domineering uncle at Blackwater Manor. Lina soon discovers that her uncle intends for her to marry his nephew, Bray, to gain control of her inheritance. She is also convinced her uncle had something to do with her father's death.

As the days pass, it becomes increasingly clear that Blackwater is haunted, and the malevolent presence seems determined to harm the siblings. To protect her brother, Lina attempts to communicate with the ghosts, all the while evading the handsome but devious Bray and crossing paths with the mysterious Max, a dashing army lieutenant with secrets of his own.

But as Lina unearths the atrocities of the past, she must now unmask her father's killer and discover the ghosts' intentions before she becomes one of them.

---

Please sign up for the City Owl Press newsletter for chances to win special subscriber-only contests and giveaways as well as receiving information on upcoming releases and special excerpts.

All reviews are **welcome** and **appreciated**. Please consider leaving one on your favorite social media and book buying sites.

For books in the world of romance and speculative fiction that embody Innovation, Creativity, and Affordability, check out City Owl Press at www.cityowlpress.com.

# ACKNOWLEDGMENTS

*The Kill Line* exists because of the generosity, encouragement, and expertise of so many people.

To my family: thank you for believing in me through every draft, deadline, and early-morning writing session. Chris, your patience, encouragement, and unwavering faith have carried me through more books than either of us can count. Mom and Dad, thank you for your constant support and for somehow always agreeing to read one more version. Dad, your work as a vision scientist inspired parts of this novel, and it was a joy to weave a little of your world into mine. To my kids, thank you for understanding when I disappear into fictional worlds. You are my greatest adventure.

To my incredible agent, Dani Sanchez, thank you for championing this story from the beginning. Your editorial instincts, strategic guidance, and steadfast belief in my work have shaped not only this novel but my career.

To Carol and Lenette, thank you for every brainstorming session, critique, and conversation that challenged me to dig deeper. Your friendship and insight strengthened this novel and improved my writing.

To Tee Tate, my editor, and the City Owl Press team, thank you for bringing *The Kill Line* to life. Your thoughtful editing, enthusiasm, and dedication elevated every page. To the cover designer, production staff, and everyone who worked behind the scenes, thank you for creating a beautiful home for this story.

To the team at Wildfire PR, thank you for your passion, creativity, and tireless work introducing *The Kill Line* to readers.

This novel would not exist without my uncle Paul Hart, a former Yellowstone National Park ranger. Thank you for sharing your stories, answering my endless questions, and generously offering your knowledge of one of the most extraordinary places I've visited. I hope I've honored both the park and your years of service with this story.

To my neighbor Tom, my friend Kala, and the search-and-rescue professionals who have shared their experiences over the years, thank you. Your stories stayed with me, found their way into these pages, and helped make this fictional adventure more authentic.

To the men and women of the National Park Service, thank you for protecting one of the world's greatest treasures.

To my friends at Land of Enchantment Romance Authors (LERA) and Killer Nashville, thank you for your generosity, encouragement, and willingness to share your knowledge. Writing can be a solitary profession, but you've made it feel like a community.

Finally, to my readers: *thank you.* There are countless books you could read, and the fact that you've chosen mine is a gift I never take for granted. Thank you for trusting me with your time, your imagination, and your hearts. I hope *The Kill Line* kept you turning pages long into the night and inspired you to seek out Yellowstone's majesty for yourself.

May we always protect the places that remind us what wildness looks like.

# ABOUT THE AUTHOR

J.J. CAGNEY writes twisty, atmospheric mysteries and thrillers where every clue is a risk and every secret comes at a price. Her award-winning novels include *A Pilgrimage to Death*, one of *Kirkus Reviews'* 100 Best Books of 2018. Before becoming a full-time author, she worked as a literary agent and with elite athletes, experiences that taught her about ambition, pressure, and what people will do to win. She lives in northern New Mexico with her family, two adorable, unruly dogs, and a suspiciously organized tank of fish. When she's not writing, she's hiking, reading, or plotting someone's next terrible decision.

jjcagney.com

facebook.com/JJCagney
instagram.com/j.j.cagney
tiktok.com/@author.jj.cagney
bookbub.com/authors/j-j-cagney

# ABOUT THE PUBLISHER

City Owl Press is a cutting edge indie publishing company, bringing the world of romance and speculative fiction to discerning readers.

Escape Your World. Get Lost in Ours!

www.cityowlpress.com

facebook.com/YourCityOwlPress
x.com/cityowlpress
instagram.com/cityowlbooks
pinterest.com/cityowlpress

www.ingramcontent.com/pod-product-compliance
Lightning Source LLC
Chambersburg PA
CBHW030336040826
49266CB00030B/255
*9781648985744*